A SLOW AND SECRET POISON

www.penguin.co.uk

Also by Carmella Lowkis

Spitting Gold

A SLOW AND SECRET POISON

Carmella Lowkis

doubleday

TRANSWORLD PUBLISHERS

UK | USA | Canada | Ireland | Australia
India | New Zealand | South Africa

Transworld is part of the Penguin Random House group of companies
whose addresses can be found at global.penguinrandomhouse.com.

Penguin Random House UK, One Embassy Gardens,
8 Viaduct Gardens, London SW11 7BW

penguin.co.uk

First published in Great Britain in 2026 by Doubleday
an imprint of Transworld Publishers

001

Copyright © Carmella Lowkis 2026

The moral right of the author has been asserted

This book is a work of fiction and, except in the case of historical fact, any
resemblance to actual persons, living or dead, is purely coincidental.

Every effort has been made to obtain the necessary permissions with
reference to copyright material, both illustrative and quoted. We apologize
for any omissions in this respect and will be pleased to make the
appropriate acknowledgements in any future edition.

Penguin Random House values and supports copyright.
Copyright fuels creativity, encourages diverse voices, promotes freedom
of expression and supports a vibrant culture. Thank you for purchasing
an authorized edition of this book and for respecting intellectual property
laws by not reproducing, scanning or distributing any part of it by any
means without permission. You are supporting authors and enabling
Penguin Random House to continue to publish books for everyone.
No part of this book may be used or reproduced in any manner for the
purpose of training artificial intelligence technologies or systems. In accordance
with Article 4(3) of the DSM Directive 2019/790, Penguin Random House
expressly reserves this work from the text and data mining exception.

Typeset in 11.5/15.75pt Adobe Garamond by Falcon Oast Graphic Art Ltd.
Printed and bound in Great Britain by Clays Ltd, Elcograf S.p.A.

The authorized representative in the EEA is Penguin Random House
Ireland, Morrison Chambers, 32 Nassau Street, Dublin D02 YH68

A CIP catalogue record for this book is available from the British Library

ISBN: 9780857529510

For Ashley

There she weaves by night and day
A magic web with colours gay.
She has heard a whisper say,
A curse is on her if she stay
To look down to Camelot.
— *The Lady of Shalott*, Alfred, Lord Tennyson

The area was famous for its hares; a traveller in the previous century, William Cobbett, had once seen, not far away from here, a field full of hares.
— *The Enigma of Arrival*, V. S. Naipaul

PART ONE

ARABELLA, 1923

8 February 1923

WE PUT CHARLIE in the ground today.

It seems heartless to write, but I could not move myself to cry, even as I cast my parting handful of dirt on to his coffin. I think I lost the ability to grieve over the past decade. Perhaps some things are diminished through practice, rather than grown. This was true of the number of mourners: there were barely ten of us present in all. Just compare that to the two hundred or so people who descended on Harfold for my parents' funeral. If only someone had warned us then that we would need to ration them out for what was to follow.

Then again, who among us would have believed such a warning? Not Charlie. Cheerful, optimistic Charlie. Even when I read the signs so clearly, he refused to listen; shrugged his shoulders or looked at me with concern, as if *I* were the one who should be worried. I wonder if he changed his mind in those last moments, or if – even as he came off that bloody horse – he still thought it all unconnected.

I will not make the same mistake as you, my sweet brother.

Poor Morry managed a few tears. He has always been such a tender soul. He will probably cry when we shoot the wretched horse, too. Mr Allen wants to sell it, but I cannot stand the thought of the thing getting away scot-free. Not that it is the horse's fault. The Reaper was always going to come calling for Charlie, and the creature just happened to be his instrument on this occasion.

I wonder what he will send to collect me.

It did not really dawn on me until the both of us were standing there in the graveyard, Morry honking into his handkerchief while I held the umbrella, that we are the only ones left. Our whole family tree stripped down to two little twigs. How lonely we have become.

'There's mine,' I told him, nodding to the bare patch of earth next to Charlie. 'Then yours, after me.'

The church tower seemed to look down on us – waiting, no doubt, to watch us go under. I can't stand to look at the thing any longer.

I keep imagining ways that I might die, from the improbable to the mundane. Will it be a falling tree? A sudden cancer? A smouldering cigarette thrown carelessly into the wastepaper bin one night?

Beneath my show of bravado, the truth is that I am terrified. As much as I try to tell myself that it is inevitable, that I must make my peace with it and wait in resignation as the hourglass fritters itself away, I do not want to die. It is as simple as that. So I must cling to my one consolation: I am <u>not</u> like Charlie, or my other brothers, or our parents, because I know what is coming. I see the distant headlights on the road. If there is any chance to avert their path, then I swear on Charlie's grave that I will take it.

I am so very tired of funerals.

VEE, 1925

ONE

THERE'S A DEAD deer in the way. No question of getting past it, not on this narrow country lane. The taxi rolls leisurely to a halt, headlights illuminating glistening clots of blood on matted fur, a mouth held in a permanent scream. The engine trundles softly.

After a minute, I lean over from the back seat. 'Can't you do something?'

The driver glances at me in the mirror. 'I don't know what to tell you, love,' he says. 'I can't get round that.'

'Isn't there another road?'

He shakes his head. 'Nah.'

'But this road has to come out somewhere, hasn't it?' I'm trying my best to keep the frustration from my voice, but he's not making it easy for me.

The man purses his lips and blows out through them. 'Not unless I go all the way back up the Warminster road and loop round.'

'Can't you – I don't know – move it?' I wave at the deer. Its eyes are stuck open in a sorry gaze, as if still trying to bargain with whatever it saw during those last moments.

He shrugs. 'I've got a bad back.'

I glance at my pocket watch, angling its face to catch the last of the September evening light. First the delayed train, now this: not a good first impression. 'All right, I'll move it, then.'

The driver guffaws, though I wasn't joking. 'Look, love,' he says, with a scratch of the nose. 'The village is just over there. See the lights? It's five minutes' walk, tops.'

I look out at the dim, muddy road. The overgrown verge. The tiny glimmer of yellow showing through the trees. 'You want me to get out here?' I'm regretting the skirt, smart hat and dress shoes I let Gladys talk me into wearing. *Just for the first day, so they know you're a nice girl, like.* After all the things that have been said about me, I couldn't help but find this funny.

'Can't be far,' says the driver. 'Be near on half an hour to go the other way.'

At least I don't have much to carry – just the one suitcase and Dad's old holdall. I climb reluctantly out of the cab.

'Straight up the road to the village, then it's a track on the left,' says the driver. 'You'll be fine, love; can't miss it.'

I was *meant* to be greeted at the station by a Mr Reacher – the estate manager I've been exchanging letters back and forth with in preparation for today. But whether because of the late train or another reason, when I arrived, I found that he'd buggered off, leaving this prepaid cabbie in his place. Must cost a fortune, the distance we've travelled. I consider making a last-ditch argument in favour of moving the deer – if only to get the fare's worth out of him – but then I look at the creature's sharp-twisted neck and think better of it. There's the grunt of a revving engine and the taxi begins to reverse, not waiting to see me on my way. Probably wanting to get home. Wife, kids, evening paper to read. Besides, even in my nice-girl skirt, something in the way I carry myself always seems to kill any gentlemanly impulses. Intentional, of course. The headlights swing round into the hedge as the taxi finds a place to turn. Then just the receding glow. Then darkness.

Once my eyes have adjusted, I heft up the suitcase and step on to the verge, trying to avoid anything that might be a bit of deer. It's not a five-minute walk. It takes a quarter-hour to find the 'track on the left' – which is, in fact, on the right. But here it is, a hand-painted wooden board: Harfold Manor. I thought it sounded rather grand when I first read the advert in the *Morning Post*, but what I'm currently seeing is a lot of mud, and I suspect the place has been misrepresented.

Still, I've been lucky to get the job; it's not as if people up and down the country are jumping at the chance to employ a woman gardener. Especially one without any formal horticultural qualifications. I didn't expect to hear back when I sent the letter of application – not least because the listing was a good few weeks old by the time I'd convinced myself to write. But then the reply came almost immediately, as if there'd been no deliberation at all. Reacher's abominable small handwriting offered me the job then and there, laying out the terms of employment. He didn't even ask for a reference.

My way to the manor is completely dark, sloping down between steep wooded banks that blot out the final wilt of twilight. I slide and stumble as I go, caught off-guard by sudden changes in texture, sudden obstacles. The fucking dress shoes. If I ever see that taxi driver again . . . Finally, I reach the end of the track, the bleat of a lantern coming into view. A pair of gate-posts part the trees. When I get closer, I see that two leaping rabbits or hares or suchlike are carved into them, one on either side. Between them, a set of cast-iron gates bear a swirling design. Shut tight.

While I'm distracted, my toe hits something unyielding and I go tripping forward. Hands and knees in the mud. Hat knocked off and lost in the darkness. My bags have landed a foot in front of me – thankfully still held closed by their straps. Scrambling to my feet, I grab my luggage, and in this frenzy almost jump out of my skin when I look up to see a man now standing on the other side of the gates.

This newcomer is middle-aged, wearing a flat cap and tweeds. Not tall, but broad-shouldered and stocky. Wellies on his feet. A weathered tan to his skin. He's holding an electric torch, the beam of which he now sweeps over me like a nightwatchman. 'Miss Morgan? That you there?' He has a proper Wiltshire accent, the syllables swallowing one another up. 'Blimey, what's happened to you, then?'

I shake my head and move closer. He's not dressed like an estate manager, so perhaps he's the groundsman, mentioned in Reacher's instructions. 'Mr Allen?' I guess.

He hesitates a moment as he takes me in, then slides back the bolt, pulling one half of the gate narrowly open. As I squeeze through, he puts a hand out for my suitcase, extends the other to shake. 'Call me Tom.' It sounds almost like 'Tam', the way he says it.

'Vee,' I say, then clarify, 'Morgan, yes.' It's clear I'm not what he was expecting. Unusual enough for a gardener to be female, but I'm also an odd age at twenty-five – too old still to be saving up for marriage, too young to have given up on the possibility. I've got my dad's ungainly height, my mam's thick, black hair worn in a messy Eton crop. A strong Cardiff accent. And I'm covered in mud. Although maybe mud comes with the profession.

Tom trudges up the drive, nodding for me to follow. 'We thought you'd be here round nine,' he says. It doesn't sound accusatory – just like a topic of conversation. Making small talk.

'The train was delayed,' I say. 'Something on the line, I think it was. Then later, just outside the village, the taxi couldn't get through. There was a deer. You know, dead.' I have a sudden urge to pull a face to illustrate, eyes crossed and tongue lolling. Thankfully I fight it back.

Tom nods as if this is nothing unusual. 'That'll be that lot from Warminster. Always tearing about the lanes, drunk as you like.' He looks me over again. 'You're best wearing white so they can see you in time to stop.'

I try not to recall the way the deer's neck had been twisted. Its sorry eyes. The crawling feeling up my spine.

'Mr Reacher said to apologize that he couldn't wait for you, only he had to get off away to London. He's often up there on business.' Tom leads me up the drive till we reach a fork. The main path continues, fat and self-assured, with a gem of light at its end. 'The manor,' says Tom, nodding at it. We turn off and take a simpler, gravelled track to the cottage. *My* cottage.

I'd hardly believed my luck when I'd learned the job came with its own place on the grounds. *Are you sure this isn't a bit impulsive?* Gladys had asked when I broke the news – which was rich coming from her – but I'd known there was no point in deliberating. It was just what I'd been after: a chance to start afresh.

In the halo of Tom's torch, I make out yellow Cotswold stone, a door that needs a paint. Crabbed windows with leaded panes. It's perfect.

Tom holds out his hand. 'Key,' he says. The metal's warm

from his pocket. 'Have the torch as well. We're not on the electrics yet, but the gas comes out for you, and I've left some water. Me and the missus are up at the manor, if you have any problems. Round the back door.'

I nod. 'And her Ladyship?' Lady Lascy's looping, fierce signature had sealed the employment contract – although it was Reacher who'd arranged everything. I imagine ladies don't bother with that kind of paperwork. They have charity galas or what have you to organize.

'Oh,' says Tom, setting down my case on the front step. 'No, you won't see much of her, I don't suppose.' Leaving the remark to hang unexplored, he heads back toward the manor.

My key scrapes inside the lock, sticks for a moment, then turns. The door opens inward. I expect a creak, but the hinges are well oiled. The smell of still air and old, chilly buildings. A narrow front hall with a side table, on which a key dish and a vase of dahlias have been set out for me. I brush a finger over one of the blooms and smile. Did Tom leave these? There's something touching in the thought of a man like him out among the flowers, delicately selecting the best to cut.

There isn't much to explore. One up, one down. The ground-floor room is squarish, the ceiling low – not so low I have to stoop, but I'll need to watch my head on the door frame. Upstairs, I find the luxury of a double bed. The sheets are white, with a pink flower pattern on thin, faded fabric. The headboard is pushed up against the chimney breast – that'll be welcome warmth come winter. A number of cushions with needlepoint designs are scattered about. They all show hares performing various antics: jumping, boxing, sleeping. The furniture looks old, scuffed and warped with poor use. When I open the wardrobe to hang up my clothes, there are deep scores in the wood on the inside, all the way round the bottom third of the door – rodents, I assume. Bloody marvellous.

From one of the bedroom windows, I spot squares of illumination that I guess come from the manor building. We're closer neighbours than I'd imagined, me and Lady Lascy. Maybe I'll pop round for a cup of tea, I joke to myself.

As I lie down to sleep, I'm struck by the change in soundscape. No women moving about, no rush of late-night traffic or drunken shouts of merrymakers staggering home. Instead, the creaks and groans of the cottage settling, the rattle of the wind. Unfamiliar animal noises from outside. Then a scritch-scritch-scritch. Maybe from the wardrobe. Maybe the attic. A creature scampering with little claws on wood. Moving in the ceiling above me – almost the sound of a rattling tin. Not so different from Cardiff after all. Wherever you go, there's always vermin.

The next morning, Tom takes me on a tour of the gardens. Even so early in the morning, the day is shaping up beautifully, with an open, cloudless sky the blue of cornflowers. A light breeze carries the cow-smell of manure from over the fields. Insects hum lazily at the edge of hearing.

I'm back in my overalls and work boots today, one of Dad's straw sun hats on my head. The familiar garments feel like a sigh of relief. Gladys is one of my best friends and I respect her opinion to no end, but that doesn't mean I have to listen every time. The fact of the matter is, I'm here to be a gardener, not a secretary. They aren't going to care what I wear, so long as I can keep the plants alive.

Harfold's grounds cover around forty acres, including the

crop of woodland I had to walk through last night. 'Used to be closer on three hundred when I was a lad,' says Tom, 'but then Lord Lascy sold a lot of it off. That's Henry Lascy, her Ladyship's late father. Lots of tenant farmers lost their homes and their livelihoods overnight, as it were.' He shakes his head in disapproval. 'Nasty business.'

'Mmm,' I say, noncommittal. Better settle in before I plunge too deep into local politics. I'm here to keep my head down, after all.

'But yours was never a farm cottage,' Tom continues. 'That's always been for the head gardener.'

From this, I take that there must once have been a team of gardeners. And now it's just me and Tom to look after all this glorious, sweeping land.

The head gardener's cottage is on the edge of the estate, a stream marking its border from open farms beyond, hills speckled with white and brown sheep. A little way off to the left, more of Harfold village – a few roofs, the church tower. On the other side, the cottage backs on to an overgrown paddock. 'Horses, is it?' I ask, nodding at what looks like a coach house and stables.

A shadow in Tom's expression. 'Not for a couple of years.'

We cross the east lawn, following an uphill slope till we catch the main driveway. Scruffy yews line its sides, their original shapes almost obscured by summer growth.

'They'll need doing, then,' I say.

'Feel free to be as artistic as you like.' Tom has a cheeky, boyish smile that peels the decades from his face. He's not too bad a sort, I don't think. Reminds me a bit of Mam – the nose for gossip. So long as he stays interested in other people's business and not mine, we'll be right as rain with each other.

Up the drive, I finally get my first proper sight of the manor. I don't know enough about architecture to date it, but I think it's a good age. Georgian, possibly. The main body is a heavy oblong of red brick, decorated with lighter stone detail that oozes the aura of Old England. Ivy clambers up its face to give it a bearded look. The hipped roof is done in dark slate, with mouldings underneath it all carved in elaborate designs. Everything would be beautifully symmetrical, down to the pair of slender chimney stacks, if it weren't for an extra wing that stretches back on the west side. Such an odd, lopsided shape for a building. And, while the window and door frames are painted a cheery white, as we approach I see the cracks and chips, the dirt and lichen. It's one of those buildings that looks less and less impressive the closer you stand.

'That's us.' Tom nods. 'Nora's in town this morning to put the orders in, but you'll meet her later on. My wife, that is,' he adds, when he sees me looking blank at the name.

'And the other staff?' I ask.

Tom chuckles. 'It's just us.'

'Only the two of you to look after this whole place, you mean?' Can't keep the incredulity from my voice.

'These days? Yup.'

'And just her Ladyship living here?'

Tom nods. 'Mr Reacher is often about, though, when he's not in London.'

I look up at the gleaming windows. Lady Lascy must rattle round in all that space like the last match in the box.

The Allens' wing overlooks a kitchen garden, the well in one corner and a henhouse in the other. A hatch against the main wall that I guess must lead into a cellar. 'You'll help yourself to eggs, mind?' Tom insists. 'Nora will do us some lunch later.' He nods in the direction of the back door. 'Just come on through at two o'clock.'

There are several garden rooms beyond the kitchen plot: a paved terrace at the front of the house, followed by a rose garden, water garden and statue garden. A crusty potting shed. A vast greenhouse plump with glossy tomatoes and massive, knobbled cucumbers. And still, there's more. Tom leads me up a set of uneven steps to the west lawn, a level rectangle that must be perfect for games. As if to confirm this, a weathered blue summer house is stacked full of ancient-looking croquet hoops, tennis racquets and folding chairs. But the grass is too long for anything of the sort at the moment, growing over my ankles.

A walled orchard separates the games lawn from the main road: a swarm of stately trees, twisted and knotted, heavy with the apples and pears and quinces of the season. There are already windfalls clogging the grass underfoot. The sweet, heady smell of decaying fruit. Finally, right at the end of the grounds, Tom leads me to a sizeable lake and boathouse. 'How big did you say your last place was?' he asks, dabbing his neck with a hanky. It's warming up now the late summer sun has climbed a way in the sky.

I try to remember what I'd put in my application letter, if I'd even mentioned it. Another strange oversight from Reacher not to have verified my references, but then I wouldn't be here if he'd thought to. 'A bit smaller than this,' I say in the end.

Tom's eyes have drifted to a nearby coot, bobbing its head up and down in the water as it looks for food. 'It's a lot, mind,' he says, 'but Lady Lascy doesn't want anything fancy doing with it.' He rummages in his pockets, pulls out a bit of bread crust.

'It was all Bruce could do to keep up with the watering, these past months.'

It's been an endlessly dry, hot summer, with record-breaking low rainfall. The entirety of Britain has been stinking to high heaven.

'He'd been here for donkey's years,' Tom goes on, 'but his rheumatism's too much for it now. He's moved in with his sister down the village. Nice woman. Bit of a drinker, though.' He chucks the bread out with an under-arm throw, so it plops down a few feet from the hungry bird. 'I'm sure he wouldn't mind having a talk, if you've got any questions. It's the white cottage by the church.'

'I'll look out for it,' I say, though I doubt I'll be making social calls round the village any time soon. I'm here to get away from the judgement of others, not to invite any more of it.

Lunch is in the Allens' quarters. Two o'clock – Lady Lascy keeps late hours, and so must we. My stomach's growling loud enough to wake the dead by the time my pocket watch has ticked its way around. I don't know how the Allens put up with it. I scrub the dirt from my face and hands, run a brush through my hair. I've only been doing a spot of light weeding this morning, but I already look a sight.

The back entrance has its own little porch and a knocker that looks – again – like a jumping rabbit or hare. I'm starting to think someone round here has a fondness for the creatures. When I come closer, I find the door's been left open a crack, propped with a stopper. From inside, I catch the faint sound of singing – a woman's voice, breathy and high. After a line or so, I recognize the hymn as 'All Things Bright and Beautiful'.

I peer inside, nudging the door. 'Hello?' I call. 'Tom?'

I'm met with a flurry of barking, followed by a large, grey blur. A dog hurls itself at me, forepaws ramming into my chest so it's all I can do to keep my footing. Hot, meaty breath in my face. Tongue flopping out. I shove its snout away.

The singing cuts off. 'Mutton! Get back here, boy!' The woman has the same countryside accent as Tom.

The dog plops back on to four legs, but otherwise ignores the order. He's a massive thing, above waist height. Scruffy face with a downward muzzle and big blob of a nose. Two alert brown eyes. His legs are strangely spindly, greyhound-ish, holding up a broad, muscular body. Oversized paws. Stubby tail wagging – at least that means *he* thinks he's being friendly.

'That the gardener?' calls the woman. She must be Mr Allen's wife. Nora, I think he said.

I snatch my fingers out of licking range, seeing as I've just washed them. 'Yes.'

'Mind you clean your boots.'

I obligingly knock them a bit on the scraper, then step in. The corridor is white-washed, lined with coat pegs and a shoe rack on one side. A stark drop in temperature where thick walls have kept the heat at bay. The dog pushes past me, skittering through to where I assume Mrs Allen can be found. I follow.

A dim kitchen, lamps not lit at this time of day. There's a rectangular wooden table, sturdy and functional, and wooden sideboards too. Cupboards, a deep basin of a sink, an enamel oven in front of which the dog has flopped down. Mrs Allen is stirring a pot on the stovetop, but turns when I enter. Like her husband, she's a sturdy build, with greying curls and soft, droopy cheeks. Blue flowers patterning her dress under a grease-specked wrap-around apron.

'Afternoon – Mrs Allen? I'm . . .' I gesture back out the door, in the direction of the cottage. 'Miss Morgan. Vee.'

Mrs Allen nods to the table, where three places are already set out. 'Won't be a minute.' Doesn't invite me to call her Nora in return. Well, I can't charm everyone right away . . . As soon as I sit, Mutton is up again, pressing his head into my lap.

'Watch your food with him, he's a greedy sod.' Mrs Allen has her eyes on the kitchen clock. Although nothing in particular has passed between us, I sense that she doesn't want me here; a stiffness in her shoulders. There's none of the warmth that her husband has offered. She goes back to stirring, ignoring me. The dog, on the other hand, won't let me alone, but I'm quite happy to ruffle his ears. His wide, glistening eyes have a certain appeal. He's got a powerful aroma to him, though.

'Is Tom not joining us?' I ask, after a while.

'He's just bringing her Ladyship her lunch.' She jerks her head in the direction of a set of service bells on the wall – a reminder of our mutual employer. 'She likes to have it sliced up for her first. He'll be back in a tick.' A saucepan lid chugs out steam in a clack-clack echo. Mrs Allen lifts it to let a cloud escape, then places it back. I wonder at the detail about Tom slicing up the food. Whether there's a reason Lady Lascy can't do it herself, or if it's simply the level of service she expects from her staff. 'Does she eat alone, then?' I ask.

'She doesn't have much choice.' Mrs Allen wipes her hands on a rag, then hangs it over the oven rail. 'She won't have anyone else inside the house these days. Just us and Mr Reacher. That's her cousin.' I hadn't realized the estate manager was a relative of Lady Lascy. Another silence. Mrs Allen doesn't resume her singing. A shame – it wasn't bad. I'm about to ask how long she's worked here at Harfold – just to stave off the boredom – when a door closes somewhere beyond. Heavy footsteps. A few seconds later, Tom comes in through a side entrance. He still has his work clothes on: flannel shirt and braces. Must have waited table in them. I can't picture it, Tom placing food down daintily in front of a lady. Can't picture yet who this lady must be.

Mrs Allen serves up. Joint of pork, small potatoes, broad beans and a celeriac mash. A little ale, malty on the tongue. The food is under-seasoned, all texture boiled out of it. Not a patch on Mam's cooking.

Now that Tom's here, the conversation is easier, picks up a natural flow. He acts as conductor, pulling me into an account of the morning's work, then summoning Mrs Allen to help deliver an anecdote about the cows up the road. It's possible Mrs Allen's earlier chilliness wasn't personal after all – with Tom for a husband, maybe she doesn't need much social skill. You get that with couples sometimes. Mam and Dad are a bit like that: Mam's a chatter, Dad's a touch more introspective. Though that might be from what happened during the war. Anyone would come back quieter after that.

'So what brung you here from Cardiff, Vee?' Tom asks. 'No gardens out that way?'

I give a slight shrug of the shoulders. 'I just needed a change.' The Allens are waiting for me to elaborate, rattle off the usual lines about the grime of city living, wanting to spend time out in nature. I impale a particularly firm bean with my fork. 'When you've been in the same place your whole life, it can feel a bit small, can't it?'

All those whispers. The people who thought they knew me, thought they knew everything about my story. The turned heads when I walked into the grocer's. The little boy who spat on my shoe that time.

Tom winks at his wife. 'That's not me, is it, Nora? I was born in the Prescotts' place up the village and I've stayed here ever since. Oh, I could never leave.'

Mrs Allen sets her cutlery down with a light clatter. 'It's a long way to come, though,' she says, not satisfied with my answer. 'Do you not have family back at home?'

'My mam and dad moved away.'

'But you must have other relations?' she presses. 'Or friends, at least?'

I try for a winning smile. 'I'm sure I'll make some new ones.'

Mrs Allen sniffs. 'There's not much in the way of social life out here.'

There wasn't for me in Cardiff, either, in the end. I've been staying with a couple of pals the past year: Gladys and Lou, the only ones who stuck with me. A camp bed on their kitchen floor, that cold in winter I'd had to sleep with my coat on. Clatter of train tracks out the window. Smell of cooking fat. Mice bold as anything – too clever for the traps, but I could never bring myself to poison them, hated to think of their little bodies in spasms, froth at the mouth. I'd been forever throwing slippers at the bloody things. Not that it was fair for me to complain. Lou and Gladys never said anything, but I knew what they were risking, taking me in. Two women living together like the pair of them, it only worked as long as nobody was looking too carefully, and people haven't been able to look away from me this past year. I'd known when it was time to move on.

Mains finished, Mrs Allen dollops out four helpings of a gooseberry fool. Sets one of them aside under a cheese cloth. Hands the others round. Passes Tom the sugar bowl so he can deposit four heaped spoonfuls over his serving. For my part, I relish the tart burst of flavour after a rather bland meal.

Tom is telling a story about Reacher, how he's exploring investments in the capital. 'You'll see him come by soon enough, I'm sure. He's hard to miss.' He raises his eyebrows, inviting me into a confidence. 'A committed bachelor, if you catch my meaning. But I expect you'd know all about that sort of thing?' His expression is casually blank. I must have misheard. I know that other people can read me as a *committed spinster* myself – I walk only the finest line of plausible deniability, after all – but this older man from a little farming village isn't the type I'd expect to state it outright. And in such a neutral tone . . . A strained silence stretches out, then Tom's expression is suddenly swept with embarrassment, and he stammers, 'Being from the city, I meant. I imagine there's all sorts there.'

Now it's my turn to look embarrassed. 'Right you are.' But it's too late to shake off the misunderstanding.

'I've always liked Mr Reacher,' says Tom, in some kind of olive branch. 'It's never bothered me that he's . . .'

The strained silence is back. Mrs Allen clatters the spoon noisily in her pudding bowl. Mutton, as if sensing a change in our mood, thuds his tail on the floor tiles.

Sudden shrilling. One of the servants' bells has gone off, its brass mouth still trembling with the memory of the noise. Tom and Mrs Allen both stand at the same time, a wordless conversation passing back and forth between them.

'I'll go,' says Mrs Allen, plucking up the last portion of fool.

She half turns to me with a sharp nod. 'See you tomorrow, Miss Morgan.'

I rise from my chair too. 'I shouldn't come and introduce myself, should I?'

Panic flickers in Mrs Allen's eyes, but then disappears again so quickly I can't be sure I didn't make it up. 'Oh no,' she says, 'her Ladyship won't want that.'

'She doesn't want to meet me, then? Check me over?' Can't help but press the point – I'm curious about her now. Want to see for myself what kind of person lives in this grand old house all by herself.

'I told you earlier,' says Mrs Allen, 'Lady Lascy is very particular.' She closes the side door firmly behind her.

As I head back across the east lawn, I feel the bulk of the manor at my back – a single window lighted on the ground floor, even in the middle of the day. A creeping, prickling itch as if I'm being watched. I glance over my shoulder. Can't spot anyone. But even as I enter my cottage, shutting the door tight behind me, that call bell continues to echo like a voice in my ears.

TWO

THE LANE SUCKS at my boots, as if the manor grounds don't want me to leave. Strange when it's been so dry of late. But then the track is on a sunken level, and – now that there's light to see by – its steep banks are revealed to me, covered in nettles and grass. The trees are just tripping into their first autumn colours: soon there'll be leaves on the ground in great drifts to clear up. That irresistible crackle underfoot.

Movement up ahead of me. Pace slowing, I turn my head to look up at the path. It's becoming steep now, the banks and boughs overhead crowding in so that it's more like a tunnel, leading up to a circle of golden morning light at the summit. And there, in the centre of the circle . . . I relax. It's just the Allens' dog again.

'Hello there, Mutton,' I call out.

His legs and underbelly are matted with sludge, as if he's been wading through deep muddy water. Must have been in the lake.

'You coming with me?' I ask him, and he seems to understand, as he plods over to my side. In spite of his mighty smell and his rude way of introducing himself the other day, I have to admit he's got a certain charisma.

Mutton and I walk as far as the red post box up on the main road. I'm sending two letters, reporting back on my time at

Harfold so far – one each to Mam and Dad. Separate addresses. Tom offered to post them for me, but I'd rather do it myself.

He's been telling me a little about the area: Salisbury Plain. It's an ancient chalk plateau – you can see as much in the soil, the pale tracks over the fields. I'll have a devil of a time keeping the gardens fertilized and watered. Apparently the War Office owns a fair deal of the land round here – they used it to prepare troops for the Front during the Great War. While I can't say I'd heard of Salisbury before, I have heard of Stonehenge, which is a near neighbour to Harfold. I'll have to make sure to take a trip to see it. Send Mam and Dad a couple of postcards next: *look where your daughter is now.*

Letters deposited, it's well past time to tackle the yews, which are supposed to be my focus of the morning. I survey the hedges as I come back toward the house. There are twelve in total, bordering the driveway in symmetrical pairs. The first five sets are small – around four feet high each – and were once geometric shapes, from what I can make out. Easy to put right.

'Get away then, Muttsy,' I tell the dog. 'You can't be running around under foot, now.' At my shooing motions, he slinks off, ears down and stubby tail no longer wagging. Glances back at me with mournful eyes, slivers of white like crescent moons showing at the edges. 'Sorry, boy, but the last thing I need is you knocking me from a ladder.'

Starting with the smaller hedges, I set at the task with my shears, snipping back the new growth to resurrect neat spheres, cuboids, pyramids. The work lulls me into a trance: the shush of falling, feathery cuttings; the overwhelming green in every direction. I love this. Up and close to nature, shaping it with my hands. It makes me feel peaceful. Powerful.

I first discovered this rush as a child, helping Dad sow cabbage seeds in our little garden in Butetown. Then the war came and, with Dad gone away, it was suddenly my job to keep it all alive. I found I had a knack for it. Dreamed of a vast garden of my own. Maybe even studying at a horticultural college, sitting my RHS General Exam. But in the meantime, I still needed serious employment, so I started work in a laundry as a receiver, then progressed on to sorter, and finally the coveted rank of hand ironer. It was boring, repetitive labour, cooped up indoors with powder constantly clogging my airways when I wanted nothing more than to be out in the sunshine. I knew that I lacked something essential in common with the other girls, though I couldn't put my finger on what it was back then.

And that was my life up until March 1917, when I saw the posters for the Land Army round town. That illustration of a young woman wearing overalls. Like a boy, but not. I'd stared at it so long that Mam had asked me what was wrong. But I still couldn't name it – I only knew there was a sudden knot in my stomach, a feeling that the picture had been somehow pinned up just for me. The opposite of how I felt around those other laundry girls. The next day, I'd gone straight down the employment exchange and asked to be put in the agriculture section. They were looking for women over twenty and I'd just turned seventeen, but I'd fibbed about my age to get in, just as all those bright-eyed boys at school had done three years earlier. And suddenly I was the one in overalls, working with a gang to plough, pick stones, cut hay.

That's how I'd first met Gladys and then Lou, both of them assigned to the same farm as me. Gladys, with her sculpted curls and a full face of make-up that they were forever making her wash off. Completely unsuited to the job. Still, she always had a cigarette to share, a cheerful tune to sing. It turned out she didn't live far from us in Tiger Bay – her father was a Jamaican docker. By contrast, Lou was a proper workhorse, capable of hefting twice what the rest of us could manage; she'd grown up on a farm in the Valleys. She wore her hair shorter than I'd ever seen on a woman before, and had a way of swaggering about that I immediately envied. The three of us were fast friends within weeks. I hadn't realized till then how alone I'd been.

The sun hovers high overhead like a bird of prey. Even with my shirtsleeves pushed back, it's too bloody hot. Sweat's running into my eyes as I work, and I have to keep reminding myself not to wipe it away with my bare fingers, covered in sap as they are. The yew is an extremely poisonous plant.

Dad didn't spend the war fighting overseas. A life-long pacifist and professed socialist, he was against the conflict from the start. So he joined the No-Conscription Fellowship. Was denied exemption. Refused his orders anyway. Ended up – as did most so-called 'Absolutists' – in prison. He never talked afterward about what happened to him in there, but he came out with a permanent squint as a souvenir.

They released him at the end of the summer in 1919, and after a while he found a position as a gardener out toward Penarth. Talked his new employers into taking on Mam as a cook as well. The Land Army had been disbanded, so I was on to odd-jobbing myself, not able to face another stint in the laundry, and I often went along to lend Dad a hand. Sometimes, if his eyes were playing up, I'd take over for him as I used to do at home, and eventually I was offered a formal role as undergardener. The family – the Reeses – were fond of me. I think it amused them to see a girl grubbing around in the dirt; Mr

Reese would stand at the window and watch me from time to time, shaking his head as if it was the funniest sight. That sort of thing did get on my nerves, but a job was a job, and they even entrusted me with spare keys to the store-shed after a time. This fact hadn't worked out in my favour, in the end.

At seven feet, the pair of hedges closest to Harfold Manor are taller than the rest, and I'll have to use the steps to get their tops. It's anyone's guess what shape these ones used to be. I take them in from a distance, visualizing my different options. Remember Tom's invitation to be as artistic as I like. For whatever reason, this thought leads me back to all the rabbit decorations I've spotted about the place. Rabbits . . . Yes, why not?

I turn my shears on them, hacking out two conical bodies, two pointed noses, four tall, upward-reaching ears. I've done them to face each other across the driveway, like they're in silent conversation. *What delicious carrots we've had lately.*

As I gather up the discarded cuttings, I think I see a quick movement out of the corner of my eye, from the direction of the big house. The upper floor. A curtain falling back into place. I pause for a moment, not sure if I'm being watched. Then, thinking *why not*, give a wave.

By the evening, I've moved on to netting weeds out of the ornamental pond in the water garden. Mutton's back once more, frolicking in and out of the central fountain, casting rainbows of droplets every time he shakes his head.

Behind me, the manor house. I'm acutely aware of every window. *Just stop thinking about it*, I tell myself. It doesn't matter if my mysterious new employer is looking; there's nothing for her to see.

But with a void of information, I can't help but speculate. Just *who* is Lady Lascy? Some kind of recluse, evidently. My imagination cobbles together a timid, mousy little woman – the kind of person who reads from a prayer book every night and is prone to nervous faints.

A crunch of footsteps on the paved terrace. Moments later, a man appears around the corner. He has a round face with puffy eyes, over-magnified by a pair of thick-lensed spectacles. Floppy, hennaed hair. A pair of binoculars hanging about his neck. In his mid-thirties, if I had to guess. He's wearing a linen suit in a slightly pinkish hue. Mam would probably call him vulgar.

'Hiyo,' he says when he spots me, with a finger-waggling sort of half-wave. He shows all his top teeth when he speaks. If his clothes hadn't given him away as a member of the upper classes, his booming, southern, boarding-school accent does the trick.

'Evening, sir.' I put my net to one side, to be polite.

'Now, let me see,' says the man, looking me up and down. 'Either you are a very under-prepared poacher, or you're the new gardener.'

'Got it in one, sir,' I say. Wipe a hand on my overalls before extending it. 'Vee Morgan.'

'Maurice Reacher.'

I've already guessed as much. We shake hands, his grip soft and slightly moist.

'I am *so* pleased to have you here with us. You can't imagine the struggle we've had to fill the role. One reads such complaints in the news about unemployment, and yet it seems that, when it comes to it, nobody actually wants to *work*.' His words are cheery enough, but a deeper complaint lurks beneath them.

'I reckon it's probably the location, sir,' I offer.

He nods, as if considering this. A little surprised to be talked back to, perhaps. Seems to respect it. 'You think? Yes, I suppose everyone does want to move to the city these days. God knows why. I'm pleased enough to stay there sporadically, but to *live* there? With all those *people* around you?' He scoffs, theatrical.

'You do get tired of them all.'

Left out of the conversation, Mutton comes nuzzling up to me, snout slick with pond scum.

'What?' asks Reacher. 'Oh yes, Cardiff, wasn't it?' He comes closer to pat Mutton on the rump. 'Wonderful.'

'No one local wanted the job, then?' I wonder aloud.

A frown at this. 'The village rabble? No, they're all hopeless. Now, *Wales*. Magnificent part of the country.' The abrupt change in subject has an artificial ring, as if Reacher's making an effort to sidestep the topic of the villagers. 'And what a beautiful language, so lyrical.'

'Diolch,' I say, hamming it up for his amusement. I don't actually speak much Welsh. Just the King's English – as His Majesty likes it.

'I took a holiday to the Black Mountains several years ago,' Reacher goes on, 'where I was fortunate enough to spot a glorious pair of red kites.' He pats the binoculars around his neck in demonstration. 'Do you have any interest in birds, Miss Morgan?'

This isn't a question I've ever given particular thought to. 'I like them well enough.'

'Good stuff. We see some excellent specimens around these parts: stone-curlew, corn bunting, hobby, quail, nightingales. You must keep your eyes open for them.'

After I've agreed that I will, Reacher goes on to ask me a number of questions about my plans for the garden, my thoughts on this and that. To begin with, I assume he's testing my knowledge as a new employee, but after ten minutes, I suspect he's just the sort who likes to have a natter. Despite all his bluster, he's rather charming. Funny. A bit naughty. I'll have to accept the fact that he won't be letting me get back to the pond work any time soon.

'And I see you've been busy with the yews,' he goes on. 'Were the hares your idea?'

I grimace at this. 'They were meant to be rabbits.'

'Ah well, easily confused. I assumed hares because we're so close to the Plain.' My expression must reflect my confusion, as he adds after a moment, 'You've heard of the Salisbury Hare?'

I have not. Shake my head.

'It's a local folk tale,' says Reacher, 'tangentially connected to the history of Harfold. Supposedly there is a magic hare that lives on Salisbury Plain. If one sees it dance under the full moon, one will enjoy good fortune for the rest of one's days – although it only shows itself to the good and innocent of heart, naturally.' Heavy sarcasm in his tone. 'It appeared to a distant Lascy ancestor, so the story goes. I thought you were trying to put a pagan blessing on the land.'

It's too late to admit that I'm not sure of the difference between a hare and a rabbit. I shrug. 'Not on purpose, at least.'

Reacher hums in consideration. 'Let's say they are hares. Bellsy will be delighted.'

'Bellsy?' I'm sure I've heard him right, but the word is nonsense to me.

'Lady Lascy. The old girl has a thing about the hare story. She's very superstitious. We probably shouldn't encourage her, but it's good for her to have something to keep the mind active.'

I could swear that Tom had mentioned being a child in the lifetime of Lady Lascy's father, but here Reacher is talking as if his cousin is geriatric herself. 'How old exactly is her Ladyship, if you don't mind my asking?'

Reacher squawks out a laugh. 'Four years older than me, and *that's* what's important.' He maintains a cheerful smile, suggesting this is all said in good nature. An established joke that he's inviting me into.

I prod at the pile of drying pond weed I've left on the side, hoping to encourage any stray creatures to scurry free. 'What's she like, then?' I ask, nice and casual, as if I haven't been wondering this for days now. 'Besides superstitious, I mean.'

He laughs again. 'Oh, she's a menace.'

I'm not sure how to slot this information into my existing, mousy portrait. A dark brown water spider takes the opportunity to flee, racing panicked back to the safety of the pond. 'I've never met a Lady,' I say, pulling my hand out of the spider's route – I've learned from past experience that these ones can bite.

'Lucky you,' says Reacher, his tone dry.

Obviously I've run into the upper classes before, but never anyone with a title. The Reeses were new money, made from the mines. And the rich children I'd known as a child, the ones whose nannies came with them to the park, would only have been middle class. Still, they felt a world away back then. I remember once I was out playing with some boys from my street – I must have been about ten – and I was wearing this old cardigan of Dad's because it was chilly that day. I can still picture it clearly: a brown, stripy thing with an orange trim that I was always stealing off him. I was tall for my age, so it just about fitted, and I liked feeling as if Dad was keeping me company. His Pears soap and moustache-wax smell clinging about the fabric. Anyway, there I was, minding my own business, when this little snub-nosed boy, who was always trotting past with his nanny around that time of day, began to giggle. I had no idea what he found so funny, until the servant tugged his arm and hissed, 'You mustn't laugh; she can't help it if her mammy doesn't have any money for a coat.'

Well, I was absolutely fuming at that! I'd never thought I was poor before – just normal. After that, I'd gone home crying to Mam at the injustice, only to find that she was having none of it. 'There's no use snivelling,' she'd told me, 'that's just the way it is. Some people get dealt the better hand. But look here, it's about what you do with your cards.' She was a regular bridge player in those days – not a heavy gambler, like, but it was a little fun to be had with the other mams on the street. 'If you're clever enough,' she went on, 'you can still win the game.'

I spent that evening thinking on Mam's words, and the next day I went back to that park and searched round until I found a heap of stinking fox shit. Using a twig, I scooped up a dollop, and then I hid in the bushes near where the boy normally came on his walk. Sure enough, after a while he appeared on the path with that hateful nanny of his. I waited until the very moment they had passed me by, then I leapt out and swung the twig in an arc so that it sent the muck splattering all over their backs. I didn't wait to see what happened next, just turned and ran, but behind me I could still hear the nanny's high, horrified scream followed by the boy's wailing sobs. They were pure music to my ears.

Anyway, here I am, still wearing Dad's clothes – or his straw hat, at least – and working for a Lady. So that just goes to show where that fox-shit nanny can stick it.

Reacher comes over now to peer at the pond, as if checking my work. 'And how are you finding it all? I hope the Allens have been treating you well?'

I think of Mrs Allen, sour-faced at the lunch table each day. The sense that she wants nothing more than for me to disappear. I wonder if there's any connection between her attitude and whatever it is that Reacher doesn't want to discuss about Harfold village. The tense meal always ends with that sharp ring of the servants' bell. The Allens hurrying to answer. Each time it happens, I picture the lady at the other end, her delicate spindle-finger pushing the brass button. Her touch racing along the web of hidden wires that vein the manor. The sound of the clapper tonguing the bell.

But what the women of the house lack in friendliness, Tom more than makes up for – he's an easy-going, solid type. Seems to have recovered from our little awkwardness at lunch that first day, and he's generally happy now to chat away without asking me too many questions about myself. Just how I prefer it. He's one of those people who can make a story out of anything; he had me listening to a long yarn about woodpeckers for almost half an hour the other day – and I was having a great time of it, too.

'Tom's been wonderful,' I say, tactful.

'He's a good man. Cracking worker.' Reacher nods at his own reflection. 'Speaking of which, I had better let you get back to it. Coming, Mutton?'

The traitor dog follows after him.

*

By the time I'm done for the day, it's nearly dark, twilight pushing up from the garden's fragrant shadows. Tools put away, I take a pail to the well for my evening's water. I'm surprised the Lascys have never had it plumbed in, but Tom says that it's not odd for countryside estates to lack modern luxuries: the gentry are resistant to change, even when that change would be an improvement.

My path back to the cottage takes me past the chickens, to which I whisper a goodnight, and around the side of the manor house, past the vacant panes of ground-floor windows. One of them is lit.

Now, I'm not a nosy woman. As long as people leave me to mind my own business, I'll return the favour. But the mystery of Lady Lascy has been eating me up. I simply have to know what she's like, this secretive aristocrat who has everyone jumping to carry out her orders. So, I reason to myself, there's no harm in taking just a little look to see if she's in there. A glance, really. You can hardly help it if you're walking past.

Placing my bucket down gently on the path, I step up to the glowing glass. A set of heavy, purple-red curtains have been drawn on the other side, obscuring most of the interior, but they don't quite meet at the centre, leaving a narrow band running vertically from top to bottom. If I press my face close and shut one eye, I can snatch a glimpse of—

A throat being cleared.

I jump back, heart smacking in my chest. Turn to see Mrs Allen. She stands beyond the radius of illumination, her face unreadable. Looming like a horrid angel of judgement.

'I – I was just . . .' Unable to think of a good excuse, I let the lie peter out. 'I didn't see anything,' I say instead, which is the truth – more's the pity. The impression of firelight and soft textures. Just shapes and shadows, no time to identify them as anything in particular.

'And what was it you were expecting to see?' asks Mrs Allen.

'Nothing,' I say. Pause. 'Lady Lascy, I suppose.'

Mrs Allen takes a step closer, causing me to move back a pace without really thinking about it. 'Your job is to do the gardens, Miss Morgan,' she says. 'You've got no business inside the main house, nor with her Ladyship neither.' Her tone's severe, but also commanding, as if she's used to people doing as she says.

'I only meant . . .' I swallow, try again, firmer. 'I have a right to know who I'm working for.'

'If you want to get along at Harfold, I'd advise you not to go poking about in other people's affairs,' Mrs Allen says, as if I haven't spoken.

'Right,' I agree. Take another pace further away, aware of the sanctuary of my cottage out there in the night behind me. 'Look, no harm done, and it won't happen again.'

'You should leave.'

I don't know what it is about the way Mrs Allen says this, but I'm sure for a moment that she isn't simply referring to this window, right now: she means that I should leave Harfold itself. The words reach right into my inner organs and squeeze. My feet stop beneath me until I make a conscious effort to move them again. 'I'm going,' I tell her.

She points to the ground. 'You forgot your pail.'

The bucket of water. Of course. I dart back to pick it up under her steel gaze, sloshing half the contents down my legs as I do so. Retreat fast as I can down the drive.

When I finally reach the cottage, my pulse slows at last.

God, that woman's a fright. I've been nothing but lovely to her and here she is, treating me like the dirt on her boot. It's not a crime to peep into a window. At least, I don't think it is . . . But I should watch out for her, all the same. I don't want any trouble.

As I open the front door, a pale flash on the side table catches my eye, reflecting the very last of the day's light. An envelope. Not posted under the door: someone has been inside, propped it up where I'll see it. The intrusion pricks at the back of my neck. I set the bucket of water down by the door, then pick up the letter and carry it through to the sitting area. When I light the main lamp, I see that it's addressed to 'The new gardener' in a calligraphic hand, bold and spidered. Taking out the paper knife, I slice open the seal. A rough scrap of fabric inside. A needlepoint picture. It's done in coloured threads, blocky but distinctive, the same style as the cushions upstairs. This one is of a woman in overalls and a straw hat.

I drop the cloth as if stung.

It's an image of me.

I pick it up again, note the slouch of the shoulders, the wide-legged stance with hands in pockets. It's not just a superficial likeness – this is *exactly* how I stand. An uncanny skin-crawl. Somebody has been watching me. Closely.

Not Tom; he'll hardly be one for needlework. Someone in the fields, then. Unless . . . I remember the twitching curtain at the upstairs window of the manor. Could this be a gift from *her*? Lady Lascy, watching as I walked up and down the lawn all day. Skewering me under a needle. Then, as I lurked about to try to catch a glimpse of her, she was darting out to let herself into the gardener's cottage, to leave the picture for me to find.

I look in the envelope again to see if there's any note. Blank, but for the brown foxing stains in one corner, as if this is a scrap of old paper that's been lying around for years before being put to use. What's the artist's intention here? Am I meant to feel welcomed? Flattered? Intimidated? Or merely confused, as I am now? *A menace*, Reacher had said.

    I run a thumb over the bumped stitches. Imagine the movement of the needle. A lady's refined fingers touching where I now touch. I lift the cloth to my nose and inhale. Dust and mildew. What is *she* doing at this moment, I wonder. Has she seen me return to the cottage? Does she assume I've opened the envelope – and, if so, how has she envisioned my reaction? How close did her imaginings get to the reality of it? Maybe we are thinking of each other at this exact moment. That gives me a strange thrill. Almost erotic, but no, more like the moment a prey animal realizes that it's being hunted.

    I wonder if Mrs Allen will tell her what I was doing just now. I'm not sure if I hope that she does, or doesn't.

    Out of the window, this side of the manor has all gone dark. Lady Lascy is in there somewhere, but no matter how long I stare, all I see is my own self reflected in little panes of glass. Oval face, thin nose, eyes a little too far apart. And Lady Lascy remains a mystery.

    With a sharp tug, I draw the curtains shut.

THREE

'NEED ANY HELP with that?'

Tom looks up at the sound of my voice, head swivelling round till he locates me leaning on the orchard gate. He's been in with the fruit trees all morning, picking up the last of the windfall apples and chucking them into a wheelbarrow. They've made quite the heap – a glorious tumble of reds, golds and greens. Tom's now seated before them on a three-legged milking stool, pawing over his spoils and variously throwing them into one of a trio of large tin tubs.

'Well, if you like.' He nods me over. 'Always happy for the company.'

'What're you doing, then?' I ask.

Tom bumps the nearest bucket with his foot. 'Freshest ones for eating,' he says. Bumps the next. 'Manky ones for juicing.' Then the third. 'Rotten ones for the compost.'

'Got it.' I squat down, waving away a sudden spate of charity in Tom that makes him offer me the stool. Take an apple from the barrow. Not too bad. I put it in the 'eating' tub. 'What do you do with the ones for juicing?'

'I've got a cider press in the shed,' says Tom. 'I'll show you later, if you like? It's a bit of fun.'

'Go on, then.' Working like this with Tom reminds me of my Land Army days: the easy companionship that springs from shared labour. He's less to look at than those girls, though! 'And what about the ones for eating? Good fresh, are they?'

'More for cooking,' says Tom. 'Nora does a lovely crumble.'

Mrs Allen hasn't brought up my spying since she caught me last week, and I'm not sure if she's mentioned it to Tom, though I think most likely not. Still, I have a suspicion I haven't heard the last of it from her. 'Can I ask you a question, Tom?'

Squelch of an apple landing in the compost tub. 'Whenever you like.'

'Have I done something to upset Mrs Allen?'

He looks confused by this, a furrow appearing on his suntanned brow. 'I can't see how you would have.'

I flick a wasp away from where it's investigating my hands. 'I get the sense she isn't that pleased to have me here, is all.'

'Nora? Nah.' Tom shakes his head. 'Tell you what, if it's anything, it's that she just weren't keen on having another live-in – she wanted someone daily from down the village. Mr Reacher and her had a bit of a disagreement over it. But fact is, nobody from the village wants anything to do with us anyway.'

Reacher had also said no one wanted the job. But if that was the case, there'd be no reason for Mrs Allen to hold it against *me*. I can't help thinking there's more to the story. 'Why's that, then?' I ask.

Tom scratches his chin with one thumb. There's a little scab from where he's nicked himself shaving. 'Now, I'm not one for gossip' – *not* the impression I've got from him so far – 'but let's just say that them lot in the village haven't always seen eye-to-eye with the Lascys. I told you about his Lordship – Henry Lascy, that is – selling off all that land. Most of it went to this chap called Gerrish, who rents it back to them at an increased cost – and even the farmers who had enough to buy their own patch off Lord Lascy outright are struggling now, what with everything.' I know the headlines: plunging post-war land value, food prices pushed down by import, repeat foot-and-mouth epidemics wiping out the livestock. 'Folks don't forget, and they blame the Lascys for it, like his Lordship knew what was coming when he sold up.' Tom shakes his head to show he doesn't buy into this himself. 'But it's not fair to hold that against Lady Lascy, either way, especially after all her hardships.'

'Hardships?' I ask, setting aside another apple for the compost. So many of them already gone to rot.

'She's had a bad run of it,' sighs Tom, expression solemn, but a twinkle in his eye to say he was hoping I'd ask. 'Her poor parents passed back in 1911 – an unfortunate accident in the lake – and since then, Lady Lascy's also lost all four brothers. A tragic waste, it really is.'

The manor house seems even larger for a moment: all those people missing from its rooms. 'That can't have been easy for her,' I say. I haven't told Tom about the strange needlepoint. There's a faint impulse to keep it private, as though it's a secret I share with my reclusive new employer. 'What were they like, her family?' I ask instead.

'I've been here for thirty-odd years, and they've always been good to me. I had some of my own family trouble a while back, you see. My brother . . . He passed away. Wife and three kiddies left behind.'

I mumble a noise in sympathy.

Tom shakes his head. 'It was a hard time for us all, but the Lascys were the first to offer their help – his Lordship paid for the funeral. Even gave me a bit of extra money to put aside for the young 'uns.'

'And her Ladyship?'

'Oh, she's been very decent to me, too. Still had my job for me after the war, and not all the men who came back could say the same.' He pauses to flick a small spider from his sleeve. 'I owe them a lot, I really do.'

Once all the apples are sorted, Tom goes to fetch the press out of the shed. We start off with me quartering the apples and Tom mulching them. He's produced yet more buckets to place under the press spout, gathering the juice as it overflows. Then we swap over, Tom showing me how to work the machine. It takes more force than it looks: I have to turn the crank round and round against increasing resistance as the apple flesh compresses, and the whole contraption is rickety with age and prone to losing its balance if shoved too forcefully. But the hard work is rewarded quickly with the froth and dribble of juice. A cloudy, deep amber-brown liquid, filled with swirling murk.

'We'll strain that right out,' says Tom. 'Bit of cheese cloth. No problem.' We've both worked up a sweat, hair clinging damp to our foreheads. Tom pats himself over for a hanky. 'Ah, that reminds me.' Pulls a small, silver picture frame from one of his pockets. He must have fetched it when he was off looking for the press. 'Thought you might like to see this, as you were asking.'

I wipe my pulp-covered hands on the grass before reaching out to take it. A photographic portrait of a family posed in a garden. After a moment, I recognize the location as the west lawn here at Harfold, the lake and boathouse in the background. There's a pompous-looking man in a suit and tie, seated at the centre. Bareheaded, squinting as if in bright light. Large gut and a face that melts into beard. A woman sits beside him, one hand touching his elbow. She wears a light summer dress, high-necked with long, lace sleeves, and a floral sun hat. Pearls at her throat. She seems to be smiling, but trying not to, as if the formality of Victorian portraits is still on her mind. Standing around this couple are six younger people, ages spanning from childhood to early adulthood. To the left are four larger boys – men, really. One has almost succeeded in growing a thin moustache. Then, to the right-hand side, another boy – definitely the proper word this time – around twelve or so. He has the gangly, awkward look that comes after a growth spurt and before bulking out. Thick eye-glasses. A young Maurice Reacher, I realize. Then finally, standing a little distance from him as if she doesn't appreciate the placement, a girl. Perhaps fifteen or sixteen. Her hair is dark, worn up in an adult woman's pompadour, and she sports a raffish necktie. Though she's barely more than a child, her self-possession sings clear from the print.

'That's her, is it?'

Tom nods. 'And there's Rex, Harry, Stephen and Charlie. And Mr Reacher, of course.'

But my attention stays caught on the girl – the same person, maybe, as the one who stitched my portrait, who sneaked into my cottage. It's only when Tom clears his throat that I see he has his hand out to take back the frame. I have been too busy staring at her face to notice.

At the north of Harfold's grounds, the stretch of woodland leading up to the main road fans out on either side of the driveway, spanning as far as the orchard wall to the west and the river to the east. This acreage is largely Tom's to look after, but a shaded footpath from the statue garden leads to a little clearing with a wildlife pond, which it's my job to oversee. Unlike its tidy counterpart in the water garden, this pond is rugged and full of character.

Leaving behind the apple juicing, I head up here to cut back and divide the plants from the water's edges: yellow flags, marsh marigold, golden sedge, water mint and reedmace. The day's cooler here under the thick leaf cover. A dragonfly drifts past my face. A calm spot.

I start piling the cleared foliage by a wide-trunked beech, the fat roots creating a convenient hollow to hold it. I put a hand briefly to the tree's smooth, silvery bark. The leaves above are turning toward their autumn russet. As I scan my eyes up, I catch on an irregularity – letters carved into the wood. Not much more than crude scratches, really. They're above head-height, just where a low branch butts out – the person who put them there must have climbed up to do it. If I stand on one of the more burly roots and go up on tiptoe, I can just about read them: RLHLSLCLAL. It takes a moment for me to read beyond the nonsense sequence and realize these are initials: Rex Lascy, Harry Lascy, Stephen Lascy, Charlie Lascy. And AL – that must be *her*. It only strikes me now that I don't know her Christian name. Reacher had called her something odd. Childish. Bellsy, that was it. Short for Annabel, perhaps? As if summoned by my thoughts, there's a crackle further up the path, followed by the sudden materialization of Mutton. He hares up to me, pushing his head into my stomach until I scratch his ears.

Seconds later, Reacher comes into view. Stops short when he sees me. 'Ah, hello again.' Despite wearing a hat, he's caught the sun on his face, cheeks glowing red with it. Again today, he has a pair of binoculars hanging round his neck. 'Always at a pondside, aren't you? Say, you're not secretly a water nymph?'

'I could ask the same of you, sir,' I say, jumping down from the beech root and batting away the dog.

Reacher puts a hand under his chin, as if posing for a portrait. 'Narcissus, more like!'

Mutton, not offended by my rebuff, skips away to the pond's edge. A startled vole leaps into the water to escape. Mutton whines after it, and Reacher just has time to say, 'Don't you dare!' before the dog is in with an almighty splash.

'Oh, blast,' says Reacher, 'Mrs Allen will have my bollocks.' He raises his voice to call after the dog, 'And she would have yours, too, if they weren't already gone!' He shares a grimace with me. 'If you aren't scared of her, you should be.'

I *think* this is a joke. 'He does belong to the Allens, then?' I ask, still unclear on this point. 'Not Lady Lascy?'

Reacher pauses, cocks his head. 'You know, I can't remember. He just lives here. We all love you, don't we, Mutts?'

Mutton rises out of the water at last, rivulets running down his flanks. The scene brings to mind folk stories of the Ceffyl Dŵr.

'Even Arabella likes him,' Reacher adds. 'And she doesn't really like anything.'

Not Annabel, then. *Arabella.* I turn it over silently in my mouth, the press of incisors to lower lip, the flick of tongue.

'What were you doing up there?' asks Reacher, nodding over at the tree.

'Oh, just having a read. Those initials up there – the Lascy children, aren't they?'

Reacher prowls closer to see. 'Looks like it. I'll bet that was Charlie who put them there. He was a real rough-and-tumble boy, always in trouble. He and Bellsy were thick as two nasty little thieves. They were the youngest, you see. Rex, the eldest, liked to think he was in charge – he was a natural despot – but he had no authority over them. Stephen was more of a stickler for rules, very boring. Nose-in-a-book sort of lad. Harry was my favourite. He had a quiet sensibility, but not in a dull way like Stephen – it was more that he was thoughtful. Much kinder than Arabella and Charlie.' He stops talking to take a tin from his pocket – silver, fronted with an enamel picture of a heavily built bird with feathery tufts around its beak. Tilts it for me to see. 'Great bustard,' he says.

'Excuse me?'

'These fellows used to live all over the country, until farmland destroyed their habitats and any stragglers were hunted out of existence. Bewick's *History of British Birds* has them down as 'excellent eating', so I don't suppose they ever stood much chance. Salisbury Plain was their last noble stronghold. I have a stuffed one, back in the manor – I'll have to show you sometime.' He opens the tin and taps out a cigarette. Offers one to me, which I accept. Lights them for us.

We stand for a while, puffing away and looking out over the pond. Mutton digs in the pile of discarded plants. The vole comes creeping bravely back out of the water. A swallow swoops down to take a mid-flight drink.

'Why birds?' I ask.

Reacher blows out a dart of smoke, watching the swallow continue on its way. 'I lost my mother when I was twelve, and came here to live at Harfold year-round.'

An unexpectedly morose turn in the conversation. 'I'm sorry to hear that,' I say.

He flicks a hand, batting off the sympathy. 'Rex and Harry were already up at Oxford by then, and my other cousins weren't exactly my friends. I was too timid to speak to the village children either, and so I was left to myself a great deal with time to fill. At first, the birding was just an excuse for wandering about the countryside alone, but I soon found a real love for it: they're magnificent creatures, endlessly fascinating to watch. It also allowed me to broaden my circle, connecting with all sorts of people around the world who share the same passion – I suppose it is as much about the community as it is about the birds, these days.'

It's hard to imagine Reacher as a shy, lonely little boy, given what a friendly face he's put on so far.

'Well,' he says, throwing down his cigarette end and stamping on it, 'I had better get on my way. Care to walk with me a little?'

I've finished at the pond edge; all that's left for the day is to cart the cuttings over to the bonfire heap, and I can come back and do that later. 'All right,' I say, stubbing out my own cigarette. 'Lead on.'

Reacher plunges further into the woods, pausing on occasion to swap his spectacles for the binoculars, or to point out a nest. We're following a path that leads eventually back to the main drive, where we have to pick our way carefully down the steep banks to reach the road. The gatehouse is visible not far ahead.

As we draw level with a collection of boulders that rest at the side of the track, Reacher pauses, nodding his head at them. 'This is where Charlie . . .' A small noise in the back of his throat. 'It was a riding accident. A terrible misfortune.'

Tom had mentioned that they haven't kept horses in a couple of years. He hadn't told me why.

'It was such a shock,' Reacher goes on. 'He was always a strong rider, and the horse was normally as docile as anything. They'd been out for a trot and were on the way back home. We think she must have seen something to spook her, knocked him off. He hit his head and . . .' Reacher's eyes linger on one of the rocks, the surface blunt and unforgiving. Then, with a shake of the head, his expression clears. 'Sorry, I don't mean to depress your spirits. Dead birds, dead boys . . . It's this place.' He sweeps his arms around to indicate the entire estate. 'It is simply brimming with bad memories. Still, it's the family seat: one has to love it, even so.'

We continue up the drive, leaving the boulders behind us. Charlie's final moments. He would have been so close to home. Could probably even see Harfold, from up there on the horse. The manor staring back at him, unfeeling, as he lost his saddle.

I can't sleep tonight. The mice are louder than ever, skittering to and fro, to and fro. I swear the ones in Lou and Gladys's house were never this active. Find myself missing that camp bed on the kitchen floor. To think, I spent the whole time I was there wishing I could be back with Mam and Dad in Butetown – yet here I am now, looking at it with nostalgia. The memory plays tricks.

In the dark, I keep seeing flashes of those faces in Tom's photograph. The Lascy family. Rex, Harry, Stephen, Charlie. Something macabre about it, the way they've been preserved right ahead of all that misfortune. Like when you hear of a dreadful accident happening nearby, and realize you'd been there only hours before. You were *just* speaking to them.

I admit defeat, heading downstairs for a slice of bread and butter by candlelight. As I chew, I pick up the fabric scrap that

Lady Lascy left for me. *Arabella*. I've kept it out on the side all this time. Keep returning to it under some compulsion.

I know I can be vain. There's a certain message I want to convey to the world, and that's what most strikes me about this picture – the artist has captured it, even in the simple needlepoint style. She's seen me in the way that I want to be seen.

I shouldn't let myself get too involved in all of Harfold's little quirks, I tell myself. Should put both myself and my curiosity to bed. But there's still a restlessness in my chest, tight and trembling. A good walk to clear my thoughts, that's what I need. I shrug on a coat, lace up my work boots. Recalling Tom's warning about the roads, back when we first met, I wrap a white scarf round my neck as a signal to motorists.

I've got my electric torch with me, but soon find I don't need it: the full moon is bright and close. Big, countryside stars. The garden's wrapped in a silver shawl of light. Maybe I'll see Reacher's magic hare, I joke to myself.

My plan is to take a loop, starting up the main road into Harfold village, then coming back over the fields. I hurry past the rocks that Reacher pointed out to me earlier, my instincts telling me not to linger. Up on the road, I see no motorists tonight, nor any hapless dead animals. An owl swoops ghost-pale overhead. I don't think I've ever seen one in the wild. The road passes a sleeping farm, the manure and milk odour of the sheds familiar in a comforting way. Me and the other Land Army girls used to hide in with the cattle for our smoke breaks when the weather was bad. I caught Lou and Gladys in there once, too. *Not* smoking. Those cows heard and saw a lot of things . . .

It's about a quarter-hour to walk into the village proper, its cottages mostly dark and the main street empty at this time. A handful of men out the front of the pub when I pass it. The sign shows a rabbity creature on its hind legs, reaching with forepaws up to a circle moon. Below it in gold lettering: *The Dancing Hare*. The Lascy legend clearly reaches beyond the manor grounds. A number of eyes track me in silent curiosity as the drinkers finish their last round. A single woman stands with the men, guarding a pram that she rocks to and fro with her free hand. Nowhere near as lively as the pubs in Cardiff.

Next I pass St Anselm's church, a Gothic-looking building with narrow windows and elaborate stone carvings up the walls. A lone clock tower is topped with decorative battlements. After this, I come to a village green, and a little further up is the white house that Tom told me to look out for – home to my predecessor – looming like a chalk cliff at sea. How did Bruce find it, tending to the manor's grounds? Must be strange now, knowing that another person has taken his place, is reshaping the gardens that he'd dedicated years of his life to. I wonder if Mrs Allen was more pleasant to him than she is to me. Or if Lady Lascy ever stitched his picture. Something in me hopes that she didn't. Then I remember I'm not letting myself get caught up in all that.

When I reach the end of the village, I veer on to the fields, hopping a ramshackle hedgerow and following the rise of the hill up, back home, dodging cowpats as I go. I turn my torch on again – don't need to twist an ankle on the uneven ground – and confused insects dart in and out of the beam. The flash of a white stripe as a badger shambles past. Lou used to swear that a badger once bit her nephew's hand clean off, but I don't think that can be true. Still, I give the creature a wide berth. Just in case.

A way ahead, I spot a glimmer of light, twin to my own torch. I don't think this one's electric – it skims the ground as if held low, like you would a lantern. Must be one of the villagers. Well, that's no bother to me, so long as they keep themself to themself, I think. But as my route progresses, I notice this person seems to be headed the same way. Up to the manor.

Perhaps Tom or Mrs Allen, come back from calling on a neighbour? But either of them would have taken Mutton on such an outing, and I don't spot him bounding about anywhere. Can't make out much in the way of detail from where I am – the artificial lights have reduced my night vision. Everything else is impenetrable shadow. If not the Allens, then who? Reacher, out looking for nocturnal birds? Or could it be an intruder? Someone creeping about in the dark. I'm sure there's plenty of value to take from the manor, if a person was so minded, and it's not like Lady Lascy employs a heavy guard. I turn off my torch. Again, just in case.

I've drawn a sight closer by now, my stride faster than the other walker's. As my eyes readjust, I see it's a woman – or at least someone wearing a skirt. I'm not one to comment. She keeps halting every so often, lifting her lantern to look about, beam sweeping lighthouse-like over the waves of grass, as if she's seeking something out. Then – apparently not finding it – she moves on. Several more yards. Another pause to search. I can't spy anything remarkable myself, but then maybe that's the problem.

Finally, the other person reaches the stream at the Harfold property boundary. After one last look behind, she crosses at the footbridge into the woods with an easy confidence. Which is when I realize who she is. I know it suddenly, deep in my chest, as if part of me already recognizes *her*.

I'm hurrying now to close the distance. She's already disappeared into the trees on the other side, but her lantern still glints between trunks. I follow over the bridge, almost slipping as I go. It's little more than a slimy plank really, a wooden railing for support along one side, the other open to the river below. On the opposite bank, I plunge into the vegetation. Branches reach out to touch my face, snatch at my scarf. Cobwebs tear before me. *She* must be able to hear my rustling pursuit at this point. I haven't thought ahead to what I'll say when I catch up.

Finally, I break out of the woods, joining the driveway at the gatehouse. She's still ahead of me, halfway up the path to the main house, passing through the recently cut yews that keep sentry. No longer stopping to look around.

I half raise a hand. 'Hello!' My voice is louder than I'd intended in the thick silence of night.

Lady Lascy doesn't react. But surely she's heard me, surely she must have seen me following behind. Determination flares in my chest. I *will* speak to her.

'Wait!' I shout, increasing my pace. I reach the first of the yews. Lady Lascy is between the final two, the hares. 'I want to talk to you!'

She pauses. Twists back to look directly at me. Her face, lit by the lantern below, appears ghoulish, eye sockets in deep shadow. And then she smiles, like a wolf baring its teeth. I'm suddenly rooted to the spot. My own breathing in my ears, ragged after my hurry to catch up. Pulse throbbing at my throat.

After a few heartbeats, Lady Lascy turns again, flitting up the steps to the manor's front door and slipping inside. Disappearing like the last fragments of a dream.

I get there only seconds later. Consider hammering on the

wood – but no, that will wake the Allens. I press myself to the door to listen. '*Please*,' I say, hoping my words will carry inside. 'I just want to know why you sent that picture. I have a right to ask!' Losing my temper, forgetting I'm speaking to the person who pays my wages.

Silence. I'm just about to give up when I swear I hear a noise from within. A laugh. High and musical, like the peal of a bell.

PART TWO

ARABELLA, 1920

3 March 1920

WE'VE JUST HAD the most horrific news at breakfast: Stephen has died. One of the other doctors wrote to tell us, though Charlie and I had to wait for Morry to come over to translate the French. You'd think they could at least have had the decency to find someone with a little English to compose the letter.

Apparently they had an outbreak of the Spanish flu three weeks ago, and it carried Stephen off with it. Where is the bloody sense in that! That he would survive through the entire war in those squalid field hospitals under the Krauts' fire, only to be taken out by the patients for whom he had stayed behind.

No: I do not think it can be as simple as bad luck. I have been thinking it ever since Harry's death: there is a pattern to this all. One every three years. Always in the early months. All leading back to that night . . . Charlie will not allow it. 'You should know by now that death is senseless, Bellsy,' he said to me this morning. 'I understand that you want to find meaning to it, but I promise you there is none.'

'What if there is?' I had to ask. What if we are to blame for this? He didn't believe me when Harry died, but look now! Charlie and I should never have done what we did, and it has come back as a curse upon us.

'You need to pull yourself together. Stephen is—' His voice choked, so that he had to try again. 'We have just lost our brother, and all you can do is worry for yourself. I wish you would let the past rest, put down those morbid hare pictures you are so fond of sewing, and join me back here in the real world. This is not what Stephen or anyone else would have wanted for you.'

I was desperate to find a way to make him see. 'But Charlie, what if what happened to them was all our fault?'

He refused to hear another word, just slammed his teacup down so hard it cracked the saucer, then went raging off to some other part of the house. He can't face the idea that we are being made to pay for our wicked actions, but Morry and I are fully agreed on the matter, at least. We cannot ignore the truth any longer: we must be ready for what is still to come.

'Charlie will reconsider in his own time,' was Morry's advice, 'and never forget that I am here for you as well, Bellsy. We must look out for each other, you and I.'

VEE, 1925

FOUR

A KNOCK ON my door. It's first thing in the morning and I'm eating breakfast, only part dressed. Groggy from my restless night, though it feels half like a dream: seeing Lady Lascy out there in the fields, chasing her up the path like a wild animal, shouting through the door. I took it much too far.

It's Mrs Allen on the front step, scowling like a gargoyle. 'Morning, Miss Morgan.' Mutton's with her, and she has to hold firm on his collar to keep him in place. 'Her Ladyship has asked for you to come up to the main house.'

'I see.' That's it, then: I'm being dismissed. The breeze works its way under my pyjamas, as if autumn has replaced late summer overnight. Mrs Allen appears to be waiting for something. 'What, right away?'

'Of course.'

'All right. I'll come with you now, in a minute. I just need to . . .' Gesturing down at my housecoat.

With Mrs Allen waiting outside, I hurry to dress. Painfully put on the nice skirt, the shoes, neither really recovered from my encounter with the muddy lane that night I first arrived.

When I emerge, Mrs Allen looks me up and down but doesn't comment, just strides off in the direction of the manor. Ignores the path to cut a straight line over the lawn. I follow behind, batting Mutton away from my stockings. He's got no clue how much these things cost.

A flash from last night as we reach the front steps. Me, demanding answers. That taunting laugh in reply.

Mrs Allen opens the door. There's an inverted horseshoe above the lintel, a folk protection from bad luck. Although I've been obsessing these past weeks over what Lady Lascy is like, I hesitate now.

'I don't have all day,' says Mrs Allen, one hand flapping in impatience.

We enter into a hall. A massive, echoing space, open right up to the second storey. A gloriously decorated dome overhead – although, now I think of it, it must be a trick painted on to the ceiling, as I didn't see a dome from the outside. Despite the room's gigantic proportions, it's so crammed with all sorts of objects that I can hardly squeeze in. It looks less like a grand hall and more like some kind of antique dealer's, or an auction house showroom. Glass cases and cabinets full of bric-a-brac. A grandfather clock, running two and a half hours late by my count. A long, low wooden cabinet almost blocking the statement staircase, its surface adorned with polished copper, candlesticks, vases of dried flowers, glassware, china, even a stuffed monkey, its face twisted in a permanent grimace. A flock of chairs, none of them matching in style but all sharing the same shabby, worn upholstery. Their seats are over-burdened with needlepoint cushions, furs draped across their arms and backs. Footstools, lamps, wicker baskets of more dried flowers. The shell of an unlucky tortoise. On the floor, a large Persian rug – a worrying dark stain at one corner, pushed half under the cabinet in an attempt to conceal it. A towering stack of empty wooden pallets in one corner. Garlands of ribbon and glass beads draped up the staircase banisters, and what look like newspapers piled all up the steps. Walls caked in frames so densely arranged that it's almost impossible to look at one long enough to make out the picture. A luxurious chandelier, its chain far too long so that it drips down to eye level. Dust and cobwebs in the corners, on the surfaces, under the chairs, hanging alongside the chandelier. Why hasn't Mrs Allen kept it clean? And this is just the entrance . . .

'She's in the morning room,' says Mrs Allen, as if I know the layout of the house already. Luckily, the instruction's accompanied by a pointing finger. Door to the right, almost hidden by a folding screen. 'Straight through that one, then you'll see it.'

I nod and pick my way through the maze of obstacles, trying to ignore the crunching noises underfoot from scattered rubbish. I place my hand on the doorknob. It's ivory or bone, yellowed with age and handling. Turn it slowly.

'Miss Morgan—' I turn back at Mrs Allen's voice. Her expression has a strange twist to it, as if she can't quite remember what she was about to say. 'Watch how you go, now.'

Puzzling out what exactly this signals, I step through into the next room. I'd thought Mrs Allen meant this was the morning room, but I see at once that it's not. A dining room: big mahogany table and chairs. At one end, two seats have place settings and silver out as if in preparation for a dinner party, with fine patterned china on display. The rest of the surface is lost to a heap of fabric scraps, all different cloths, patterns and colours, from plain cottons to elaborate printed silks. Scattered candelabras on the table bear mismatched candles, and in places globs of wax have dripped down on to the textiles, soldering them together. Yet more picture frames teem on the walls. Needlepoint samplers fill some of these as well. All around the table, more random items are stacked haphazard: hat boxes, a broken spinning wheel, a knee-high wooden hippo. Multiple doors lead out to other parts of the house, so Mrs Allen must mean for me to pass through, as if this were a corridor. I skirt carefully round the table and chairs, wary of getting tangled up. When I accidentally touch one of the fabric scraps, it's damp under my palm. I fight back the urge to retch.

Not sure where I'm going, I try the first exit I come to. A wood-panelled chamber on the other side, stale with the smell of old tobacco. Nobody in here either. There are rusted swords and spears and guns mounted on the walls. Horrid. On to the next door, and this one gives me a tingle, right here behind my navel. I can almost sense that Lady Lascy is in the room beyond. Is waiting for me. Has maybe even heard my footsteps as I approached. I place a palm against the white-painted wood of the door as if feeling for vibrations. This is the last moment of not knowing. After this, all of my speculations will be answered one way or another. A sadness in my chest at the thought, like a gentle bereavement.

But that's not what's important here, because I'm about to get my marching orders. Don't know what I'll do next. Can't go back to Cardiff. There's a cool, icy resolve in my chest to stay calm, not to submit to the degradation of begging for my job. The humiliation of watching Dad plead with the Reeses to keep him on is still fresh. Their indifferent expressions, as if his years of hard work meant nothing to them. I'd wanted more than anything to slap them across their unfeeling faces. No: I'll keep my head and my dignity. I open the door. Very bright – the flickering glow of oil and candlelight. The day outside is overcast, and the hall and dining room have been in relative gloom, so the contrast when I step into the morning room is dazzling, and this is all I can register at first. Then shapes begin to form and I realize there are multiple light sources: wall sconces, floor lamps, open-flamed candles blazing away. Every textile surface seems to have some kind of design stitched into it, as if the artist can't bear to have a scrap of clear fabric in sight. And so many different objects and patterns, so many oddities and luxuries and reflective surfaces, that I can barely locate the woman I've come to visit.

I feel more than see the eyes that are watching me. And then I find them there, amid it all. A faded gunmetal blue. Sharp face. High cheekbones. Pointed arch to the eyebrows and thin, flat lips that tilt up at the corners as if in a private joke. Flecks of silver on a head of wavy, chestnut hair – this worn unfashionably long, like an old woman, though she must be in her thirties. Without the ghoulish effect of the lantern light from last night, she could be called attractive. It's clear that this is the girl from the photograph. Arabella Lascy, two decades on. She's sitting on a low settee, legs crossed at the ankle and tucked beneath. An elbow is propped on the armrest, so as to support her chin in one hand. The immediate air is of assessment, deep consideration.

Well, I'm evaluating her right back. Too much jewellery for this time of day, sitting alone at home: pearls round her neck and in her earlobes, gold bangles, glittering rings – three to a finger, not necessarily complementing one another. A frothy gown, more suited to a party. She can't have put this all on just for my benefit . . . Can she? I've never seen anyone this dressed up in my life.

The silence stretches to an unbearable weight. Well, I think, if I'm going to lose my job anyway, I may as well speak my mind. 'Look here, I'm not going to apologize for last night, if that's why you've called me in. I may be your employee, but that doesn't give you the right to spy on me, or to come into my private quarters without my knowledge. It's a violation, that's what it is, and . . .'

I trail off, because Lady Lascy has started to laugh once more. Those thin lips stretch wide over broad, white teeth. Her shoulders heave with it.

'Have I said something amusing?' I'm determined not to lose my temper again.

Lady Lascy shakes her head, helpless. 'Oh, I am sorry. It's just – Welsh! I had forgotten!' Wipes an eye with the palm of her hand. 'You will have to forgive me.' Flutters her fingers. 'It's not often I speak to anyone new.' A full smile this time, stretching to the corners of her eyes. 'I was curious to see if you were what I expected. Up close, I mean.'

An uncertain moment of silence. 'Well . . . here I am,' I say, stepping further into the room. This space is a little clearer than the previous two, making it easier to move around.

'Here you are.' She gazes at me with unabashed interest, her eyes glittering. Not at all the mousy woman I'd first imagined.

The way she's looking at me gives me more confidence. 'So am I what you expected?'

'I'm not sure yet.' Her voice, like Reacher's, is all round vowels and over-pronounced consonants.

I jut my chin. 'Good, cos I'm not sure about you either.'

Lady Lascy twists one of her rings, meditative. Not offended by my bold tone, but meeting it with the calculating look of a card player who sees what her opponent is doing with that ace and plans to intercept it. 'Would you like a drink? I believe I have some whisky.'

'It's eight o'clock in the morning.'

'Is it really?' Tone doubtful, as if I might be lying. 'Tea, then.' She points behind me, and I turn to look. Don't see what's being indicated until Lady Lascy says, 'The bell there by the door. Would you ring it for me, please?'

I wonder again if she has an ailment, a condition that keeps her in the house. But then, she'd been walking about last night without trouble, so it seemed. Is she now too weak to stand, or simply too entitled to do it for herself? I wonder if this command is some kind of test.

Still, I do as she asks, crossing to the call button and giving it a press. Somewhere in the Allens' quarters, the bell marked 'morning room' must be ringing away. Lady Lascy's instructions from my hand.

When I turn back, the woman is *still* watching me. *Enough of this malarkey*, I think. 'Will you just tell me plain: are you giving me the sack, or not?'

'Not. It was enough trouble to hire you in the first place.'

A tension I hadn't even known I'd been holding melts out of my limbs. I move a little closer again. 'It *was* you who did that picture of me, wasn't it?'

'I often stitch things that I see out of the window. Whatever catches my eye. Things I find interesting.' She suddenly smiles again, as if to reassure me this is meant as a compliment. 'Just like the Lady of Shalott. *The curse is come upon me.* Do you enjoy Tennyson?'

We did 'The Charge of the Light Brigade' in school, but I don't say this. The conversation keeps veering away from what I'm expecting. 'My Lady . . .'

'Why don't you call me Arabella. Tom and Nora both do.'

I don't know that I believe her. I've only ever heard the Allens use a formal address – behind her back, at least. I press on: 'I still don't understand why you *sent* me the picture, in that case.'

Lady Lascy – Arabella – holds my gaze. 'Maybe I wanted to see what you would do.'

A rattle at the door, then Mrs Allen comes in with a tea-tray. Thin bone china, green motif like abstracted ivy. Tarnished silver spoons and sugar tongs. A plate of biscuits, garish yellow. They've been cut neatly into tiny squares, each one just a mouthful in size. It's unclear if Arabella requested this all in advance, or if Mrs Allen simply knows her well enough to predict whatever request is about to arise.

As Mrs Allen walks over to us, she keeps glancing at me, as if nervous. Perhaps worried that I haven't been behaving myself. 'Hold this.' She shoves the tray at me, and I take it by reflex. Mrs Allen moves a side table right up next to Arabella, clearing its ornaments away in a practised sweep so that I can set the tray down. Pours out the tea.

'These are my favourites,' says Arabella, pointing to the biscuit pieces. Catches my curious expression. 'I only eat in small bites these days. I had a nightmare once about choking to death on my food. One can't be too careful.'

After Mrs Allen has retreated, with one last, lingering stare cast in my direction, we're in silence again. I examine a cabinet, the objects arranged on it. Three little china pigs, a framed photograph that I recognize as Arabella's mother, a silver snuff box, a dead wasp.

'We have an Epstein bust somewhere in here,' says Arabella, waving over her shoulder without turning. 'My second brother, Harry.'

Epstein . . . I may have heard the name before, but I'm not sure. Following Arabella's direction, I walk round behind the settee to look, and yes, there it is beneath a discarded shawl, a young man's face set in bronze. A squarish jaw and full, fishy lips. Could be any one of the four from the photograph. The house must be filled with relics of all these dead brothers. Dead parents, too. Doesn't Arabella find it morbid? 'It's a good likeness,' I say. Then, realizing I have no reason to know this, add, 'Tom showed me a picture of you all, posed in the garden.'

'Oh yes,' says Arabella. 'I think I know the one. I was quite the thing back then, wasn't I? Time is so cruel . . .'

'Go on, you aren't so bad now,' I say, before remembering again that I'm speaking to my boss. Keep forgetting it. Her attitude is too informal, as if we're on the same level. 'I mean to say, you've aged well. And you're not exactly old anyway, are you?'

'Hmm,' says Arabella. She sounds amused. 'It's kind of you to say so.'

I clear my throat. She keeps steering the conversation away from the subject of me and my employment. 'Your family must have been here a long time,' I try, following her lead as I return to claim my tea. Sit on the sofa opposite Arabella's. Immediately regret it when I hear rustling beneath me, some small animal shifting around under the seat. A footstool to my side is decorated with yet another needlepoint hare, the same as the furnishings in my cottage.

Arabella takes a biscuit. 'We built the house, you know. In 1709 – James Lascy, the second Viscount. But of course we can trace the family further than that – on Daddy's side at least, as far as the Norman Conquest. We lose Mummy's side sooner, around the Tudor era.' She gives a casual shrug, but her eyes dart to my face, as if wanting to be sure she's impressed me.

'That's a shame.'

'I must show you the family genealogy one day. We have it on a wall upstairs. The room is normally closed up, though, so I will have to get Nora to ferret out the key first. I don't mean today – I am not . . . quite up to it. But you must come back to take a look; it really is most interesting.'

Sipping my tea, I wonder how it must feel to be so anchored to your ancestry. To see the roots of your family tree dug into the soil like this, the country house bold evidence of an innate belonging. I assume my own family are Cardiff-born a fair way back, but we dwindle into obscurity after a couple of generations. I don't even know the Christian names of my great-grandparents, let alone some chap from the 1700s.

'Of course, the grounds were much more extensive, back in their era,' Arabella goes on. 'And the house in better shape, I'm sure. It is simply impossible to run a country estate these days . . . In any case, I look forward to seeing what you can do with our depleted gardens. Maybe you could plant more hedges along the east boundary.'

I'm relieved to be back on comfortable ground, but this strikes me as a strange request: the east garden has the best outlook over the fields down to Harfold village. 'Wouldn't that block the view?' I ask.

'Exactly. I cannot abide that church tower – so ugly.' She touches one hand swiftly to her neck, as if she has just felt something there, then frowns. There are biscuit crumbs scattered over her breast. 'Well . . .' A long pause. 'I *am* glad we've met.'

It's clear this is a dismissal. I set my cup back on the tray, before standing. Half expect Arabella to stand too and wish me goodbye, but she doesn't. 'Thank you for the tea.'

'I hope I shall see you again soon. Tinkle the bell again on your way out.'

Going back through the dining room, I meet Mrs Allen, who is forced to reverse into the hall so that I can get through. 'On your way?' she asks.

I nod.

Her eyes flit over my face. 'And how did you find her Ladyship?'

'She was all right,' I say. Hesitate. If I don't ask now, I'll never be able to. 'Well, I don't want to pry, but . . . What exactly is it that's wrong with her?'

'Nothing's wrong.' The reply comes sharp and quick.

'I thought . . . She hardly leaves the house, does she? And the way everything's . . I thought she must be ill.'

Mrs Allen shakes her head. 'No, she's perfectly healthy. Just a bit peculiar.'

'But,' I say, in a last feeble protest, 'she didn't stand up at all . . .'

Strangely, Mrs Allen lets out a snort at this. 'No, I expect she didn't. That old dress has a great big tear up the back, and she won't let me mend it for her. She was probably worried about showing you her arse!'

This doesn't strike me as funny, though. I'm touched with a surge of pity for Arabella, in her sham finery. Trying so hard to impress me – just an employee, after all – without letting on that she's doing it. Desperate to talk about the past. She must be very lonely. Maybe this is what Mrs Allen has been trying to hide from me until now, feeling ashamed on behalf of her dilapidated employer, not trusting me as an outsider to keep her secrets. But if that's the case, why tell me about the dress?

'Mrs Allen,' I try again, 'if you don't mind my saying, I've had the sense that you don't particularly want me here. If it's not about Lady Lascy's health, then have I done something to offend you?'

She seems surprised by this, although it's unclear whether it's because of what I've said, or the fact that I've said it. Her chin twitches. 'No,' she says at last. Pauses to think. 'If you must know, I don't like to see someone new getting sucked in.'

It's not the answer I was expecting. 'Sucked in?'

'To Harfold, I mean. Especially someone so young – and live-in, as well.' She shakes her head. 'It's not a happy place, this.'

That makes a kind of sense. The tragic history of the Lascy family must weigh heavy on everyone who knew them, not just Arabella. 'Well, thank you for your concern,' I say, 'but I think I'll be all right.'

Mrs Allen gives a smile that doesn't quite reach her eyes. 'Of course.'

I can tell this isn't the end of it. And the blaze of my curiosity has only been fanned brighter after meeting my strange employer.

Now that I can put a face to the name, I no longer get those goosebumps when I sense Arabella's gaze through the blank windows of Harfold Manor. Sometimes I stare back, seeking her out. I find myself charmed now by her awkward interest in me. The tentative wave she'll give out of the window if I spot her, the way she will call down from time to time with a question about my work. *Do you have enough compost to be getting on with? When do you think those dahlias will go over? Does that type of spade have a special name?* It's clear she has no real care for the answers – these questions are just an excuse to start a conversation. Eager to impress with a story about the expense of such-and-such statue, the history behind a remarkable architectural feature. It's all strangely endearing. And it's not like I have a whole queue of other people waiting to speak to me.

A couple of weeks after our first meeting, Arabella remembers her invitation to show me the Lascy family genealogy. 'Nora found this at last. I don't know *what* she had done with it,' she says, dangling a key from her little finger. She's standing in the front doorway, having just waved me over from across the lawn.

I wonder if Mrs Allen had lost the key in the chaos of the house, or whether she was intentionally withholding it in an attempt to keep me out of things. Either way, she isn't around now to observe us: she and Tom will be down at the Sunday church service. Of course, I'm also on a half-day, but I don't have plans for my free afternoon, so I think *may as well* and knock my muddy boots on the doorstep, before following Arabella into the entry hall.

'We're this way.' Arabella leads me up the main staircase. Her dress today is a bright yellow velvet, over which she's layered several shawls with various beads, frills and fringes. The result is a strange, top-heavy silhouette. No shoes or stockings on her feet. As I follow, I have to tread carefully around the teetering stacks of newspapers that appear to live permanently on the steps. Some seem fresh; others are faded, caked in cobwebs and dry mouse shit.

At the top, we reach a wooden walk that encircles the entire upper half of the open hall. Arabella taps a framed watercolour painting of the Dover cliffs as we pass it, the shading done in pretty pinks and blues. 'My brother's work – Harry.' There are entryways leading off the left- and right-hand sides of the walkway, further corridors branching away. Arabella turns left. 'We don't use this wing any more,' she tells me. The passageway we enter is curiously empty of clutter. More dust and cobwebs. Very dark – at the far end, the lone window is shuttered, so only thin bars of light creep through. 'You'll have to forgive the mess,' Arabella remarks. I can't tell if this is meant as a joke, or if the irony has passed her by entirely. 'I never come this way these days.'

'Why's that, then?'

Halting in front of one of the doors, Arabella struggles in the half-light to slip the key into the lock. 'It's just so expensive to keep up, and too much work for poor Nora. She used to have three maids under her before the war, did you know? It seems frivolous when it's only me – and Morry on the odd occasion. Ah, here we are.' The crunch of protesting metal.

This room is as plain as the corridor: just a bed and some bulky item of furniture, shrouded under white fabric. Bare boards on the floor. It's as if we've stepped into a completely different house. There's only one wall hanging – the promised family tree.

Arabella wrests open the shutters, letting in a slap of daylight. Her face is touched suddenly with gold. She's quite handsome from certain angles. 'This was my parents' room,' she says. 'Mummy used to let us up into bed with her on a Sunday morning – all five of us children – and we'd loot her breakfast tray like a family of brigands. She always stayed in bed late on a Sunday.' A fondness in her voice, as if she can still see them all tucked up together.

'It must've been nice having so many siblings. I always wanted a brother. Someone to run around and play boys' games with.' I'm not sure why I say this.

Arabella looks over at me, lifting her eyebrows. 'I don't imagine that stopped you.' The tease in her voice is a surprise. It doesn't have any malice to it, though: it's familiar, almost intimate.

I find myself smiling. 'No.'

'My brothers were wonderful. Charlie, in particular. I wish you could have met him. We were the best of friends, Charlie and I.' She crosses to where the genealogy hangs, now illuminated enough to be read. 'I wouldn't have liked a sister, I don't think; I enjoyed the attention of being the only girl. Mummy's little pet.' She taps one finger delicately on the picture frame. 'Here, come and look.'

I move to stand beside her. The writing isn't particularly large, so I have to get close, our shoulders a breath away from brushing.

'Don't be shy,' says Arabella. 'Lean in, do.'

As she promised, the genealogy begins with the Normans – Robert Lascy, born approximately 1042 in Poitiers. A decorative title reads: *The pedigree of the Lascy family of Harfold, 1774.* And indeed, stylistic differences appear from around the late 1700s as later hands have extended it. Subtle variations in tone where names have been added over time – I imagine done by the hired help, rather than the ladyships recorded here. The overall design is simple, not much in the way of illustration save for one of

Harfold's omnipresent hares tucked into a corner – a striking contrast to Arabella's own lavish needlework. Still, the deep green cloth it's made from must have been expensive back then. The lines of connection are picked out in gold thread, names embroidered in white. The flow of blood across all these centuries, all these dead ancestors. Twenty-nine generations. What a weight to have over you. The final one standing of an age-old breed, like the last great bustard of Salisbury Plain.

Arabella points out a handful of the various characters – this one was accused of witchcraft; this one lost his eye in a duel. James, second Viscount Lascy (born 1668 in Canterbury), the man responsible for building Harfold.

'Have you heard the story?' Arabella asks. 'James was riding through the countryside by the light of a full moon when a hare came into his path. He only managed to draw his horse to a halt at the last moment. He expected the small creature to flee in fear, but instead it stood up on its hindlegs and started to dance, circling around him, faster and faster, thumping its feet to a mystical rhythm.' As she describes it, a dreamy delight spreads across her face. 'When James stopped at a local village and shared his tale, he learned that the creature he had encountered was no ordinary hare, but an ancient pagan god of the land. There had been stories of it appearing as far back as the time of the Plantagenets. In showing itself to James, it had honoured him with a blessing of good fortune. He returned to that same spot the following day, and there he placed the first stone in the construction of Harfold Manor.'

I understand now the reason for all the hare iconography about the place. Reacher hadn't made the connection quite so clear in his version of the tale.

Arabella traces a finger from James through the generations until she reaches the bottom of the genealogy, where her own name is stitched. 'And that blessing is meant to have travelled from one owner of Harfold to the next, all the way down to me.' Next to her name, a row of brothers, their lifespans cut short in thread. 'I had to do these dates myself,' she says, indicating her parents and the boys. Was that with the same needles and thread she used to do my portrait? The thought puts a cold feeling in my bones. The open space where Arabella's own date of death will be entered – as if the family tree is holding its breath for it. 'There's Maurice.' Arabella adds. The only child of her mother's sister. 'And nobody after us – not unless Morry has an extremely drastic change of heart.' Not turning her head, she slides her eyes sideways to glance at me. 'I assume you'd guessed that about him?'

I'm smiling again. 'What about you, though?'

Arabella chuckles. 'Am I a homosexual?'

'Oh, I didn't mean—' I start to correct myself in a panicked rush, before realizing she's teasing me once more, and laugh as well. A lightness in my chest at this moment of connection. '*Children*, Arabella! You don't think you'll have any?'

'Look, there isn't much space down here,' says Arabella, indicating the blank area at the base of the genealogy. 'It's as though they knew it would end with me. No . . . it is too late for children.'

'You think so?' Arabella's birth date is listed as 1887, which makes her only thirty-eight years old.

'I haven't the time for it,' she says.

It strikes me as a strange statement from a woman who doesn't actually appear to *do* anything. No work. No travels. No

83

social engagements, apart from Reacher and myself. I'd think Arabella had all the time in the world to fill. Instead, her life is vast and empty – at least it seems that way, looking in from the outside. A yawning loneliness as her family tree has been whittled down and down. Perhaps this is why she feels the need to cover every surface with needlepoint decoration: to fill the gap. And maybe that's what the picture of me was really about, and the invitations into her home. She is trying to make friends. I see my own solitude of the past years mirrored back to me, and my heart goes out to her. It may be that we each have something we can offer to the other.

FIVE

SO LIFE AT Harfold goes on, the year creeping forward. When I first came here, it felt like the long, dry summer would never break, but now the air is increasingly chill, the weather turned grey and wet. I move my attention to all the things that need doing in preparation for the winter months, putting the garden into hibernation. I collect seeds and cuttings for storage, plant in the spring bulbs, sow early kitchen garden vegetables, transport the faded remains of tomato and cucumber plants from the greenhouse to the compost heap – the glorious richness of decay already hanging about them. Next year, they'll nourish the new plants. I love the cycle of it, the repetition. Whatever changes in life, wherever I end up, the patterns of the garden will always be the same. There's a comfort in that. Mrs Allen reveals several recipes for gourds that are no more flavourful than her summertime fare – another thing that doesn't change. A fraction of her chill against me has lifted since I confronted her about it, but we still aren't precisely amicable.

Arabella doesn't invite me into the manor again, but we continue with our chats at the windows. She might show me her latest needlepoint project. Sometimes I'll bring her a sprig of garden blooms. She doesn't seem to leave the house much; that night I followed her over the fields is the only time I've seen her outside.

By contrast, Reacher is always in and out. He joins us at Harfold fairly often, normally staying several nights at a time, a large trunk strapped to the back of his car and a covered cage in the passenger seat beside him. I haven't yet caught a glimpse of whatever feathered friend he keeps in there, but I can sometimes hear it singing down from his open bedroom window, a mournful sort of tune. He spends his days either dashing to mysterious meetings with reams of paper poking out from his briefcase, or dressed more casually for a spot of birding. Always makes a point to stop and share a joke with me, though.

November arrives in a cold snap, and with it, Guy Fawkes Day. 'D'you want to come down to the village with us tonight?' Tom asks, catching me at the well in the morning. 'Me and Nora were going to see the Guy getting burned.' He stamps his feet in the cold. Even from here, his big, shapeless coat smells as if Mutton has been using it as a bed, which – knowing the dog's habits – is likely the case. 'I could do with that bleeding bonfire now, mind you.'

'Maybe,' I reply. 'If you think they won't mind. I don't really know anyone, like.' I'm only realizing now that I haven't spent much time in Harfold village at all, apart from to walk through it a handful of times. I've been so preoccupied with the manor. With Arabella. I should have made more of an effort to meet my new neighbours. Go to the pub, to church. Not to get overly familiar, but enough to establish myself as a trusted figure in the community. 'You know what? Yes, I'd like that.'

'Smashing,' says Tom, punctuating this with another heavy stamp. 'I'll come by and knock later, then. After supper.'

It's been years since I did anything to mark the occasion. I've avoided public gatherings ever since what happened with the Reeses, always afraid someone will recognize me from the papers. And before that, there was the war: the Defence of the Realm Act and its ban on anything that might be used to signal enemy forces. The lighting of fireworks and bonfires was forbidden. There was a short period of grace in between those two events, but even so, I've spent fewer years celebrating than not celebrating over the past decade.

I have the sense that Arabella hasn't had much cause for celebration recently either, so when I spot her through the morning room window later in the day, I step over to the glass, thinking I might invite her along. Pause for a moment to watch her. She has an open notebook in her lap, into which she's scribbling with an ink pen – too far away to see what, but it looks like words. Shoulders hunched, expression completely engrossed. Her hair's loose, so she has to keep tossing it back to keep it from falling over the page, and I find myself smiling at the impracticality of not just tying it up – that's Arabella all over, that is, the same as the torn dress she refuses to let Mrs Allen mend, the food she won't eat until someone else has cut it into pieces. She's so stubborn in her ways, even when the smallest change could make her life that much easier.

When I rap, she jolts up in shock, looking round before her eyes fall on me. The alarm in her face gives way to a relaxed welcome, and she presses the book closed – not pausing to blot – and places it to one side. A green leather binding. Rises to come to the window, pushing up the sash so that we can talk. The ill-maintained wood sticks, squealing, so she has to force it.

'Sorry to bother you—' I start.

'It's no bother at all.' She smiles, releasing the sash and standing back experimentally to see that it stays. When it doesn't immediately come slicing back down, she leans forward over the sill, resting her elbows there. The morning sun plays pale over her face, a silver wash catching the ridge of her upper lip, the fine hairs and the frown lines. She has an ink stain on the right index finger.

I nod down at it. 'What were you writing just now, then?'

'Writing?' She half glances behind her, back to the notebook. 'Oh, that. It's nothing. A diary of sorts. Self-indulgent habit.'

Propping myself with one shoulder against the wall, I raise my eyebrows. 'Would you let me read it?'

A barbed flash in her pupils. 'You must *never* touch it.' The words are fierce and sudden, like an animal lashing out in panic.

'I'm sorry, it was just a joke . . .'

As if catching herself, she laughs. Scowl melts away. 'No, *I* am sorry. How ridiculous of me. It's just that it is personal, isn't it? It was not written for other people to read. It would hardly make sense, I really just write down whatever I am thinking in the moment – no matter how trivial.' She runs her finger absently over a pad of moss that's growing on the windowsill. A woodlouse scuttles away, its nest disturbed. 'It would be dreadfully depressing, anyway: just lots of people dying. There is nothing titillating, I can assure you.'

I shrug. 'Oh well, still plenty of time for that.'

This seems to tickle her, as she laughs again, throwing back her head. A vein shows blue through the exposed skin of her throat.

'Speaking of which . . .' I say, flicking my gaze away from her and out over the lawn to the distant church tower. 'Me and the Allens were going to see the fireworks this evening, if you fancy a trip out? Could be a bit of fun.'

'How thoughtful,' says Arabella. When I turn back to her, she's watching my face. 'But I shall regretfully decline. The village folk will hardly want me there. It would be like having one's parents at a birthday party.'

'I'm sure they wouldn't—'

'Anyway, I don't like to leave the manor grounds these days, if I can help it.' She shifts her position, back straightening. 'I know how this sounds, but it puts a dread in me to go beyond them. I can't bear it.' Her voice has an artificial lightness, as if trying to conceal the depth of this statement.

'What about that time I saw you in the fields?' I ask. A quick flush of heat in my chest as I remember my behaviour on that occasion, chasing her down.

'That was an exception. The full moon . . .' She touches a hand to her mouth, pulling down on the lower lip. Flash of white teeth. 'Would you believe me if I said I was looking for the lucky hare?'

'You mean that folk tale about James Lascy?'

Arabella pulls a scrap of moss off the windowsill, flicking it down to the ground below. 'I know it's just a story, but it was something we did as children — Mummy would take us out on the Plain to look. We did see hares, of course, but never a dancing one. And in recent years, since everything that's . . . Well, I like to keep up the tradition. It helps me to remember them all.'

I picture her again on that night, with her lantern. Her search had seemed so determined, so methodical. It wasn't simply light-hearted reminiscing and, if she really had been looking for the hare, then finding it was much more important to her than she was admitting.

'Well,' says Arabella, breaking the silence, 'you enjoy yourself at the bonfire, Vee. I shall be quite all right up here on my own.'

I eat a quick supper of bread and butter, then prepare myself to go out, putting on a clean set of overalls layered with a woolly cardigan, coat, scarf and hat over the top. There's a frost in the air tonight.

Tom, Mrs Allen and I take the shortcut over the fields, our breaths misting white. Clouds scud across a gibbous moon. It would have been full a few days ago, and I wonder if that means Arabella had been out again, searching for her hare. I can't see the difference – why she could face doing that, but not this.

Mutton bounds about us in ecstasy, not believing his good luck to have a walk with *three* people at once. 'Watch he doesn't eat those sheep turds,' says Tom, without much severity in his voice.

In the direction of the village, I spy the orange glow of the bonfire. Can't help but glance behind me, reflexive, to see the few twinkling lights of Harfold Manor. They're sorry and lifeless in comparison. I feel suddenly sad at the idea of Arabella sitting up all alone – she may have insisted that she doesn't mind, but surely she must feel a twinge of unease at being the only living soul in the house. 'Will she be all right up there?' I wonder out loud. 'Her Ladyship, I mean. I wish she'd have come with us.'

'She wouldn't want to, either way,' says Mrs Allen. Disapproval in her voice, as if she thinks it inappropriate that I'd even suggest it. I hope that Arabella didn't mention my invitation to her.

Tom gives a hunch-shouldered shrug. 'They used to come down, mind, when they was children, with their governess. Remember her, Nora? Miss Yates.'

Mrs Allen makes an opaque noise in response.

'She was a funny one,' Tom goes on. 'Lord Lascy ended up having to fire her since she was overly fond of cocaine tablets. Not that I'm one to judge – I took my fair share of Forced March during the war – but she got silly with it and ended up stealing some brooches to pay for the stuff. Then when his Lordship searched the nursery, he found she'd put a false bottom in one of the cabinets to make a cubby-hole and hidden masses of pill bottles under there. So that wasn't on. What if the children had got into them?'

Well, that's quite the story. I'm not sure what to say in response.

We walk in silence for a bit, then Tom starts up again: 'Anyway, Guy Fawkes Day is for the littluns really, isn't it? Me and George used to get *that* excited about it.'

'Who's that, then?' I ask. Not a name I remember hearing before.

'George? My brother.' The one who'd died. A flicker of sadness on Tom's face, but then he chuckles to himself. 'One year, he was in disgrace for something or other, and Dad said he couldn't go. So I tried to sneak him out in a wheelbarrow, all covered up in weeds and whatnot. We both thought it was a fine plan, till we got to the bonfire and old Mr Pearson said, "Great work, my lad, throw that on to burn, then."' He guffaws again, slapping his thigh. 'George was out of there like a shot, I can tell you!'

I laugh along with him. 'Are his wife and the family still in the village, then?'

'Nah, they moved off to Somerset to stay with her parents.'

'They were lovely children,' says Mrs Allen, suddenly

rejoining the conversation. 'I keep saying to Tom we should move out that way to be near them.' There's a flash of tenderness in her voice – so she's not all steel, then. This knowledge makes me like her a little more.

Tom rubs his nose with the back of his hand, sheepish, as if this is an ongoing point of disagreement. 'Well, they're all grown up now, aren't they? They won't want us old codgers hanging around.'

The smell of woodsmoke hits as we draw near to the village. Harfold isn't a large place – there can't be more than thirty or so families who live here, and tonight, it seems like every one of them is gathered on the green. Backlit by a roaring bonfire, people of all ages huddle in groups, talking, laughing, drinking from mismatched mugs. The mouth-watering whiff of cocoa. True to Tom's word, a number of children are running around underfoot, playing a chase game which Mutton joins immediately, his appearance met with squawks of shrill excitement.

Ignoring the canine chaos, Tom points out various notable people to me. There's the vicar, a tiny, unfortunate-looking man with thin, reddish hair and large ears. Sue Barnes – dressed all in blue and carrying a baby on her hip – is a distant cousin of Tom's. Mr Wight the churchwarden. The tweeded Farmer Watts, who works the fields directly over the river at the east of Harfold's grounds, though he doesn't own the land himself; Mr Gerrish from Warminster way has that honour. Next, Tom waves at an older man with a large, tufty beard. 'There y'are, Bruce!'

When the man waves back, we go over to meet him. I assume this must be the former gardener.

'Good to see you,' says Mrs Allen, treating him to a broad smile. 'How's your sister?'

'She's around somewhere, Nora. She's got a bit in her already, though, I warn you.'

'Have you met Miss Morgan yet?' asks Tom, ushering me forward.

Bruce leans in to squint – it's a struggle to make anything out in the low light. 'How d'you do,' he says. His accent is thicker even than Tom's, almost hard to understand for a newcomer like me. 'That garden running you ragged yet?'

'It's a lovely spot,' I reply.

'I have to say, I couldn't believe my ears when Tom here said they was getting a female in to replace me. I've never heard the like! Especially with so many lads in the village here who'd have been glad for the extra pay.'

I feel my smile grow thin. 'That's not how I heard it. Tom said they couldn't get anyone local – didn't you, Tom?'

'You know what people think of her-up-there,' Tom agrees, jerking his head back in the direction of the manor.

Bruce snorts. 'Silly superstition, the lot of it. *I* never had any trouble with her, or with any of them, for that matter. You know me, I loved that post; I'd have kept going till I dropped if I'd had my way about it.' He squints at me again. 'Well I never . . .'

'Miss Morgan is doing a good job.' This praise, coming from Mrs Allen, is so surprising it distracts me for a moment from the curious talk of superstition. Is it possible I've made headway with her?

Chastened, Bruce lifts his hands in surrender. 'I didn't mean no offence, Miss Morgan.'

'You should call in and see the garden,' I say. 'I've done a lot with it already. It just needed some hard work and attention.'

Before Bruce can register the implied insult, there's a commotion from further up the green.

'The Guy!' shouts one of the children, and sure enough, a pair of adolescent boys emerges through the crowd, carrying a stuffed figure between them. This Guy has been made with a certain attention to detail: he's smartly dressed, with a lace collar and conical hat, and someone has taken the care to fashion his moustache and pointed beard out of what looks like wool.

'Throw him on!' shouts another child, and then all of them take it up as a chant: 'Throw him on! Throw him on!' The boys are clowning: swinging the doll back and forth, as if preparing to chuck it into the fire, then snatching it back at the last moment. A collective groan of disappointment. 'Get on with it!' hollers an older boy – perhaps a brother or cousin, from the similar features. At last, the Guy is released into the blaze. The villagers cheer as licks of fire curl up its limbs, blackening the clothes, the carefully made lace collar. A small girl starts to cry. Some of the other children laugh at her.

Looking around, I realize I've been pulled away by the spectacle and have lost Bruce and the Allens. I wander for a bit, nodding greetings at anyone who looks my way. Buy a cup of the cocoa. It's sweet and thick, warming me through as I sip it. Not as good as Mam's recipe, though. A mournful pang in my chest as I remember winter evenings together with my parents, the three of us huddled by the stove with our steaming drinks, swapping the news of the day. I return the empty mug.

I've ended up near the little girl who was crying over the Guy. A woman of about my age is stroking the child's hair, soothing.

'Is she all right?' I ask.

The woman glances up in surprise, eyes taking a moment to

land on me as the source of the question. 'Oh. Yes, she'll be right as rain. Just a little sensitive, aren't you, my love?' She directs this last at the girl, chucking her on the chin, then looks back to me. 'We haven't met, have we?'

I stick out a hand. 'Vee Morgan.'

'Peggy Wight.' She reaches out to shake, with a twinkle in her smile that would be hard not to like. 'And this one here's Ellen.' They both have the same fair hair and round, ruddy faces. Sisters perhaps, or mother and daughter.

I crouch down to shake Ellen's hand, saying a formal, 'How d'you do?' which delights her.

'You're the new one up at the big house?' asks Peggy.

'That's right.'

'Rather you than me.'

I think back to what Tom had said, about the villagers not wanting to work for Arabella. Bruce's comment about superstitions. 'Why do you say that, then?'

'No one's told you?' asks Peggy. She leans a little closer, lowering her voice. 'There's something not quite right up there at the manor. All those deaths.'

'What about them?'

Ellen tugs at my sleeve, barging into the conversation: 'She's a witch.'

'What, Lady Lascy?' I ask.

A nod. 'She's a witch, and she put a dark magic on her whole family so they'd die and leave her all the money and that.'

I look up at Peggy, ready to share a smile over the girl's imagination. But Peggy just widens her eyes. 'I mean, it's not natural, is it? I'm not saying I believe about the witchcraft, but folks round here say the Lascys must've done something bad . . .

Sold their souls kind of bad. And now the Devil's coming to collect them, one by one.'

The genealogy. All of those Lascys already in the ground. A shiver runs over my skin.

But then Peggy and Ellen burst into sudden laughter, grave expressions melting away, and I realize I'm the butt of a joke. 'Your face!' wheezes Peggy, wagging a finger at me. 'I bet you were thinking, "These countryside fuckers, they'll believe anything!" We do have *some* learning out here, you know.'

Now I'm embarrassed – not because they've caught me out in a prejudice, as they think, but because, for a moment there, their talk managed to unnerve me. The only thing I can do to mask my discomfort is try to laugh along with them, join the joke. 'As it happens,' I say, crouching down again to Ellen's level, 'I've met Lady Lascy, and she's definitely not a witch. And she hasn't lost her soul, either, so far as I can tell. She's a bit odd, mind you . . . but she seems a good sort to me.'

Peggy snorts at this.

'What?'

'They might not have dark magic, but none of that lot are any good, if you ask me.'

I feel a sudden defensive urge at this. Arabella's advances of friendship may have been bumbling, artless, but I've appreciated them all the same. I don't like to hear someone insult her. Still, my curiosity pushes me to dig further. 'The Lascys, you mean?'

'All of them lords and ladies. You don't get to be where they are without walking over a pile of bent backs, you know what I'm saying?' She shrugs. 'They're on their way out, I reckon. Look what's happening all round the world: I'll bet by the end of this century, we won't even have a king or queen.'

I feel myself relax: this isn't about Arabella personally, then. Besides, I'm warming to Peggy's sparky optimism. It's as if you could almost be convinced by her vision, if you listen to her long enough. Reminds me a little of Dad. His hopes for a better world.

'It's not just the lords and ladies,' I say, thinking of the Reeses. There were plenty of bent backs behind their wealth, too.

Peggy hums in agreement. 'The Allens are good people, all the same. Though they've had their fair share of trouble. Not too far, Ellen!' This last, shouted. Bored of the politics talk, the little girl has wandered off a way, where she's picking up damp leaves from the grass and weighing them against unknowable criteria, before either chucking them or gathering them in her skirts.

'You mean with Mr Allen's brother?' I guess.

Peggy looks surprised. 'He told you about that?'

'Only that he died. Why, is there more to it?'

Glancing over her shoulder as if wary of being overheard, Peggy leans in closer. 'Did he say how?'

I shake my head.

'He was the churchwarden at St Anselm's before my dad – I don't know if Mr Allen already told you that? Well, he let himself into the church one night and climbed all the way up the bell tower. He fell right to the bottom of the stairs, neck broke clean in two. His face was hardly recognizable when they found him – he must have hit all the beams on the way down. Dad heard all this first-hand from the vicar, so you know it's true.'

A sudden image flashes into my head of the deer on the road, that first night I arrived. Its neck snapped to a right angle. I can tell from the gleam in Peggy's eye that she's trying to impress me with these gory details, in the same way the girls used to tell horror stories in the laundry about stomach-sickening injuries – always claiming to know someone who had witnessed them first-hand, of course.

'The police said it must've been an accident, but Dad always thought he did himself in – why else would he be there so late? Still, there's no way of knowing, either way.'

I look for Tom in the crowd on the green but can't catch sight of him. It must be awful not knowing the truth – to live with the possibility that his brother was *that* unhappy, and Tom didn't notice in time to help him.

It's grown even colder as we've been speaking, and I have to stick my hands in my armpits to keep them warm, wool gloves not doing enough to fight off the chill. My fingertips are slowly losing sensation – a circulation problem I've had since childhood, all my winters spent in thick mittens, no feeling in my extremities. 'Anyway, how come you took the job, then?' asks Peggy, suddenly brightening. George's story is clearly just that to her – a ghastly tale to tell, no emotional weight to it. 'You didn't want to stay closer to home?'

'No, thank you!' I aim to match her joking tone, but it doesn't land.

Peggy's eyebrows rise and she drops her voice low again. 'Why? Were you fired from your last place? Go on, you can tell me.' A mischievous grin. 'What did you do?'

'Excuse me?' The words come out blunter than I mean them to.

Peggy raises her hands in surrender. 'That's what happened to my brother Daniel, is all. He had a good job up near Marlborough, but they caught the bugger stealing, so what can you do? He's back home with us now, twiddling his thumbs all day.' She grimaces at me. 'Sorry, I didn't mean anything by it.'

'It's fine,' I say. Clear my throat.

Something new is happening: a fresh ripple of excitement through the crowd around us.

'I think that's the fireworks,' says Peggy. 'Come on, Ellen, let's find Daddy and see if he'll put you on his shoulders.' She throws a guilty smile back at me as she leaves.

Hunting around again, I finally find Tom. He's been reunited with Mutton, who's lounging on the grass to enjoy a nice large stick, presumably saved from the pyre for his benefit. Someone hushes the gathering, and then there's a countdown from ten. A shared thrill bubbling. At 'zero', the first rockets are lit. Everyone cranes their necks back to follow the hissing path. Then the bursting lights, the explosive *boom*.

Mutton jumps to his feet in an instant, a deep growl rumbling at the back of his throat. 'It's all right, Muttsy,' says Tom. But another flash of light from above and the dog is off, racing down the green like his life depends on it. Headed in the direction of the main road. 'Mutton!' Tom takes chase, me not far behind him. 'Get back here!' But Mutton won't listen, fear more powerful than what has only ever been a tenuous obedience at the best of times. Younger and faster than Tom, I pull ahead, but still can't gain enough ground to catch Mutton. He's nearly at the road already. And worse: a glint of light through the trees further along. There's a car approaching, at speed.

'Stop!' I scream, not sure if I'm speaking to the dog or the driver. Knowing that neither will hear me. I reach the hedgerow as Mutton disappears through it. No time to find a way around; I launch myself at the same gap, trying to force myself through.

I'm just in time to see Mutton, caught in the headlights as he darts across the carriageway. The blare of a horn. The car swerves. Skids on the newly frosted surface. At the last minute, the wheels find purchase, and the car rights itself before it hits the ditch.

But Mutton is safe. As my eyes readjust to the darkness, I see his guilty face looking back at me from the other side of the road. Just a second slower and he would've been flattened.

Tom wheezes up behind me. 'Is he . . .?'

'He's fine.' However, before I can do anything to tempt the dog back over, he turns tail and continues. 'Oh, bloody hell!' Unable to get through the hedge fully, I reverse back out to where Tom's waiting. 'He's just taken off again. Look here, we're never going to catch him this way. How about we head back to the green and rustle up a couple of helpers, get some torches, then we can go searching properly?'

Tom, normally so chipper, is clearly at a loss, but he agrees to my plan, and we head back to where the celebrations continue. I wouldn't know who to start asking, but Tom manages to find a few recruits quickly – one of the lanky adolescents who'd been in charge of the Guy; two middle-aged men who I gather are related to Bruce; Farmer Watts; and, of course, a pinch-faced Mrs Allen.

We round up an assortment of electric torches and someone provides chunks of sausage for us to use as bait, the meat still hot and popping from the fire, its grease seeping into my gloves. Then we strike out over the fields, fanning out in a loose line to cover the ground. We start in the direction I last saw Mutton run – away from Harfold Manor. Our voices call his name hoarsely into the night. Artificial beams piercing the sleeping landscape. Boots crunching over a layer of frost. It makes me think once more of that night I saw Arabella in the fields with her lantern. Looking for her lucky hare. At my back, the tiny lights of Harfold twinkle, dwarfed by the fireworks that continue overhead. Showers of yellow, red, blue, purple, green. How much of them can Arabella see? I feel again a guilt at having left her behind.

After a futile half-hour, we bunch back together. No Mutton, nor any trace. Either he's outrun us or else circled back, slipped past us to hide somewhere familiar. 'We'll look for him again in the morning, Tom,' says one of the men, patting him hard on the shoulder. 'I'm sure he'll turn up just as soon as he gets hungry.'

The tears on Tom's face make me think of his lost brother, George. When did the family realize he was missing? Did they go searching for him, before he was found at the bottom of the bell tower? Perhaps even some of the same people – Bruce's relatives, Mrs Allen. How long before they realized they were too late?

Mutton hasn't returned the next morning. My early walk-around's eerily quiet without his company, and every rustle of the garden has my ears pricked in expectation. Around ten o'clock, I'm in the shed when I hear commotion up the drive. Stick my head out. Heart lifting. It's the woman I spoke to yesterday – Peggy – leading a thoroughly-sorry-for-himself Mutton on a bit of rope.

'You found him!' I call, jogging over to meet her by the yews.

'He was dug into the manure heap,' she tells me. 'Absolutely filthy! We tried to get it all off him, but he didn't make it easy for us.'

I kneel down to rub Mutton under the chin. 'You gave us a proper fright, boy.'

We take the dog round to the rear entrance, where Tom's left the door propped open all morning in hope. Before we can even untie the rope, Mutton is inside, dragging Peggy with him through to the kitchen. A shout of delight from Mrs Allen. Jubilant barking.

'Mutton!' Tom's voice. 'You bad dog! You bad, bad dog!' But when I walk in, I find Tom with the largest grin I've ever seen, arms wrapped round Mutton's neck. 'You naughty bugger. I thought that was it. Oh, Christ.' Mutton gives Tom a moist kiss on the chin. Clearly not an inkling of what all the fuss is about. Tom laughs, wiping his face. 'What am I like, getting all worked up over a sorry mutt like you?'

Then chaos as Mutton jumps up on the kitchen table, rope still swinging from his collar.

'Aw, let's do him a bit of breakfast,' says Mrs Allen, dabbing her eyes with a hanky, though I'm sure any other day she'd have skinned him alive for getting up there. She nips into the larder to fetch bacon rashers, setting into a cheerful hum as she cooks – 'The Lord is my Shepherd', I think it is. Then it's tea and bacon rolls all round. Mutton licking his chops in delighted disbelief when three whole rashers are placed in his bowl, enough finally to tempt him back to floor level.

After the first course, Mrs Allen brings out a plate of spiced teacakes. Offers one to me. Then a second. 'That was good of you to help, last night. It meant a lot to Tom.' Then she actually *smiles* at me! She's got a heart in there really, I can see that now.

Once our feast is over, I accompany Peggy back out to the drive, since I'm headed in the same direction anyway. 'You've made their day,' I tell her.

'It was my brother Daniel who found him really,' she says,

giving a shy smile, 'but I wanted to bring him up. Actually, I wanted to apologize. About what I said last night. Sorry again if I offended you – I never think before I speak. Gosh, what must you think of me, spreading all that gossip and rattling on for ages about politics and that?'

'No harm done,' I reassure her. 'And when the monarchy falls, drinks are on you, are they?'

She stares blankly at me, then catches up to the joke and laughs, swatting my upper arm. In the light of day, I can see the dimples in her cheeks. 'All right, that's a deal.'

I stand at the top of the drive for a minute, waving her off. When I turn back round, I almost jump out of my skin. There's Arabella at the window. Watching our conversation. I give her a smile. She doesn't return it and I'm left with the sense that, somehow, in speaking to Peggy I've hurt her feelings.

SIX

REACHER IS BACK today, his motorcar left in the turning circle, full in the way of where Tom and I are trying to pull weeds. He drives a modest Singer Ten – not what you'd imagine for an aristocrat. The paintwork's a pretty forget-me-not blue. Undercarriage splattered with the inevitable countryside mud; I'm sure Tom will be called on to clean it soon.

'He used to live here, did you know?' Tom says, nodding at the car as if it's a symbol of its owner.

'Yes, Mr Reacher mentioned that before.'

'His father died before he was born, then his poor mother passed away when he was just a child. She was the former Lady Lascy's sister – always very close to the family, spending her summers here, so they made sure that Mr Reacher had a home after she passed. Mr Reacher took it hard, mind; he was such a fragile boy, and the older children weren't always that nice to him. But he and Lady Lascy are close as anything these days, which just goes to show . . .' Tom doesn't specify what it shows.

I wrestle with a stubborn dandelion. 'But he lives half the time in London now?'

'That's right.'

'And manages Harfold for Lady Lascy?'

'Yes, she leaves all of that to him. She's never had a head for numbers.' His voice drops, so I have to lean in to hear. 'Between you and me, the numbers aren't nearly so large as they used to be. After all the misfortune the family's suffered, to rub salt in the wound, they had to pay the death duty every time – since those boys died in inheritance order. That's been a real blow. I'd hate to see her Ladyship have to sell Harfold, but I wouldn't be surprised if it went that way in the end.' I'd guessed some of this from the manor's shabby gentility, the small and informal staff, the closed wing, but I didn't realize things were as bad as that. 'Not to mention—'

Footsteps approaching. We both straighten up as Reacher draws near. Conversation over.

'You two *are* a pair,' says Reacher, smiling broadly. 'We have been watching you go up and down, up and down, just like clockwork. And what a divine clock that would be!'

'Oh, get on with you,' Tom laughs.

Reacher presses a solemn hand to his chest. 'I swear it. Perfectly picturesque. But listen, I do have an ulterior motive. Are you aware we have mice?'

Tom shrugs with an air of apology. 'There's no keeping the blighters out, sir.'

'Yes, well, out of the dining room at least would be ideal. There I was, eating my toast, and one of the chaps ran right across the table. The cheek of it!'

'They're too clever for the traps, that's what it is.'

A pout from Reacher. 'Don't we have poison?'

Spasming bodies. Froth at the mouth. I hold back a wince.

Tom pauses to think. He's still clutching one of the dandelions, absently pulling fragments from the leaves. 'If we have any, it'll be in there somewhere' – he nods to the old coach house and stables – 'but I reckon we're out. Can't remember when I last did the rounds. Let me have a look.' Beckons to me. 'You might as well come and see the collection while I'm at it, Vee.'

'The collection?'

Tom doesn't elaborate, just leads us over to the block of outbuildings.

'Do you like motoring, Miss Morgan?' asks Reacher, as Tom unlocks the doors.

'Love it,' I tell him, though I can't imagine why the question's just come to his mind. I still remember the first time I rode in a car. I'd been around eight years old and Dad's boss at the time had driven his Rolls-Royce through town for Easter, inviting all the children to have a go in the passenger seat. I'd been too frightened at first – with the man's round goggles and leather driving gloves, he'd looked like a strange insect creature that might eat little girls for dinner. But Dad had told me not to be silly, pushed me up into the carriage with an exaggerated groan. My fears had disappeared as soon as I was in that seat. That feeling of power as the engine rumbled through my bones.

Mr Reese had a lovely car, too: a new Austin Twenty in white. It looked ever so smart when it was clean, but it would get smeared in dirt almost the moment Mr Reese started it up. I was forever washing it for him, then he'd take it right back out and get it filthy again. He had that sort of careless attitude. It was a beautiful motor, all the same, and his little boy, Kenneth, would often come out to watch me at work on it. If the child was good, I'd lift him into the seat when I was done and we'd pretend he was driving, me doing the noises for him. If I ever had the money for it, I think I'd get an Austin.

When Tom opens the coach house, I see why Reacher was asking my thoughts on the topic: inside, there are five cars, huddled together like nesting chickens. Unlike Reacher's Singer, these are a higher quality of automobile: a Rolls-Royce Silver Ghost, a Renault race-car, an American Cadillac, a Daimler, a funny old steam-powered Serpollet.

'These all Lady Lascy's, are they?' I ask.

Reacher laughs. 'They would be wasted on her. No, most of them were Charlie's.'

'They could do with a wash, mind,' says Tom, rummaging through a set of shelves behind the cars. 'There's bats in the roof, so . . .' As I look closer, I do indeed see the bat shit, but even so the cars maintain a certain dignity.

'I don't know about that,' says Reacher, 'they have been very well cleaned over the years.' An odd way to phrase it – not 'well kept', but 'well cleaned'. His smirk implies a private joke – although not one he shares with Tom, who is too engrossed in the search to be listening.

'No poison,' Tom confirms at last, coming back over to join us.

I'm still stuck on the motors, though. 'Her Ladyship never takes them out?' I almost feel sad for them, as if they're aware that they're languishing among the bats. If I had such a collection, I'd be driving about every day, even just to go up the track. That's the problem with rich people, though: they never put their money to the right use. Reacher must catch my dejection, as he pricks up all of a sudden, like Mutton when he's excited.

'Tell you what,' he says, 'I need to run up to Warminster for a meeting later – how about we take one of these old beasts for an outing, and buy that poison while we're at it?'

I realize he's still speaking in my direction. '*Me*, come with you?'

'Why not?'

'Oh, that'd be brilliant, that would! But you're sure Lady Lascy won't mind it?'

Reacher waves a hand. 'Pish-posh. They're as much mine as they are hers.'

Tom looks like he may argue, but a clap on the back from Reacher is enough to win him over. As Reacher moves his own motor out of the turning circle, Tom sets about refilling the tank, oil and water in the Renault for us. Winds up the clock, setting it against my pocket watch. Checks the kerosene tail light. Adds a little fuel to the primer cups.

The vehicle is really quite beautiful – a doorless two-seater in cherry red, with a bronze stripe on either side of its sloping snout. 'Charlie's favourite,' Reacher tells me.

Once the engine is readied and we've cleared the worst of the bat shit, Reacher lets me turn the car's crank. It takes a few attempts to coax her into asthmatic action, but then we're purring away up the lane, Tom receding behind us, waving his hanky in a comic farewell.

When we reach Warminster town, Reacher parks up in the marketplace. He has a meeting at the bank, he says, and will meet me back here in an hour. He's gone before I can say I don't know my way around. Apart from the night I arrived by train, this is the first time I've been here. Still, it shouldn't be hard to find a chemist's in the town centre. I pick a direction and walk.

Warminster's a small market town, nowhere near as large as Penarth, although next to Harfold village it seems sprawling. The high street's a hodgepodge of three-storey Georgian and Victorian buildings, fronted with soot-blackened limestone like rows of grubby urchins. There's an aura of decay: missing panes of glass, faded signs, shuttered shop-fronts. The day's overcast, flattening everything further to a dreary grey. Even so, a fair number of people are out and about. In all the excitement over the car, I hadn't thought to de-muddy myself, and now I can sense curious eyes all over me. Harder to blend into the crowd here than in Cardiff.

Up East Street, I'm thrilled to discover a seed grower's, Wheeler's. Takes me a moment to realize it's *the* Wheeler's, of the renowned Wheeler's Imperial cabbage variety. I have to tear myself away from a twenty-minute conversation with the proprietor during which I place several orders on the Harfold account, and I'm still riding that good mood when I find the chemist's. The shop window stacked high with colourful bottles sends an immediate chill through my guts. It's just started to drizzle, but even so I hesitate before I enter. Take a handful of deep breaths.

Inside, a short queue prolongs my agony. I find myself rehearsing my order as the woman in front coughs wetly into a sleeve. *Good morning, I need to deal with some vermin.* Does the shopkeeper's expression flicker when I ask him for the arsenic? Just my imagination. It's not a crime to buy rat poison. Still, a cold weight of guilt as I carry the tin back to the Renault. People looking at me. Whispering. *No, they're not,* I tell myself.

A trio of pubescent boys has gathered around the vehicle in our absence, eyeing it over with obvious appreciation. They don't remark on me as I approach, then turn and goggle when I march up to the car and stow the tin.

'That ain't yours, is it?' one of them asks, voice breathy in wonder.

'My boss's,' I say. Normally I'd be encouraging their admiration, but I'm too on edge at the minute, so I ignore their chatter, craning my neck round to see if I can spot Reacher. It's not so long before he reappears, whistling what sounds like a dance-hall tune.

'All in order? Excellent.' He glances at the boys, who have moved a little distance away but are still very obviously taking notice. 'Now, I've been thinking, Miss Morgan, why don't you drive us back?'

Still wrapped up in my own thoughts, I wonder if I've misheard. 'You're joking!'

'Why not?' Beaming, he tosses me the key. One of the boys gasps.

So now *I* climb up to the driver's seat as Reacher turns the crank. I had a go with some of the farm vehicles, back in the Land Army days, but it's been years since then. I place my hands on the steering wheel with reverence. The polished wood is sleek as a rose petal. This time, she purrs into life first try, the engine loud but smooth as you like. It takes a little instruction from Reacher to get a handle on the controls, but then we're off, the three boys chasing after us a while, shouting their delight.

I take us back the way we came, following Reacher's gestures to navigate the country lanes. Push through the gears. The speed meter ticks up, needle wobbling first past fifty, then past sixty. The damp air hitting my face until it looks like I've been crying. Reacher throws back his head and howls like a wolf.

Coming to a series of sharper bends, I slow our speed. Move back down to third gear. 'How come Lady Lascy never goes motoring?' I shout over the wind.

'She's afraid!'

I recall what Arabella confessed the other day. 'To leave the manor grounds, you mean?'

In the corner of my eye, Reacher shrugs. 'She was afraid of driving long before she stopped going out. It *is* dangerous, on that main road.' His next words are lost to the elements.

'What?'

'I said, you never know what might jump into your path.'

The drizzle gives way to a shower along the Harfold road, and soon we're both drenched through, laughing breathless with delight. I turn us up the drive and, as the manor looms into sight, Reacher leans over to sound the horn with a couple of jolly hoots. For the first time since moving here, I feel almost as if I'm arriving home.

Tom meets us at the coach house, ready to get the car under cover and start drying it off. 'How did she go?' he asks.

'Like a dream,' says Reacher, wiping droplets from his spectacles. 'And Miss Morgan brought us back in fabulous style. How did you find her, Vee?'

'She drove *beautifully*,' I agree. Run a hand over the wheel-arch, now clagged with fresh mud. I'm reluctant to part with the Renault. Will likely never have another chance like this to drive it. I wonder again how Arabella can bear to leave it neglected here. I sigh, 'I'd better put this poison away, then.'

'Try the potting shed, will you?' asks Tom. 'It'll be easier to get to in there.'

However, when I step outside, I'm stopped in my tracks, because here's Arabella, outside, in the daylight. Storming across the lawn in a yellow housecoat, raindrops staining the silk. Carrying, absurdly, a cup of tea, as if in such a rush that she's forgotten to put it down. Headed in our direction.

'Maurice!' she shouts, as she draws into earshot. 'Come out of there!'

I feel Reacher appear behind me, but I can't look away from Arabella. Her flushed face, the twist of fury in her jaw.

'Bellsy, my dear . . .'

'*Bellsy, my dear!*' Arabella's lisping imitation of Reacher is not flattering, though there's a certain accuracy to it. 'I'm not listening, Maurice! Why did you let her drive that car?' Then, with more emphasis, '*That* car?'

Reacher raises his hands, palms facing out. A gesture of surrender. 'It was just a bit of fun.'

'You know *he* wouldn't like it! As if we are not cursed enough already!' She's barefoot, mud and grass spattered up past her ankles from where she's run across the lawn. A crazed look in her eye. I've no idea what she means about curses, but I assume that 'he' must be Charlie, the unfortunate former owner of the Renault. 'And *you!*' Turning her rage now on me. 'What were you *thinking?*'

'Look here, I was only—' I begin a defence, but am interrupted by the teacup, sailing through the air at an alarming pace and into Reacher's forehead. Arabella had been so fast that I didn't even register her throwing it.

'Fuck!' Reacher staggers back, clutching his brow. '*Fuck!*'

Arabella looks at her own hand in surprise, as if wondering what's just happened, and then slowly sinks to her knees in the damp grass. 'I didn't . . .' Her breathing is ragged, as if fighting back tears. 'I didn't mean to . . .'

'You're all right there, my Lady.' Tom has appeared at her side. 'Come on, let's get you up.' He bends to place an arm around her shoulders, coaxing her back to her feet. The housecoat has fallen open at the chest. I avert my eyes. Not quickly enough to see nothing.

As Tom leads her away, Arabella mumbles to him, the words I catch not making any sense. Something about Charlie. Something about her hair.

'Christ,' says Reacher, examining his fingers. They've picked up a smear of blood.

'Does it hurt?' I ask. 'Here.' Hold out a hanky.

'No, no. That was my fault. Sorry you nearly got a whipping too.' He presses the hanky to his head. 'I think it's just a surface wound.'

'Let's get Mrs Allen to have a look,' I suggest. The housekeeper and I have thawed to one another since Guy Fawkes Day, bonded by the experience of Mutton's misadventure.

Reacher seems about to protest, but eventually lets me usher him in, where Mrs Allen dabs him with alcohol. Tuts when he flinches away. None of us comment on Arabella's behaviour, but I can't stop thinking over it. Yes, she'd been angry, but – more than that – her primary emotion after throwing the teacup had been distress. Was the car too strong a reminder of her youngest brother? Again, I catch myself feeling sorry for her. She has so many layers: the awkward recluse, over the grief-stricken orphan, over the playful woman who still shows through in flashes. Something about her makes me want to reach out and help.

Once Reacher has received his medical attention, I finally take the tin of arsenic over to the potting shed. Clear a space on the top shelf. Hope I never have to think about it again.

The next morning, I'm summoned once more by Mrs Allen. A trudge over the muddy garden to the manor. 'Her Ladyship's in a bit of a state,' she says, as we enter the hall. 'She won't come down today.' Nods at the stairs.

'She wants me to go up?'

Mrs Allen starts climbing in answer. If anything, the stacks of newspapers on the stairs have multiplied since my last visit. At the top, we turn right – away from the closed wing with the Lascy family genealogy.

The corridor we pass through now is, like the downstairs rooms, packed with furnishings, artwork, ornaments, oddities. Everything is far too large for the space it occupies, so I have to weave and sidestep, copying the well-practised route taken by Mrs Allen. I can't even guess the value of some of these items, yet it's clear they've been treated without any care: a delicate vase with a crack down the centre; a wall hanging with water damage; an antique cabinet with wax melted all across the top; a broken mirror, shards of menacing glass still strewn over the floor.

Mrs Allen stops at one of the doors, knocks. Peers in without waiting for a response. 'Here she is, my Lady.' Her tone almost maternal. A reply that I can't hear, and Mrs Allen tuts and says, 'Nonsense.' Pushes open the door so we can both shuffle inside.

The room is a pigsty. There's no other word to describe it. The clutter of the rest of the house was a pale precursor to this, the beating heart of the chaos that reigns at Harfold. The walls are pink; the dark pink of the inside of a cheek, which seems to suck out the light despite the multiple candles and gas lamps blazing. Furniture crowds every corner, and multi-coloured embroidery threads unspool across any available surface. Open shelves line one wall, with books, papers and ornaments spilling over as if desperate to escape. A vast bed stands in the centre – not against any wall, but in the very middle, like an island. The floor underfoot is a sea of debris. Discarded sewing needles, clothes, jewellery, make-up, knick-knacks, papers, stationery, perfume bottles, ribbons, buttons, balled handkerchiefs, plates, shoes, game pieces, spectacles, unlit candles, money, the sheets and pillows from the bed; I have to stop looking else my head will explode. A perfumed smog chokes the air, as if half a dozen scent bottles have just been upturned on the rug; this must be coming from the mass of cut flowers piled up in one corner, all in various stages of decay. I realize suddenly, with a melting feeling in my chest, that these are the bouquets I've been bringing to Arabella from the garden. She's kept every single one of them.

Arabella is at the eye of this storm, sitting upright in her bed. She's still wearing the yellow silk housecoat. A brown stain at the breast, as if she's spilled tea down it. 'Thank you, Nora.'

Mrs Allen cuts a concerned look at me, then exits the room. I still can't imagine why she doesn't do anything to fix this abominable mess – unless Arabella won't let her.

'Come, Vee, sit down so we can talk properly.'

The only chairs in the room are piled high with dusty books. I pick a trail across the floor – cigarette carton, orange peel, thimble, single glove, trinket box – and make my way to the bed. Perch on the very corner. I've got no idea what to expect from Arabella, have given up on trying to predict her. 'Look, about yesterday . . .'

Arabella holds up a hand to silence me. 'I wanted to apologize for my behaviour. I was upset about the car, but it was Maurice who should have known better, not you. And I ought not to have lost my temper either way.'

I shake my head. 'I should have thought . . .' But I *had* thought. Wondered whether Reacher really had permission to drive the Renault. Then I'd ignored that doubt. 'How are you feeling now?'

A shrug. 'Morry knows I don't mean anything by it; he's used to me. But I realize it must have sounded alarming to you. It's just that I am cautious of motorcars, and the roads around here are so dangerous. Animals run right across before you have the chance to stop. A hare darted out in front of me once.' She shudders. 'Horrible. The way the bones crunched. It was *that* car I was driving. You would think you wouldn't feel it, but you do, right up through the steering wheel. I haven't driven since.' She fixes her gaze on me, intent and searching as if looking for a particular response. 'Listen, I didn't mean to alarm you with that talk of curses.'

Another abrupt change in topic. I haven't given Arabella's comment about being 'cursed enough' any further thought since yesterday, had assumed it was off-handed hyperbole. 'I wasn't alarmed,' I say.

Arabella tilts her head. 'No, I don't imagine you were. Sensible woman like you. You are very straightforward, aren't you?' The mattress sags as Arabella leans closer. Lifts a hand as if she is about to reach out to me, to touch, but then thinks better of it. 'I like that about you, Vee. But we are cursed, here at Harfold, whether you believe in that sort of thing or not. How else do you explain it?'

'Explain what, Arabella?' I feel the need to whisper it, though she's been speaking at a normal volume.

'One every three years, in inheritance order. Each death a tragic accident or stroke of bad luck. And on top of that, all our other misfortunes: rising debts, falling rents, foot-and-mouth in the livestock, the cost of death duties. Put it all together, and it becomes clear that there is more to it than meets the eye. Something is out to get us, and whoever owns Harfold has an expiration date on their head.'

A prickle on my neck, just at the nape. 'You mean figuratively?' I ask.

Arabella doesn't answer. 'It wants nothing more than to extinguish our line. Topple Harfold Manor. Leave us as a pile of anonymous ash.'

I'm struggling to find the metaphor in this language, but don't see it. The troubling conclusion that Arabella is talking literally. A supernatural evil is stalking her – if only in her mind. Reacher had called her superstitious, but this is more like madness. Except that Arabella is fairly lucid, in control of her functions, seems – at the moment, at least – to be rational and composed. Can such a person be mad? So maybe she's just a normal woman who has been alone for too long, sad for too long. The mind can invent strange things under those conditions.

'You know that what you're saying's impossible, Arabella?'

Arabella sighs. Rubs the back of her hand against her nose. 'You don't believe me. I knew you would not.'

'You do hear how it sounds?'

'Never mind,' says Arabella. 'I should not have said anything. I was only trying to explain why I was upset about the car. Why I find it hard to . . . get close to people. I know I can be odd.'

I don't point out that, even if I could accept the existence of a curse, nothing Arabella has just said relates in any obvious way to yesterday, or her other strange behaviours. 'Look at it this way,' I say, 'why would something be out to get you like that? You've not done anything to curse yourself, have you?'

I meant this to be reassuring, but Arabella takes it as a question. 'How confident you are.' A sad smile. 'You barely know me, Vee; you have no idea what might be in my past.' Her gaze is unsettling. I can't hold it: have to look away, eyes falling on the debris scattered across the floor.

'I'm not interested in the past,' I tell her. 'I know who you are today, and that's enough to tell me I'm right.'

This time she does touch me: a quick squeeze of my forearm. The physical contact a shock – but not entirely unwelcome. 'You don't know how pleased I am to hear that.'

I may not know all of Arabella's history, but in return, my own is a mystery to her. And if past actions could trigger supernatural consequences, Arabella wouldn't be the only person who needed to worry.

Downstairs, I meet Reacher by the stuffed monkey in the hall. There's a red welt at his hairline where the teacup struck him. Mutton is by his side, snuffling at his toes. They both look surprised to see me appear from the upper storey.

'Were you with Bellsy?' Reacher asks, eyebrows rising.

I shrug. 'She wanted to apologize.'

'That doesn't sound like her.' Reacher pulls that tobacco tin from his pocket, shakes out a cigarette and places it at the corner of his mouth.

I lean down to ruffle Mutton's fur. He's a little damp, and my hand comes away with a smear of green. 'Been in the lake again, have you, boy?'

'I can't help myself,' says Reacher, pretending to shake off as if he's the one covered with lake water. 'I think she's rather taken by you, you know.' Runs his hands over his pockets. 'Blast. Do you have a light?'

I find a matchbook in my overalls. 'What makes you say that?' I ask, striking a flame and holding it out. Reacher leans closer, puts the cigarette to it. Draws in, cheeks sinking into hollows, till the tip starts to glow red. 'About Arabella, I mean?'

He takes a moment to exhale. 'Well, for starters: "Arabella"?'

'I . . . She told me to call her that. Said that's how the Allens address her.' But I've already realized this isn't true. I think of Arabella. Her hand on my wrist just now. 'Maybe,' I concede. Feel a flush in my face.

Reacher smirks, but makes no further comment.

'All right then: what does she mean about a curse?' I ask.

He considers this. 'A way of understanding it all, I suppose.' He holds his cigarette with a European affectation, between index finger and thumb. 'Arabella has lost a great number of things over the years. Four brothers and both parents. Most of a fortune. The mind needs to create a reason for it.'

Mutton's found something edible on the floor. His tongue makes unpleasant, moist noises as he scours the area.

'She can't really think she's cursed though, can she?'

'Maybe. I thought it was a joke at first. She would mention it after any spot of bad luck. Small things, you know? One year the stream burst its banks and flooded the paddock. "It must be the curse." That sort of thing.' He opens the front door a crack to flick out his ashes. 'But sometimes – well, you saw her yesterday. She gets into these moods, and then I think she does believe in it.'

To be convinced that a malevolent force is watching over you, ready at any moment to pounce, must be a terrifying state of existence. No wonder Arabella's a recluse . . . 'And what about the house?' I ask, gesturing round to indicate the clutter. 'Sorry, I don't mean to pry, but all this isn't exactly normal either.'

Reacher takes another pull of smoke. Blows it out. 'Your guess is as good as mine. She won't let us throw anything away. You should see the rage that gets into her if someone dares to clean. Well' – he gestures to his own forehead – 'maybe you can guess at that. My theory is that it's another response to all her losses. She refused to clear out any of her parents' old possessions after they passed on, and things just spiralled from there with each new death. She hasn't been able to keep her family at Harfold, but she can cling on to everything else, at least.' He grimaces. 'Then again, I have lost just as much as she has, and you don't see me filling the rooms with old junk, do you?'

I don't see him doing anything to stop it either, but I imagine it won't go down well if I point this out.

'She has this idea,' Reacher goes on, 'that she's caused it all. I told you about the magic hare, didn't I? Bellsy was obsessed with that story as a girl – she used to go looking for it on the Plain with her brothers. Then one night, driving back late—'

'She told me about that,' I interrupt, 'hitting the hare.'

He pauses. 'Yes. Well, she thinks it put an evil spell on her. Reversed the blessing it had originally bestowed on our ancestor, James Lascy. I've never heard anyone else say the story works in reverse – that the magic hare can curse a person instead of bless them – but there you have it.'

'You haven't managed to convince her otherwise, then?'

'I find it's easier not to argue.'

'You encourage it?' I can't keep the judgement out of my voice.

Reacher frowns. 'No, no, I wouldn't say that. I have never pretended that I believe in it myself.' He sighs. Bends down to snuff his cigarette on the doorstep. Mutton, taking this as an invitation, lumbers over to him. 'I just mean that she has been sinking for a long time, and I've run out of energy to keep her afloat. Sometimes you have to prioritize keeping your own head above the water.' He tickles Mutton under the chin. 'And take that as advice for you as well, Miss Morgan: don't let yourself get pulled under.'

PART THREE

ARABELLA, 1917

28 March 1917

I CAN'T BELIEVE that Harry is <u>really</u> gone. I had a letter from him only a fortnight ago with one of his lovely watercolours of the coast, done so cleverly all in pinks and purples. Even as a child, he always loved the sea, and it brings me a modicum of comfort now to think of him resting for eternity beneath the briny waves, even as it breaks my heart that we have nothing of him to bury. I have asked Morry to have the picture framed for the landing, so that at least part of him can remain with us. If only there were a way to fix every fond memory in place the same way, keep them here with me for ever.

Although one hears all the time of our brave lads lost to the war, I never expected one of my own brothers to be among their number. It sounds so foolish to write this now, but I had almost convinced myself that, after everything that has happened here, the boys would be safer away from Harfold, as if the house were to blame for our misfortune. Yet it seems the bad luck will find us wherever we go. It is almost enough to make one think that it is intentional, as if there is something out to get us . . . Now, that <u>is</u> foolish. It was a bloody German U-boat; there is nothing mystical about that.

I just had to put down my pen for a moment to deal with

Mr Allen's puppy, who is hell-bent on getting into the main house and tangling itself up in all my sewing supplies. The thing is a real terror, although I suppose it is rather sweet when it's behaving. Morry had to come to my rescue to help shoo it from the library.

Thank God I have him to help me through this, what with Stephen and Charlie off fighting God knows where; three cheers for myopia! After all the time I used to spend trying to drop him, pretending I had missed his letters or already had other plans, I never thought I would one day be so grateful to have him hanging on. And he has been such a guide in managing the estate with the boys away. I am in half a mind to leave the business side up to him and be done with it. I find it all so hard to make out, but it seems as though our finances are under strain – Morry says the war just keeps driving the death duties up and up. We may have to close off some rooms to save on costs. Perhaps I will move to one of the chambers on the other side of the building – not Harry's room, of course, but I might borrow Stephen's while he is away. I shall welcome the change: I cannot stand to look out of my bedroom window and see that church tower any longer. It has become a constant memento mori to my eyes. I have rediscovered an old needlepoint cushion, left half finished in my childhood, and have been working on it once more. It feels good to have something purposeful to do with my time; even though I have no control over anything much in the world, it is reassuring to be able to leave my mark at least on these few inches. The picture is of a hare under the full moon, as in the old family story. We could use its protection now.

I mentioned to Morry this silly idea about calamity following us around, but he didn't laugh at me. 'You mean like a curse?' he asked. I was ready to pass it off as a joke, but he was serious. 'It could explain it all, couldn't it?' he said. 'And remember Rex's last words . . .'

I had not been thinking of a <u>curse</u> exactly, but now that Morry has planted the idea in my skull, I can't seem to shake it. It makes a twisted sort of sense . . . Because everything always goes back to that blasted night. To what I did.

VEE, 1925

SEVEN

IN THE QUIET of night, my mind often drifts to those years I spent working for the Reeses. Dad started with them in 1920. He'd been out of prison for almost half a year by then, and out of work with it. Every time he'd interview for a job, it would all be coming up roses until they reached that final, inevitable question: 'And what did you do during the war?' Then he would have to tell them. And that was that. A permanent stain on his reputation. Finally, Mr Reese took him on. He made it very clear that he considered it a big charity to Dad, who would be expected to behave with nothing short of perfect conduct at all times. Still, by 1921 Dad had more than proved himself, and I was offered the post as undergardener, working alongside him at the Reeses' townhouse in Penarth. They had another place in the countryside not far from Llanelly, but Penarth was their main residence for most of the year. It was a neat Victorian home with three storeys, attics and a basement, and a decent patch of land. Nothing in comparison to Harfold Manor in terms of size or grandeur, but it was far better kept and had a deal more staff. The Reese family was made up of Mr Reese, his wife 'Young' Mrs Reese, his mother 'Old' Mrs Reese, and the son Kenneth, who was around three years old when I started there.

It was as good a place as any, and the staff were generally

happy – or at least grateful to have the work. Of course, there was the normal grumbling about 'upstairs' – that's only natural. Mr Reese spoke down to us as if he thought we were all ignoramuses, and his wife seemed to invent chores just for the joy of it. Old Mrs Reese could be a right cow, too, when she had the mind for it. She had this habit of marching around like a general with her walking cane, bashing it against anything that displeased her – whether that was a poorly scrubbed floor tile, a wilting begonia, or the legs of an unfortunate housemaid. In private, Dad used to do a good impression of her using the garden rake, sucking in his cheeks and walking with her crabbed, close-footed gait. These were only harmless antics, the likes of which you'd find in fine houses up and down the country.

But little Kenneth was a different matter; I adored that boy. He looked a real cherub, with this lovely head of curly hair and cheeks so round that his face was almost wider than it was tall, and he had the sunniest disposition you could imagine. Yet his parents never seemed to want to spend any time with him. I could never understand it! It made me wonder sometimes if they had any hearts at all. This meant that he'd often come out into the garden to play, and I occasionally abandoned my work to entertain him, playing horsey or chasing him round with a tatty glove that I used for a puppet. He could never manage my first name – shortened it, in that way children will, to one syllable. I can still hear his sweet voice, demanding, 'Chase, Vee, chase!' I still have dreams about that Penarth townhouse. The sweet-smelling honeysuckle by the garden gate. Speckle-bellied starlings preening in the birdbath. A sea breeze whipping salty through my hair. Kenneth's laughter as he ran. The shushing of the surf. But all the while, a dark shadow over it, a clenching dread in my throat. A storm is coming. And I realize I'm in the store-shed. And there's something in my hands.

Somewhere now, the sound of water. A burbling – glugging, sucking, almost tidal, like the lapping of waves down Tiger Bay. I wake to it. Think at first I must still be dreaming. But as I stare at the square of paler night where my bedroom window is, feel the scratch of sheets around me, my stale mouth, my heavy bladder, I know I'm not.

Fighting muddled thoughts, I slip out of bed and jab around with my feet till I find my slippers. Light the candle at my bedside. Go over to the window and pull back the curtain. It's too dark to see anything beyond it, just my own face reflected back, a gentle yellow in the glow of the flame. See also the rivulets rushing down the other side of the glass. A heavy rainstorm with howling wind, the lash of drops, the patter of it on the roof. But this isn't the sound I was hearing. The bubbling, lapping noise comes from downstairs.

On to the landing. Louder now. Hazed outlines of furniture come into view as I descend. At the bottom of the staircase, the gurgling fills my ears, and as I reach the final few steps, I put my foot down into a shock of water. With rising panic, I hold the candle overhead and squint as it reflects back from places it shouldn't.

A good half-foot of water is carpeting the floor, licking at the table legs, the sofa, the walls. Wellies over by there, bobbing at the front door, uselessly out of reach. Gritting myself for the unpleasantness of what's coming next, I push forward. The water's so cold it's not like stepping into water; it's like having my feet instantly removed. All sensation leached in a moment.

Don't panic, I tell myself. Deep breath. I need to wake Tom. Need to grab my wellies first, for the walk across the garden.

They may already be wet, but they'll still be better than going barefoot. I make my way to where I last saw them, using the wall for a guide.

An object bumps against my shin, and I stoop down to touch it. Rubber. I pick up the boot, then feel about for its twin. One-handed with the candle, it's a struggle to tell which is left or right. I jam my feet in at random. The wrong way around. Well, no time to struggle with swapping them over now. My raincoat is easier to find, still hanging on the stand by the front door. I pull it on over my nightclothes. Manage to locate the electric torch in the kitchen drawer, although, once I can see the churn of water by its brighter light, I almost wish I hadn't. Hesitate for a moment, then take Arabella's needlepoint from the drawer as well and tuck it into my pocket.

Outside, the lower lawn has become a second lake. The wind threatens to bowl me over as I splash through the flood. The rain continues, driving almost sideways, stinging nettle-like at my bare face and hands. Its noise, too, is ungodly: the shriek and howl, terrifying groans from the trees, a hammering of water against earth. Every step is a battle, and the manor seems further away than it ever has. I can't look up to check my progress: a single tilt of the head wins me an eyeful of water. My nose is streaming – too numb to feel it at first, but then I taste the salt on my lips. But as I climb the gradient of the lawn, the ground underfoot goes from completely submerged to a shallow puddle, then simply boggy. When I reach the front wall of the manor, the sturdy stone feels like an anchor – no, like a harbour wall. I consider heading round the back of the house to the Allens' quarters. Then I ring at the front door instead.

It takes a number of tries before the hall window finally

illuminates, dazzling my eyes so I have to cover them. I have an arm still held in front of my face as Tom finally opens the door.

'Vee?'

When I try to speak, I realize my teeth have been chattering together the whole time. My syllables come out with a percussive accompaniment: 'It's all bloody flooded.'

Tom digests this swiftly, the only sign of alarm a gentle, 'Blimey.' He's in his nightshirt, blue-and-white striped flannel. Felt slippers on his feet. He opens the door further. 'Get inside, come on. Let me fetch a torch and I'll take a look.' His reassuring calm makes me feel almost as if his 'taking a look' will be enough to solve the problem.

I wait for him on the hall rug, watching a puddle spread around me and trying to stop shivering. The stupid stuffed monkey grins at me as if it finds the whole situation hilarious. 'You can shut it, you can,' I say. Talking to a dead monkey. Must be tired.

Tom re-emerges from the corridor, now wearing his own raincoat and wellies. Wielding a heavy electric torch. 'Come on, then,' he says gruffly.

With Tom's more powerful light, the lawn's now visible – or, rather, the swamp where the lawn used to be. I was lucky to have made it across without slipping over and falling face-first into the muddy churn.

'Blimey,' says Tom again.

About twenty feet behind the cottage, where the paddock's supposed to be, a torrent of water rushes past. As we watch, it rips a fresh clod of earth from its bank and gobbles it up. Like a beast feasting on its surroundings. 'Fucking hell!' I say.

Tom looks perplexed. 'The stream's burst its banks before, but never so bad as this.'

We splash over to the front door, left ajar in my rushed exit. An assortment of my smaller possessions have escaped: more boots bobbing around the lawn. It finally hits that my home is flooded, that there's nothing I can do about it. A lump in my throat, hard and choking. 'What do we do?' I ask.

'Wait for it to stop,' says Tom. 'You can sleep in the manor tonight . . . though the upstairs servants' quarters have been shut off for so long, I don't reckon they're safe for use. I'll have to make up a bed for you in the kitchen. Just for tonight – we'll find something better tomorrow if you can't go back in the cottage.'

Inside the manor again, I shed my raincoat and wellies, let Tom put them out in the porch. The neck and hem of my nightgown are soaked through, my bare feet grubby with circles of black-green dirt under the toenails.

'You'll want to dry off,' says Tom. 'I'll wake Nora.'

'Oh no,' I hurry to say, 'please don't. I don't want to be any trouble.'

'Well . . .' says Tom.

'I'll be fine. Honest.'

'But you'll be needing dry clothes to wear to sleep,' says Tom. Then, seeing my fearful expression, 'All right, I'll find you something of mine for the time being. I can't imagine Nora's clothes would fit you anyway.'

A sudden creak from overhead. We both freeze as a pair of pale legs appear at the top of the stairs. A white cotton nightdress, ratty at the hem. Then Arabella in full sight. 'Is that Vee?' Her face is pinched with confusion.

It's been a few weeks since the incident with the Renault. Since then, Arabella has seemed more jumpy than usual: flinching at loud noises, complaining that the view of the church tower is giving her headaches. There's been no further talk of curses since that day, but still I can't help feeling since our conversation that a change has happened between us. In letting me see her vulnerability, Arabella has invited me into something private. And without really knowing it, I've accepted the invitation.

'Sorry to wake you, my Lady,' says Tom. 'There's been a flood.'

'A flood?' Arabella's eyes are two dark points of contrast as she takes in my sodden appearance, my mud-spattered nightgown. Lingering on my bare arms and shoulders. I feel suddenly exposed, bashful in a way I haven't been since childhood. I cross my arms over my chest.

'I'll put her in the kitchen,' Tom says, this silent exchange completely passing him by.

'The kitchen?' Arabella takes a few more steps down, hand hovering over, but not quite touching, the barister rail. 'Don't be ridiculous, Tom, there are plenty of empty rooms. Put her in Charlie's. It will be nice to have the company.'

Tom hesitates. Glances over at me. Arabella's eyes still on me as well, watching for my response.

'That's very kind, Arabella,' I say. 'Thank you.'

Arabella twinkles a smile before turning back up the stairs. Tom shrugs and beckons me to follow.

Charlie's room is a couple of doors down from Arabella's. 'It never used to be,' Tom explains, as if concerned for what I will think of the Lascy family's morals. 'When she was younger, Lady Lascy was in the other wing with her parents, but we had to shut that off after it got too expensive – during the war – and she moved over. It was only ever meant to be temporary, but . . .' He trails off as we reach the door, standing to the side so I can enter ahead of him.

At first, the space seems eerily empty, but then I work out it's just that Charlie's room is furnished to a normal level, unlike the rest of the house. There is the definite sense of a young man's tastes about it – dark wood furniture, school trophies on the windowsill, a framed set of medals over the headboard – which suggests Arabella has left it as it would have been when her brother was alive. A portrait of boyhood interrupted first by war, then death. The bed is made up with dark woollen blankets, a paisley-patterned counterpane folded at the foot. A threadbare teddy bear nestles against the pillows. I try to remember which brother was Charlie. The one with the horse, I think. The motorist. First his car, now his bed . . . 'Here you are, then,' says Tom. 'I'll fetch those clothes up for you in a jiffy.'

While I wait for him, I turn to look out of the window over the dark, bedraggled gardens. Rain still pattering outside, although perhaps a little softer now, a little less biblical in its wrath. My breath fogging the panes like a creeping ghost.

Tom brings me up a nightshirt, a towel and cloth, and a jug of hot water. When I pour this last into the washbasin, the steam rising off it is heaven. Moves me almost to tears.

Once he's gone, I struggle to remove my damp garments. The cold has transformed my hands into rigid claws, digits turned a bloodless white. I know better than to plunge them straight into the heat – a sure way to get chilblains – so just dampen the flannel and run this over the worst of the mud. Catch a glimpse of myself in the large mirror that hangs opposite the bed. I look a sight: a bedraggled, half-drowned stray. Once I'm about as clean and dry as I'm going to get this side of morning, I pull Tom's nightshirt over my head. It's a shabby old thing, the fabric soft with pink stripes faded from wear. A little large on the shoulders and short at the hem for me, but comfortable enough.

As I'm struggling to fasten the buttons, there's a light tap at the door and – before I can answer – Arabella pokes her head in. I only just have time to clasp the shirt closed over my breasts. Heat rising in my face.

'Sorry to interrupt,' says Arabella. 'I wanted to see that you had settled in.'

'Yes, thanks. It's very kind of you to let me stay.' I think I've already said this.

She tosses her head. Her hair, worn back in a long braid to sleep, swings to and fro with the movement. 'The least I can do. What's the point in all this space, otherwise?' Her eyes rest on my discarded clothing on the floor, and she chuckles quietly to herself.

'What?'

'Oh, nothing. I was just thinking that Charlie would have quite liked to have a young woman in his bedroom.'

I try surreptitiously to do up a button, but still can't get my fingers to cooperate. 'I would've disappointed him, I think.'

'Hmm. Well, not to look at, at least.' She steps full into the room, nodding down at my fumblings. 'Do you need help with that?'

'I'll be fine once I've warmed up. The blood goes from my hands, that's all. It'll be back in a tick.'

'Here, let me.'

She closes the space between us and – as if it's the most normal thing in the world – reaches out to fasten my shirt. Caught off-guard, I'm stuck still as an animal lit in the approaching beams of a car, feeling more than watching her fingers move graceful and quick over the buttons. Her face is angled down so I can see the crown of her head; the pale, unsteady line where her hair parts. It's been a long time since I've been this close to another woman. The moment stretches out, thick and elastic as toffee. I hardly dare breathe. 'There you go,' she says softly, as she closes the collar. Knuckles brushing for a moment against the skin of my throat. She must surely feel how my pulse is rushing there, more violent still than the waters outside. I don't know myself if it's in fear or misguided excitement. She steps back a tread. Then, just when I think it's over, she takes one of my icy hands. 'Poor old Vee,' she tuts, chafing it between her own.

'I'm used to it,' I tell her. Can't think how else to respond, made stupid by the turn of the situation.

Arabella brings my hand up to her mouth and exhales. Her breath hot and humid against my skin. When the blood begins to flood slowly back, I can't help but wince, the deep joint-ache no less painful from years of familiarity.

Seeing the colour return to my flesh, Arabella finally releases her grip on me. 'Better?'

'Thanks,' I nod, shaking out my hands.

She's already drifted back to the door, but she turns to look at me as she exits, her expression perfectly straight. 'Sleep well, Vee.'

After a minute or so, I realize I am still standing in the middle of the room, dazed. I hurry to tidy up my things, comb out my hair. The interaction repeats over and over in my mind. Arabella seen in a new light. Was that really nothing remarkable to her, or was there more to it? And, if so, could her previous advances also have been about more than a search for friendship? But maybe this is all the product of my own imagination; one-sided desires projected outward . . . I climb into Charlie's bed, elbowing his teddy bear aside as I go. Listen to the weather prowling round the window. Wonder if Arabella has fallen back to sleep yet. Still feel her fingers at my throat, the last thing I think of as I slide into unconsciousness.

The dawn is flat and grey when I wake, a bank of clouds in the sky and the sun not yet over the horizon. Distances look confused, shadows falling where they shouldn't and dimensions not yet rendered in full. An alien effect, made worse by the sheet of groundwater clogging the lawn, its surface ruffled by the breeze so all reflections are oddly disjointed, refracted. My cottage looks small and miserable. The front door still open, like a gut-wound exposing its organs to the air. An ache in my joints, my temples and chest. Can't breathe through my nose. I hope it's not the start of a cold.

In the light of day, I take a quiet look around Charlie's bedroom. His clothes are all still in the drawers, neatly folded. Pressed suits hang in the wardrobe, as if waiting for him to step back into them. I run my fingers over tweeds, flannels, silks. Glorious materials. A startled moth whizzes past my face. There's a damp patch on the ceiling. If I squint, I can see a ghoulish sort of face in it. There must be a leak from the roof above. A set of bookshelves under the window hold old annuals and comics: a childish selection, the kind of thing I used to beg Dad to buy for me. We rarely had the money, so Dad would make up his own stories and tell them to me instead. I take one down and thumb it open. Recognize Ally Sloper, his bulbous red nose and bristled eyebrows – a character I haven't thought about since before the war. The real plots never involved quite so much socialist messaging as Dad's versions.

I've always looked up to his political convictions, though he didn't make it easy for me and Mam. Many of the men who were denied military exemption were offered a non-combative role instead: building, cleaning, stretcher bearing. Dad refused even that. Said it would be helping the war effort all the same. I didn't disagree in principle, but it was hard to stay proud of him when all our neighbours looked down on us for it, seeing me and Mam either as traitors to the nation, or as pitiful victims of a thoughtless man. Then there were the money troubles: we had barely a whisper of the allowance that families of fighting men received. The strain of it on Mam. Her hair was full grey by the time he returned. Still, he wouldn't have been the man we loved if he had given in. A stubborn streak that Mam always complains I've inherited.

At the dressing table, I find a small, framed watercolour of a horse. Picking it up to look closer, I note that the signature on the front marks it as another of Harry Lascy's works. Sweet: the older brother painting the younger's beloved mount as a gift. But looked at now, with the knowledge of how Charlie met his end, there's a sad aura about it, as if the painting had always foreshadowed the accident. Placing it back down, I leave Charlie's things behind and start the morning. I have to borrow more of Tom's clothes, then the pair of us go out to investigate the cottage, looking, I'm sure, like a comedy duo in our matching outfits. The flood has gone down by the time we get there, but water is still pooled everywhere inside.

Tom shakes his head. 'I reckon we've still got a hand pump from last time this happened. It will need a good long time to dry out proper, mind. I don't reckon it'll be safe to live in for a while. Should at least check for structural damage first.'

'You mean I can't just move back in?'

He rubs the back of his neck, lips pressed in a tight line. 'Not really, no.'

A concerning outlook. Tom reviews the upstairs servants' quarters and – as he'd predicted – finds rotted boards, fuzzing mould and sagging, damp-stained ceilings. There'll be no moving into them. He says he can ask around to see if there's somewhere in the village that can take me. But Arabella is having none of it: she insists that I remain in Charlie's room. 'Really, you will be helping me out, Vee. I hate how empty the house feels, especially when Morry's away. You forget that I grew up here with four brothers! No, stop arguing, I won't hear any more about it. You are staying.' There's a desperation in her tone that makes me believe she isn't just saying this to be kind. A glimpse of that same lonely desire for connection that I've noticed in her before.

Later in the day, Tom helps me to salvage my belongings and bring them over, make room for them among Charlie's old things. As we're carrying the last armful to the manor, Reacher's car appears up the drive, moving slowly around leftover puddles. 'Hello!' he calls, pulling up in the turning circle. 'What's all this, then?'

Tom starts to fill him in, shouting to be heard over the noise of the engine.

'Pardon?'

'A flood, Mr Reacher!'

Frowning, Reacher leaps down from the car, before leaning back into the passenger seat to pick up the covered birdcage he always brings with him. 'Oh dear. So Miss Morgan will be in with you, will she, Tom?'

'Lady Lascy has her up in Charlie's room.'

Reacher's frown deepens. 'In the main house?'

'It was Arabella's idea,' I cut in, not wanting him to think I was the one to insert myself uninvited.

'Ah yes, *Arabella*.' Reacher puts particular emphasis on the name – a reminder that this familiarity's strange in itself. He seems about to say more, but cuts himself off with a smile, although his expression remains strained. 'Well, in that case: what fun!' Does he disapprove of accommodating the help in the main house, or is there another objection working away at him? Perhaps he's simply envious – he's been the closest person to Arabella for years, from what I've heard. He may see me as a threat to this intimacy. I think of yesterday night, Arabella's easy air as she helped me to dress, warmed my hands. But no: I'm sure I'll be back in the cottage soon enough, and Arabella's whim will be long forgotten.

On my way to bed in the evening, I have first to pass the corridor to Reacher's room. Walking past it tonight, I catch birdsong again, and glance to see that his door is open, spilling warm light out over the floorboards. I must pause without realizing, as Reacher's voice drifts out a second later: 'Is that you loitering around, Miss Morgan?'

'Sorry,' I reply. 'I heard your bird.'

'Come in and meet him, if you'd like?'

Well, I have no reason not to, so I enter the corridor and draw up to Reacher's doorway. As with Charlie's room, his appears to have been left untouched by Arabella; it's neat as a pin inside. Simple furnishings, no clutter beyond a dog-eared book on the bedside table. I find Reacher himself lounging in a cushioned armchair facing the corner, where a wooden stand displays the cage, now uncovered.

'This is Finchley.' He gestures to the smallish, round-chested bird perched inside. It has blue-grey and deep brown plumage on its back, reddish-pink on the breast, with a flash of white striping the wing feathers. Stepping closer, I recognize it as an ordinary chaffinch, the type you can see in any garden.

As if in greeting, Finchley repeats his song, a series of fast notes ending in a lively flourish.

'He's sweet, isn't he?' I say.

Reacher nods. 'He's a cheerful chap, wonderful company. Would you like to feed him a mealworm? He'll take it right out of your hand.'

I accept the brown paper bag and pluck up one of the dry yellow grubs, before holding it out on my palm against the bars of the cage. True to Reacher's word, Finchley hops closer on his perch to consider it, then jumps to cling to the cage bars by the feet, poking his beak out to peck up the offering.

'You're not strictly allowed to keep them any more,' Reacher tells me, 'but he had a broken wing when I found him, and I couldn't very well leave him out there to get eaten, could I? Give him another, go on. I do spoil him a bit.'

'How come he sings at night, then?' I ask, holding out another mealworm.

'You can train an animal to do almost anything you like if you are persistent enough,' says Reacher. 'When I first got him, I kept him covered up night and day until he forgot what the difference was between them. Now he sings whenever he sees light, no matter whether it's the sun or a candle.' He nods to the lamp burning at his bedside. 'People used to poke out their eyes with a pin, but that strikes me as barbaric. I couldn't do something like that to you, could I, Finchley dear?'

I crouch down to the bird's level. His eyes glimmer like two black gemstones, and I can't help but imagine what it would be like to push a pin into them. The moment the sharp point breaks the surface. I swallow back nausea.

Unaware of the dark turn in our talk, Finchley lets out a new sound, a *pip-pip*, turning his head to and fro.

'I wonder what he's saying.'

'That particular noise is known as "pinking",' says Reacher. 'It's a contact call – the cry birds use to signal out to one another.'

'So he's asking, "Is anybody there?"'

'Exactly.'

Finchley gives the pinking call again, then cocks his head, listening out for an answer that will never come.

'Isn't he lonely?' I ask.

'No,' says Reacher. He runs a finger over the cage bars, creating a musical noise of his own. 'He doesn't remember any other life than this.'

Wishing Reacher goodnight, I make my way back to Charlie's bedroom. On my pillow, I find a folded cloth. Another needlepoint work, Arabella's style familiar by now from the number of times I've re-examined the first one. In this picture, I'm in my sodden nightgown, dripping water like some kind of river sprite. My contours rendered in remarkable detail where the fabric clings. Dark shadows of nipples over the chest.

Flushed with swift heat, I shove the embroidery under my pillow where it can't be seen. I can still hear that pip-pip from Reacher's bird carrying faintly through the walls. It makes me feel a sudden wave of loneliness myself.

EIGHT

IT TAKES ME a couple of weeks to master the floorplan of the main house, the way that everything cobwebs out from the central hall. It's far too easy to get turned around, and I've blundered into my share of cupboards since moving in.

On the one hand, this is the grandest place I've ever lived. Such high ceilings; such tall, bright windows. Glorious views over my gardens. A home built for lords and ladies. But despite this grandeur, these sheer dimensions, the place is a ruin. I hadn't realized until now quite how much Harfold is falling apart. Rising damp, moss on the windowpanes, mouse droppings, cobwebs, silverfish scattering in every opened drawer, freckles of mould if you move a piece of furniture out of place. Not to mention the relentless, inescapable clutter. I can't take a step without almost knocking something over.

When I finally ask Tom about this, wondering if he'll have a different explanation to the one Reacher gave me, he says it's all from the closed west wing. Beyond the room with the genealogy, this is the one part of the house I've not had the opportunity to explore, painting it with the glamour of mystery in my mind. When they shut it off, Tom says, Arabella couldn't bear to part with all the treasures that were kept there, and insisted on having it all moved into the main house. But that only explains the objects of value. What about the broken ornaments? The stacks of newspapers? The rubbish strewn carelessly on the floor? Arabella must not have thrown a single thing out in years. More than a decade, even: Reacher had said it started not long after her parents' deaths.

And Arabella, of course, is in such close proximity. There to say good morning and goodnight. Inviting me to share her meals at the dining table, to 'give the Allens their privacy', she says. But I keep catching myself thinking there's more to it than this. The way she looks at me every so often . . . I can't deny that this new thought of Arabella's admiration is flattering. The chest-tightening thrill of possibility. This feeling of anticipation whenever I see her, a crackling charge that races through my body. I have to remind myself of Penarth – the danger in believing you're more than just an employee. How, after three years of service and supposed friendship, the Reeses threw Dad out without so much as a by-your-leave. All because a dinner guest had accused him of giving a 'filthy glance'. Even though the Reeses knew Dad's squint was permanent, a memento from whatever he faced in prison.

I write to Mam and Dad regularly. To Dad, detailed letters about the garden, knowing how much he must miss the time spent outside, surrounded by greenery. He's not a man made to be cooped up indoors. He must ache for the feel of soil under his nails. With Mam, I mostly share any gossip I've heard from Tom. No matter that Mam knows none of the people involved; she loves nothing more than snooping into strangers' lives. However, I haven't told either about the change in my living arrangements. Nor have I mentioned Arabella much, not since those first couple of months. I don't want them to worry about me.

I'm carrying fresh letters for Mam and Dad up the track one December morning when a deluge of grey fur and canine stink shoots past me. Moments later, Mutton loops back to block my path, dropping to the floor. He wriggles about with his belly up, mouth gasping out hot breaths that cloud in the air.

'What do *you* want, Mutters?' I ask.

He flops his head to one side and pushes his chest out further.

'You want a scratch, do you?' I evaluate the matted fur on his underbelly, the clinging scraps of mud and grass. Poke the toe of one boot at him. Mutton wiggles with delight. Then, after a few seconds, he twists away and is back on four legs, cantering ahead.

Despite his speed, there's no danger of losing him: every so often he doubles back to make sure I'm still following, runs in loops around me and sometimes gives a yip, before heading off again. I find the moment of return charming – the feeling of my company being wanted by this large creature, who could just as easily complete his route alone and in half the time if I wasn't there. But here he is, running back to check on me.

The track is full mud at this time of year, so deep it threatens to overflow the top of my wellies, and I have to hop from clod to clod. Mutton ploughs through indiscriminately: air, water, muck; it's all the same to him. I stop to breathe in the cold, fresh day, the smell of cows and woodsmoke. There's a swathe of it rising from over by the village, glimpsed through bare tree branches – someone starting a bonfire, I guess.

Mutton's caught a scent and scrambles up the track's bank, nose low to the ground, letting out huffed growls.

'What've you found, Mutts?' I call up to him. A sudden flurry of feathers, and a pheasant comes billowing out of the depths, clicking in alarm. Plain brown feathers: a female. Mutton's after it like a shot. 'Leave it!' I shout. 'No, leave it!'

Mutton loses it in another hedge, the growth too close for him to push through. He whimpers and looks back at me.

'I know, boy,' I say. 'You almost had the bastard.'

At the top of the track, I'm just pausing to blow my nose when Reacher's Singer Ten rumbles around the corner. He's been out in town this morning – an early meeting, Arabella had said. I give him a wave, and he toots on the horn in response, before pulling up on the verge.

'Morning, Mr Reacher.'

'Quite, quite.' Reacher climbs out of the car, stepping gingerly into the mud. He's wearing an ostentatious fur coat, its hem brushing the tops of his boots. High colour in his cheeks from the cold air. 'Are you off to the village?'

I shake my head in the direction of the post box, thirty feet or so further along the main lane. 'Posting letters.' I lift my hand to show them. The envelopes are heavier than normal, each one containing a handful of dried chrysanthemums, gathered just before the flowers died off. This used to be a favourite craft of Mam's, and the two of us would collude on our choice of blossoms from the garden, before picking them to press between the pages of the family Bible. A month later, they'd be ready to mount in glass and hang on the wall. A little colour to brighten the home.

Reacher gives a wink. 'Ooh, not love letters, are they?'

'No.' I think suddenly, for some reason, of Arabella's needlepoints. 'My parents. For Christmas, you know.'

'Pooh!' Mutton chooses this moment to push past me, shoving his face into Reacher's midriff. But as the dog knocks against me, my hold on the envelopes slips and they fly from my hand, spiralling down into a swampy puddle.

'You beast, Mutton!' scolds Reacher. 'Here, let me.'

'Oh, there's no need to—'

But Reacher is already squatting, and – before I can stop him – he beats me to picking them up.

'Thank you, sir. Here, let me—'

Reacher ignores my outstretched hand. Holds the letters to the daylight. 'Not too much harm done, I don't think.' A pause. He is reading the addresses, I realize. Spike of panic in my chest. I shouldn't have said parents. A stupid mistake to make! 'HMP Cardiff and HMP Aylesbury,' Reacher reads out loud, before raising one eyebrow at me. 'Prison wardens, are they?'

'Cleaners,' I say. 'My mam, that is. Dad's a gardener.' No: wrong thing to say. My throat is closing up.

'I wasn't aware that prisons normally had much in the way of a garden,' Reacher says flatly. It's clear he's caught me in the lie. 'Mr and Mrs G. Owens. Not Morgan, then?'

'Morgan was Mam's maiden name. I . . . prefer it.'

'Do you, now?'

He knows I'm hiding something, but he has no way of finding out what. It's been years since the newspaper reports, if the story even made its way as far as Wiltshire. My parents' names mean nothing here . . . I take a deep breath. 'May I have those back, Mr Reacher?' I ask, with the most confidence I can muster. 'I'd like to catch the morning post.'

Reacher looks at me a moment longer, then smiles knowingly. 'Of course, Miss Morgan.'

It takes all I have not to snatch the letters out of his hand. Instead, I accept them with an attempt at composure, and walk sedately to the post box. A wash of relief as I watch them tumble into its empty maw.

When I turn back, Reacher places a finger to his lips. Miming the promise to keep my secret.

These late December nights at Harfold are so long it feels that they'll never end. Back in Cardiff, there was always something to do of an evening – the cinema, the dance hall, the pub down the road. True, I've avoided all of these in recent times, opting to sit at home as my friends headed out in their finery: Gladys with her paste pearls and scandalous lipstick; Lou's hair freshly shingled. Both of them looking back at me in pity. But there had at least been the feeling of having the option – that I could have gone out, if I wanted.

One evening, Arabella invites me to join her and Reacher in the drawing room for a game. Clearly the pair of them are as bored as I am. As I enter, I'm greeted by a sea of glass eyes. The sneering monkey in the entrance hall is only one of the many stuffed specimens at Harfold. One wall of the drawing room is taken up with heads. Mostly deer, but exotic animals too: a lion, a zebra, a bear. Bats in a glass case. Two badgers, one on each side of the window. Several birds on top of the bookcases – these, I suppose, have been installed by Reacher, which is confirmed when I recognize the great bustard from the picture on his cigarette case. Finally, seated on a fussy velvet pillow by the hearth, there's a bedraggled tabby cat. Its painted eyes point in opposite directions.

Arabella follows my line of sight. 'Miss Moppet. Hideous, isn't it?'

'Oh, tosh,' says Reacher, from where he reclines on a threadbare divan. 'She adores that kitty.'

'I shall throw the damn thing into the fire one day,' Arabella sniffs.

Reacher winks at me. 'And have you seen the hare's foot?'

I turn to where he points behind me, over the lintel of the door. Just as he said, there's a forlorn, sandy-brown paw pinned up there. I try not to grimace. 'Isn't it rabbits' feet that are meant to be lucky?'

'Is it?'

'No matter,' says Arabella, 'this one is lucky too. It's said to come from the same dancing hare that James Lascy found on this very spot.'

Unless I'm forgetting something, this doesn't line up with the story she told me before. 'Now hang on a minute,' I say, 'you never told me he caught the creature. Why would it grant him good fortune if he cut its bloody leg off?'

Arabella shrugs. 'Maybe it came back later, when it was ready to die. I don't know.'

'We must not question the authenticity of the blessed hare.' Reacher pulls a comical face behind Arabella's back.

'It's one of the possible roots of the name "Harfold", you know,' Arabella continues, ignoring her cousin. '"Har" as in "hare". But the Middle English "harre" is also an option, from the Old English "heorra", meaning "hinge". We *are* in a sort of hinge here at the bottom of the valley. Or it could be from "here" – "this place". Or a truncation of "half". Then there's the question of the "fold". Possibly as in something that has been folded, which again could connect to the shape of the valley. Or the archaic "fold", meaning simply "land" or "soil". Or the fold where sheep live – metaphorically a home. So many possible combinations . . .' She stands abruptly then, crossing the room to run her fingers over the taxidermied paw. 'Well, I say it is the home of the dancing hare, and this is its lucky foot.'

The blaze of the open fire casts shadows over the lifeless zoo. It disconcerts me when she gets on to this hare stuff. I clear my throat. 'What're we playing, then?'

Arabella turns from the paw. 'We haven't decided yet.'

'Cards?' suggests Reacher. 'We must have a pack somewhere.'

As he goes to hunt one out, Arabella tries to extricate a card table from beneath a stack of empty picture frames, before giving up and pouring herself a sherry. The talk of legends seems to have been forgotten, replaced with a silence that I, at least, find comfortable. She measures out a second drink for me without asking, then sits down in the middle of the floor, where a few feet of space are free from clutter, setting her own glass beside her, directly on the rug. She smiles at me like a child who knows she's doing something naughty, daring the observer to tell her off. Holds out my glass in an invitation.

Joining her on the floor, I reach over to take the drink. Arabella's hand twitches at the last moment and, for just a heartbeat, our fingers brush. The tingle of unexpected contact runs up my skin. I take a sip, watching Arabella from the corner of my eye. Did she move her hand like that on purpose? She gives nothing away if so, apparently engrossed at the moment with a drop of sherry she's spilled on her skirt, close to the knee. She takes out a hanky and dabs it, with no effect.

'Here,' I say, placing my glass down and leaning over to pluck at the fabric. Stretching it taut, I wet one of my thumbs on my tongue, then press the pad to the stain. Feel the soft give of her thigh beneath the material. Swiftly pull back my hand. Clearing my throat, I take the handkerchief from Arabella and use it to scrub again. This time, the discolouration shifts.

'Thank you,' says Arabella. She presses her own thumb to the same spot, as if retracing my touch. I hear her swallow. 'Your hands are still cold.'

'Cold hands, warm heart, I think they say.' If I'm right about this, I shouldn't be encouraging it. An endless list of reasons not to. But I'm so fed up with this isolation I've been living in. Suddenly, a shout from a nearby room. The sound of objects falling. A torrent of swearing.

I move back from Arabella's space, just as a red-faced Reacher comes striding into the room, his jacket askew and his hair all ruffled. He brandishes a pack of playing cards. 'Why can't you put things in a sensible fucking place for once, Bellsy?' Practically spitting.

Arabella's lips are pressed in a thin line; she's clearly trying not to laugh.

'What are you both on the floor for?'

I make the mistake of meeting Arabella's eyes, and that's it: she bursts into giggles. Not her high-pitched tinkle this time, but a full-bodied, breathless sound of genuine mirth. Then I'm laughing too.

'Oh yes, very funny! I could have done myself real damage!' But his protests only make the hilarity worse.

'I'm sorry, Morry,' Arabella gasps eventually, 'it's just—'

Reacher throws the cards down on the rug, between the two of us. 'There you bloody go.'

'Don't wet your knickers over it.'

'You're always making fun of me.' There's a bitter edge to his voice, the hint of a genuine grievance.

Finally managing to get myself under control, I pick up the cards. 'We're sorry, Mr Reacher,' I say, fighting to adopt a straight face. 'Sit and play a game with us, sir, come on.'

'Yes, do forgive us,' says Arabella, putting on a hangdog expression.

At last, Reacher relents and lowers himself to the ground, before plucking up Arabella's sherry. He takes a pointed sip.

'A shame there aren't four of us, or we could have played bridge,' says Arabella, ignoring the goad. She turns to me. 'It was Mummy's favourite.'

'Let's do Old Maid,' says Reacher. 'You've always been good at that one, Bellsy.'

Arabella narrows her eyes at him. 'As have you.'

'I know how to play,' I interrupt, quickly. One of the many games Mam taught me. 'I'll be dealer, shall I?' I pick up the pack and flick through. This deck appears to be European, the face cards all graceful old-fashioned court figures in powdered wigs, pearls and velvet. On the reverse side, a pretty pattern of roses is interrupted by spots of damp. Small nibbles around the borders. Eventually, I fish out three of the queens: all droopy-eyed women with plump, vacant faces. This will leave the remaining one – the queen of diamonds – as the Old Maid, the one you don't want to end up with in your hand.

I shuffle, then deal out the remainder of the pack.

'These bloody mice,' says Reacher, examining a card that has been particularly maimed. 'I wonder if Tom put that poison out in the end. Will you check with him, Miss Morgan?'

Arabella frowns at her spread. 'Not now, Morry, she's playing with us.'

'Well, I didn't mean this moment, of course.'

'Not to worry,' I say, 'I can ask him later, sir.' I haven't ended up with many couples in my hand, but I don't have the Old Maid, either. I slide the cards about, sorting them by number. Lay out the few pairs before me.

As the game advances, Reacher seems to forget his bad mood. Probably helps that he has more cards down than Arabella. Placing two red jacks on the rug, he says, 'Isn't it funny that you pair off the boys with the boys and the girls with the girls?' Raises an eyebrow. 'I wonder what these two lovely knaves will get up to. The mind boggles.'

'Don't be lewd, Merry,' says Arabella, but she's hiding a smile behind her cards. 'Did you know,' she goes on, herself placing down the two black jacks, 'in a French pack, they're called valets? Represented by a V.' She smiles at me, teeth flashing in the firelight.

'Making me the lowest-ranking of the court cards, is that it?'

'Oh, I didn't mean—'

'Kneeling before the queen?'

Reacher snorts. 'Isn't that how you like it, Vee?'

'I'm sure I don't know what you mean, sir.' I keep my eyes turned away from Arabella.

More pairs are set down. The shush of moving paper. One of my legs has gone to sleep from sitting on the floor. I try to wiggle it, then experience immediate regret as pins-and-needles shoot up to my knee. I take a card from Reacher's hand. Reacher takes one from Arabella's. Another match.

Down to the last few cards now. Arabella puts down her last pair, safe from becoming the Old Maid. I take one of Reacher's cards. That gives me a couple of red sevens – I set them down. Just three unmatched cards remaining in my hand.

Reacher takes a black ace from me. Places it down on the floor with its double. Pauses. 'Hold on a tick,' he says, turning his cards around – not a normal part of the game. He shows the six of spades and the nine of diamonds.

'Oh.' I turn my own cards to reveal the six of clubs and the nine of hearts.

The final queen is missing from the pack; there is no Old Maid.

A moment's silence, then Reacher throws his remaining cards down in disgust. 'Just for once, I would like to be a winner.'

Arabella regards him impassively. 'You are aware that one can't win at Old Maid? The best one can hope for is simply not to lose.'

He isn't listening. 'Can't a man have anything? Fuck! Those damn mice have gobbled it up.'

'It's only a game, Mr Reacher.' As soon as the words leave my mouth, I know I've gone too far.

Reacher's nostrils flare. 'Is it, Miss Morgan? *Thank you*, I hadn't realized.'

'There's no need to be like that, Morry,' says Arabella.

'No, no: Miss Morgan has imparted her wisdom. Who cares if our home is riddled with vermin? Not Miss Morgan! But that is fine – she will be back in her cottage soon, won't she? Where she belongs.'

Gritting my teeth against the flurry of retorts that come to mind, I push myself up from the floor. Shake the remaining numbness from my leg. 'I'll go and ask Tom about that poison, then.' I look at Arabella, wondering if she'll say anything more. She doesn't.

As I leave the drawing room, I hear Reacher say behind my back, 'I won't have you ganging up on me like that.'

Pausing in the corridor, I hold my breath to hear how Arabella will respond. 'I'm sorry, Maurice.' She speaks in a wheedling, babyish voice. 'It was only a bit of fun.'

'I don't care for how chummy the pair of you have become.' Arabella scoffs. 'Green doesn't suit you.'

'I'm not jealous! I am looking out for you. Yes, of course, be friendly, share a laugh, there is no harm in that. But she is just a gardener, for Christ's sake. Don't mistake her for more.'

A long pause. 'I know that.'

It's not Reacher's words that sting the most, but Arabella's casual acceptance, her tone light, almost dismissive. As if all these signs I've noticed have only been in my head. I take a number of deep breaths. Try to squash down the stab of injustice, the humiliation. Hands trembling. The stinging reminder that I can join Arabella and Reacher in their games, but I'm not one of them. Just like with the Reeses. That same anger again, sharpening my breathing, pounding at my temples.

I go out to the shed for the rat poison and set out dishes of it in likely places: the back of the larder, behind the stove, in a corner of the dining room. Little piles of greyish dust. This isn't even my job. My eyes sting with frustrated tears.

When I finally go to bed, I have fitful dreams of poisonings. Arabella and Reacher in spasms, hacking up red bile. The acid scent of it. And underneath that, the garlic whiff of arsenic. Still clinging in my throat when I wake.

The rose garden is one of my favourite parts of the grounds. Nestled between red-brick walls, it has a secret quality to it, as though it exists in its own world away from everything else. The labyrinth of paths have been designed in a geometric spiral, leading through a complicated series of arches to a central stone bench. Even in the dead of winter, there's a grace to it all. The spikes of dormant rose bushes reaching out like fingers.

Since the ground isn't too hard today, I'm taking the opportunity to dig in a few bare root plants for next year. Bruce clearly had a preference for vibrant reds, but I want to bring in more pale pinks and whites. Madame Hardy, Cécile Brünner, Maiden's Blush.

Once those are done, I get out a ladder to refill the bird feeders. There's a rotund robin already watching with interest. I'm hoping these feathery friends will keep the bugs off my plants while they're at it.

The ladder's leant up against the back wall of the rose garden – part of the boundary of the grounds. On the other side, a public footpath, then farmland. Shortly, I hear voices, and stick my head over the top to see two figures coming into view. It's the woman I met on Guy Fawkes Day. Peggy. And the little girl Ellen. They're hand in hand, Ellen skipping as she goes.

I do my best wolf-whistle down at them. Peggy halts, looking all round in confusion, but Ellen spots me right away and waves with a big, gap-toothed grin. 'Look up there, Peg!'

Peg. So they must be sisters after all. I file that one away for later.

'On a walk, are you?' I ask.

'Just getting some air,' says Peggy. She's had her hair bobbed since last time I saw her – only an inch or so peeks out from her woolly hat.

'You've been chopped,' I say.

'What? Oh, yes.' She touches her head, self-conscious. 'I liked yours, but I'm not brave enough to go as short as that.'

'She said she didn't want to look like a boy,' says Ellen.

'I did not!' Peggy's blushing now.

'Tell you what,' I say, overcome with sudden charity, 'why don't you two come in for a bit? I can show you round the garden. Cup of tea. See the chickens.'

'We've got chickens at home,' says Ellen.

Peggy shushes her. 'That'd be nice,' she says. 'If you're sure *her Ladyship* won't mind?'

'What? Her? No, she won't give a fig.'

Arabella possibly *will* give a fig, and the rest of the fruit bowl besides. But I'm in a rebellious mood since the card game a few days ago. If Arabella doesn't see me as her chum, I think, then I can bloody well make some of my own.

I let them in through the back gate into the kitchen plot, and we take a loop round. Through the roses, where I explain my vision for the new plants, then the water garden, then up to the games lawn and the lake.

'I still remember when that Lord Lascy drowned in there,' says Peggy.

'Me too,' says Ellen.

'You weren't alive yet.'

Ellen pouts. 'But I remember!'

'You must be thinking of one of the boys. Anyway, we all had to go up the church for his funeral. Most of the village couldn't stand him after what he did with selling off the land, but then we all had to pretend like we were sad about him dying – so there you are.'

Ellen's afraid of the dark, open mouth of the ice house, so we hurry past that into the orchard, where I lift her up so she can clamber on to a low apple branch. She's far heavier than she looks. After monkeying around in the trees, I take them down to the greenhouse to look at the overwintering plants, the tiny pots of new-sown beans and lettuce, the cyclamen seeds left to soak in water. I explain how to check for rot and fungus, and Ellen dutifully inspects each container for me. Then we talk a bit about the differences between Wiltshire and Cardiff. Peggy's never met anyone from Wales before, and is it true that there's a place there with eighteen syllables in its name?

In the statue garden, we all pick out our favourite. Mine is a gargoyle with a lion-like face and a remarkably plump arse – he's called Albert, or so Tom told me before. Ellen picks a little boy playing the fiddle. After a moment of deliberation, Peggy's choice is a nude woman with a pensive, far-off expression.

'She's lifelike, isn't she?' says Peggy. 'Like you could touch her and she'd be warm.'

'Now, that'd be something,' I say.

Peggy grins, showing her dimples again.

I'm enjoying myself – it's a welcome change to speak to people from beyond the manor's walls. Reminds me of the uncomplicated sort of friendship I shared with Lou and Gladys: cheap tickets at the cinema, gin cocktails, tennis, laughing ourselves silly over Lou's terrible new haircut. Back before everything in Cardiff went to hell.

We head into the trees to find the woodland pond. Unlike the lake, this is in permanent shade, so a thin layer of ice on the surface hasn't managed to thaw yet. I find a selection of stones for Ellen to throw in. The satisfying crackle as it breaks into shards.

Next, I take them up the drive, pointing out my cottage as we pass. I recount the night of the flood, spurred on by Ellen's wide-eyed concern to inflate my own heroics. I may imply that I saved Tom from falling in.

'You mean to say you're living up at the main house now?' asks Peggy.

I shrug, as if it's nothing for a gardener to share close quarters with the lady of the manor.

'Isn't that a bit . . .? I don't know. I wouldn't like it, I don't think.'

'I know what you said before, but she really is all right, Lady Lascy,' I say, then remember I'm cross with her at the moment. 'Most of the time.'

Peggy shakes her head. 'You'll never convince me to trust any of that rich lot. They always show their colours in the end.'

I think, again, of Penarth. Dad thrown out for nothing more than a squint. Completing the loop, Peggy and Ellen admire my topiaries, then follow me back to the rear of the house. We bypass the hens, since Ellen has made her feelings on those clear.

'Sit out here, and I'll bring you a cup of tea now in a minute,' I say, depositing them in the kitchen garden. I nip inside and put the kettle on. Fuss over Mutton while I wait for it to boil – he's been taking a nap by the looks of things – then make up three cups of tea. Lots of milk and sugar for Ellen, as a guess. Then I put an extra sugar in for Peggy, too. She seems the sort.

Mutton joins me as I head back out, much to Ellen's delight, and we take it in turns to throw a stick for him as we sip our drinks. It's a bit of a squeeze to fit all three of us on the single bench by the back door. Ellen's in the middle, and she keeps accidentally kicking me as she swings her stubby legs.

'Thanks for inviting us,' says Peggy, twisting round to look at me over the top of her sister's head. 'I hope we haven't kept you from your work too long. Though I'm sure Lady Lascy's such a saint she wouldn't care.' She gives a cheeky wink.

'Not at all: you were dead helpful. Ellen, I've never seen a more thorough greenhouse inspection. Maybe you'll be a gardener when you grow up.'

Ellen shakes her head. 'I'm going to be a telegraphist.'

'Are you, now?' I say, trying not to sound too disbelieving.

'I've been learning Morse code.' She starts tapping her mug with a fingernail, lips pursed in concentration. 'There, that one was my name.'

'That's incredible,' I tell her.

Peggy sticks her tongue out at me behind Ellen's back. 'You should come down to the village more often,' she says. 'Pop by for a cuppa any time. We owe you one, now. It's two doors down from the pub, with the green windows – you can't miss it.'

'All right then, I will.' After they've said their goodbyes to Mutton, I let Peggy and Ellen back out on to the footpath to finish up their walk.

I'm just returning from waving them off when I hear a rattle-rattle from above. A window on the upper storey is opening. Arabella sticks her head out. 'Vee. Get up here. Now.' It's one of the rooms on the closed wing. I can only assume she's been following my progress round the house, as there's no other reason for her to be in there, and with the shutters open.

Sighing, I scrape off my boots and slink inside, through the Allens' kitchen and into the main hall. Arabella is waiting for me at the top of the staircase. She does not look best pleased. Her lips have gone all pale and she's frowning up a thunderstorm.

'How can I help you, your Ladyship?' I ask, bobbing a curtsey from the bottom step.

Her frown deepens. 'Come up here. Why are you speaking like that?'

'I'm your employee, aren't I?' I ask as I climb. 'Vee for valet.' Peggy's talk has only brought back memories and fanned my anger.

'You're not upset about the other night.' Coming face to face with her on the landing, I cross my arms. 'As a matter of fact, I am.'

'Fine.' She squares up to me, standing to her full height. I'm still the taller one, though. 'Speaking as your employer, then, I don't pay you to spend your afternoon flirting with girls from the village.'

'I don't know anything about that. I was just being friendly.'

'And I was born yesterday.' But it's clear that I've wormed under her skin with this: her breaths come quickly, a vein twitching at her temple. 'I really can't imagine what you see in that Peggy Wight. I always found her exceptionally rude.'

She's jealous, I think with a thrill. I knew I hadn't imagined it all. 'Look here,' I tell her, 'everything that needed doing has been done. I have a right to entertain guests from time to time.'

'Not on my property, you haven't.'

'Well, I don't have my own property, do I? Or even my own living quarters. Because you haven't lifted a finger so far to fix up that cottage.' Almost a month, and there hasn't been a whisper of moving me out of Charlie's room.

Arabella looks away first. 'We don't have the finances at present.'

I hadn't been attracted to Arabella, not at first – she was too odd, too distant, too eccentric. Yet, ill-advised as it was to let my guard down, I allowed her strange courtship to win me over. The awkward flattery I found charming. The intimacies we've shared. But I'm tired of this ambiguity, I realize now. I won't be thrown scraps. Either she can admit what I am to her, or we can draw a line under it all here and now. I lift my chin in a challenge. 'That's the reason, is it?'

Her shoulders twitch. 'I don't know what you are suggesting.'

So she wants to pretend she was never chasing me to begin with – a cat toying with its prey. Still, I'm certain now that I haven't been misinterpreting her.

'Listen, Arabella,' I sigh, taking a step back, 'you say whatever you like. All I ask is that you make your choice, and stick to it. I've had enough of the game.'

She continues to feign that she doesn't understand my meaning, but I can see from the way she's fidgeting about that she does. 'You have to understand,' she says at last, 'it is not so simple for me. I cannot live as other people do. This curse . . .'

I have to shake my head at that. 'Haven't you had enough of that excuse?'

Don't wait for her answer, just head down the stairs and back out of the door. It's up to her whether she'll go away and reflect further. Either way, I've said my piece, and though Arabella may not be happy to hear it, I certainly feel much better to have it off my chest.

NINE

ARABELLA AND I treat one another very civilly after our encounter on the landing. The fire of her passion has gone out. I keep catching myself regretting having said anything to her. Missing her attention. But then I remind myself that the uncertainty had been driving me doolally. A little boredom never hurt anyone.

Christmas Day arrives with a stiff, frosty breeze. I get a nice card through from Lou and Gladys – handmade, with a Welsh dragon done in silky red ribbon – and one from Peggy and Ellen, too. Nothing from Mam or Dad. After breakfast, we all gather in the morning room to exchange presents. Arabella hands Mrs Allen a belt of cloth – the traditional gift for female servants. The fabric is a deep blue colour, bringing out Mrs Allen's eyes when she holds it up in front of her. 'Oh, that's lovely, that,' she says. For Tom, there's a tin of high-end tobacco, which I intend to persuade him to share later in the day. In the meantime, he shakes first Arabella's and then Reacher's hands appreciatively. Last, Arabella comes to me, presenting a brown paper package. It has a textile squash to it, but it's smaller than the one Mrs Allen received. 'I didn't think you would want any cloth for a pretty dress,' says Arabella.

'What gave you that idea?' I quip, allowing the familiar joke since it's Christmas. Pulling back the wrapping, I reveal a pair of gloves. They're made of a buff capeskin, with a simple embroidered pattern on the wrist-length cuffs. When I dip my fingers inside, I find warm fur, softer than a bed of dandelion seeds.

'Russian rabbit,' says Arabella.

Reacher snorts. 'Not rushing enough.' Despite his warm manner, I can't help but remember what I overheard him say to Arabella after the card game. He'll spend his Christmas Day cracking jokes with us, but – deep down – he doesn't see the Allens and me as anything more than the staff. A little of the warmth I'd previously felt for him has died.

Arabella ignores his interruption, tilting her head at me. 'Try them on, do.'

They're a perfect fit. I flex my hands, enjoying the creak of new, creaseless leather.

'I sewed the pattern myself,' Arabella adds casually, as if this is nothing, something any employer might do for her staff.

I re-examine it, noting that what I'd first taken for abstract shapes are in fact stylized flowers and foliage. 'They're beautiful,' I breathe, holding them up for Tom and Mrs Allen to admire, then down for Mutton to sniff. I can already tell they're ten times warmer than the wool gloves I normally wear through winter. 'Thank you, Arabella. I love them.'

Arabella shrugs. I note she's folded up the brown wrapping paper, will most likely be keeping it even though I've torn it quite a deal. 'It's more a gift for myself,' she says. 'I can't have my gardener losing her digits to frostbite, can I?' But she can't hide how pleased she is that I like them.

'I've got a present for you as well,' I say.

'Oh, you didn't have to.'

'Well, for everyone, really,' I add – though that's not strictly true. 'You all have to follow me. It's outside.'

'God, it's not a treasure hunt, is it?' mutters Reacher, but he dutifully files along behind the others as I take them to the front door.

I nod at Arabella to open it. 'Go on. You just need to stick your head out.'

She gives me an appraising glance, then does as I command. The four of them cluster in the doorway, looking out over the yew bushes. I had a busy Christmas Eve, out there with my shears. The two largest plants have been transformed – no longer hares, they're now a pair of fine hounds, modelled after our very own noble beast.

Tom, Mrs Allen and Reacher step outside to admire them properly. Grinning in delight, Tom grabs Mutton around the neck and asks, 'Who's that, then?' The dog catches the excitement and starts up an ear-splitting series of barks, his wagging tail threatening to knock Tom over.

I sidle up behind Arabella, who has remained on the front step. 'I hope you don't mind,' I say, 'but I thought it was time to turn over a new leaf. Let's start again. No more blessings, no more curses.'

She turns her face slightly, so I can just see part of the profile. I'd worried she might be upset at the desecration of the hares, but no – she's smiling. 'No more games,' she whispers. Then, before I can properly register the words, she strides out on to the path, clapping her hands. 'Mutton, you are honoured!' Laughs as the dog bounds over to her.

Now I'm the one left watching on the step. This fizzing in my chest. A hope I've not been allowing myself to feel. Warm all over – not least in my hands, held tight in their new gloves.

*

Later in the day, we all head to St Anselm's church in Harfold village – even Reacher. Even *Arabella*. She's dressed almost soberly for once, in a smart grey suit and hat. A simple green necklace round her neck – only one chipped bead at the back. Something appealing in the severity of the outfit. It's clear neither she nor Reacher has graced the flock with their presence in a long time, as there are many turned heads and whispers when we enter, some hurried shuffling near the front as villagers evacuate what must be the Lascy family pew.

The church is far smaller than I'm used to seeing, and the pews are crammed together, with room for only one arch on either side of the nave. I suppose it was designed centuries ago for an even sparser congregation – the very first Lascys, Allens, Wights and so on. The walls are done in pale grey limewash, but festive sprigs of holly, green ribbon bows and tapering red candles have been arranged to bring in Christmas colour. There's just the one stained-glass window in the chancel, depicting a white-bearded man – presumably Saint Anselm – carrying a curling, golden staff. On second glance, I notice the face of a hare peeping out from behind his robes, as if hiding.

Arabella and Reacher take their seats impassively, not once looking round to meet all the eyes on them. As servants, the Allens and I sit at the back with our fellow common muck. Bruce is here with a woman I assume is his sister – she has a flushed face and is letting out a stream of discreet hiccups, in any case. Peggy and Ellen spot me and give a wave. I wiggle my fingers back, feeling a bit bad on account of using them to wind up Arabella. Peggy's a nice girl: she doesn't deserve to be shuffled around like a playing card.

I haven't been inside a church in a while. My family were never regular attendees, though Mam liked us all to go for the main holiday services. For several months after what happened with the Reeses, I started going at least once a week, thinking I'd better put on a show of godliness. Looking back on it, though, that probably made me look more guilty – like I was warring with my own conscience.

I'm tall enough that I can still see Arabella's hat from here, over the heads. I barely listen to the service. All I can think about is how Arabella must have turned me over and over in her mind as she deliberated on what gift to give me, must have picked these gloves out from a catalogue, imagining me wearing them. Sketched up the design to add to the cuffs. Then what she said to me this morning, on the doorstep. 'No more games.' I keep turning the phrase over, trying to find the meaning. Some kind of promise. An answer. A decision. Or just another game in itself? My mouth is dry as sand.

I pull my eyes away from Arabella, trying to concentrate as we rise for a hymn. Mrs Allen sings with gusto at my side, making up for my weak contribution as my attention wanders over to the door to the bell tower. That's where George Allen drew his final breaths. Peggy had said that he was the church-warden before her dad. For those who remember George, his presence must still be felt all around this building. That door always a reminder at the corner of their vision. I glance at Tom, suddenly self-conscious, as if I'm intruding on something private by thinking about his brother. His expression is peacefully attentive, nodding along to the words of the song. A soft smile on his face. If he *is* thinking about George in this moment, it must be a happy memory.

After the service, Tom and Mrs Allen turn into the churchyard. 'Me and Nora are going to visit that lot,' says Tom, nodding in the direction of the graves, 'if anyone wants to join us?'

Reacher looks to Arabella, as if waiting for her permission. Arabella shakes her head. 'I have spent enough of my time in that awful graveyard,' she says. 'I will not be going back there until I'm in my own coffin.'

'Merry Christmas,' says Reacher, pulling a face at the rest of us.

Tom shrugs. 'We'll catch you up then, shall we?'

'I'll come with you,' I say to the Allens. 'That is, if you don't mind, Arabella? I'd like to thank Charlie for lending me his bed.' I've heard so much about these dead Lascys that I have a morbid need to see them for myself.

Arabella tilts her head at me, amused. 'By all means.'

Parting ways with our employers, Tom, Mrs Allen and I head into the church garden. We visit a patch of bygone Allens first of all. Tom's people have been living and dying in Harfold village for almost as long as the Lascys, it seems. He points out his grandparents, parents, a favourite spinster aunt. George. The former churchwarden's resting place has been kept impeccably tidy, with fresh flowers already laid out when we reach it.

'George must have been a pillar of the community,' I say.

'Oh yes, he was very well liked,' Tom agrees. 'He knew everyone. Always had time for a chat.' He nods at the headstone, an elaborate affair that stands out from the surrounding Allen graves. 'Lord Lascy paid for that, in George's memory.'

Whatever the rumours, George's death had clearly been generally accepted as an accident rather than a suicide, since he's buried here on church ground. I wonder if Henry Lascy's generous financial assistance greased the way for that ruling – it certainly couldn't have hurt matters.

'Are your family here too, Mrs Allen?' I ask, turning to her. She's in a festive mood today, cheeks rosy as she smiles at me.

'I'm from Marlborough way. Cherhill, if you know it?'

'We met at the Marlborough Mop, didn't we, Nora?' Tom adds. 'Lord Lascy had me along with him to help pick out a new housekeeper. Well, when I saw Nora, I thought there's a woman I wouldn't mind talking to every day.' He winks at her. 'Mind you, I was too twisted up with nerves to speak one pip for the first half-year she worked here.'

Mrs Allen chuckles. 'I thought he hated me.'

'Well, I worked up the courage eventually, didn't I?'

'And you've never shut up a day since,' she retorts, batting him playfully on the shoulder.

After Tom's family, we move on to the Lascys, their headstones far more ornate. I seek out the ones from this century: Arabella's parents, Henry and Caroline (1911); then her brothers Reginald (1914), Harold (1917), Stephen (1920), and Charles (1923). A bare patch of earth to one side, waiting hungrily to one day receive Arabella and Reacher. Laid out like this, it gives me a shiver. Almost easy to believe the talk of curses.

We head back up to the manor via the main road, the fields far too boggy for our Sunday best. 'You've both worked for the Lascys a long time, haven't you?' I ask.

'Oh yes,' says Tom, rubbing his chin. 'That must have been about 1898 you came here, weren't it, Nora? And I've been at the house since '95 myself.'

'You've never thought of leaving, then? Exploring the country a bit?' It's not usual for servants to stay on as live-ins after they marry: most people want to put down roots and start a family of their own.

Tom shakes his head. 'Where would I go? This is my life.' A pull in Mrs Allen's face. I remember what she said on Guy Fawkes Day, about moving nearer to Tom's brother's widow and children. Seems she doesn't quite share Tom's loyalty to Harfold. 'Besides,' Tom goes on, 'this is where George is buried. I can't go off and abandon him.'

Behind his back, Mrs Allen looks at her husband with something like pity.

I'd been hoping to catch Arabella alone back at the manor, but Reacher has other plans, keeping his cousin to himself for a round of duets on the piano, followed by an intense match of chess. Later, we sit down to dinner. As it's a special occasion, Tom and Mrs Allen join us at the dining table, which Mrs Allen has been allowed to clear fully for once, though we still can't quite get our feet under due to a number of boxes that are stored beneath it. There's a great big goose, its skin crisp and shining with oil as Tom serves up, and mounds of roast potatoes, parsnips, carrots, sprouts and stewed apples from the garden. Liberal lashings of wine.

Then comes the Christmas pudding, and we put out the lights as Tom sets fire to a spoonful of brandy, all cooing at the blue flames. Mrs Allen has hidden silver charms throughout, a tradition to predict what awaits us in the year ahead. I find an old tuppence in my portion – a sign of coming riches, Arabella interprets. Tom receives an anchor (safety), Mrs Allen a boot (a journey) and Reacher a button (continued bachelorhood).

'There's a surprise!' Reacher pouts. 'Tell you what, Nora, can

I share yours instead? I could use a holiday. Shall we go and seek out exotic birds somewhere warm? I have been thinking of Southern Rhodesia, or Brazil.'

'That sounds lovely,' Mrs Allen agrees.

'Although I may need to borrow Miss Morgan's tuppence to finance the trip.'

'You can't just pass your fortune on to another person,' says Arabella, still searching her helping for a glint of silver.

'Why not?' asks Reacher. He's already in the middle of accepting Mrs Allen's loot.

But Arabella's attention is on her own bowl again: no amount of mashing at the chunks of pudding will reveal a charm. She's managed to pick a piece with nothing in it. 'Bloody marvellous,' she says. 'No future for me, then.'

'Or maybe you get to decide your own,' I suggest lightly.

She flicks me a glance. Calculation behind her eyes, as if summing something up.

'I'm keeping this tuppence, though,' I add, praying no one else can see the flush of heat that's just come over me.

To end the meal, we have a round of cheeses, biscuits and pickles. By now, we're all glowing merrily. Swapping dirty stories. Mrs Allen wearing Reacher's spectacles for whatever reason. Tom plants a kiss on her chin and they both giggle like lovers half their age. Mutton vomits in the corner from too much goose. 'All good parties end in someone puking,' laughs Reacher.

Finally, it's time to turn in for the night. Tom and Mrs Allen wish us sweet dreams. They practically have to drag Mutton away – he's nowhere near ready for the jollity to end.

The rest of us head upstairs. I hadn't noticed it until now, but Reacher is staggering drunk. Takes a deal of coaxing to get up each step, me in front holding the candlestick, Arabella behind, nudging him on. Halfway up, he knocks over a pile of newspapers. They avalanche down the staircase, sending a fat brown spider scurrying away. Reacher sniggers, then puts a finger to his lips and shushes, as if he doesn't want us to tell what he's done.

'You should move these,' I say to Arabella. 'Someone will break their neck, one of these days.'

'Death by tabloid,' she replies. 'That would make a headline.'

'I'm serious. Maybe it can be your New Year's resolution, how about that? Get the house in order a bit. I don't mind helping.'

But Arabella doesn't look convinced. 'I'll think about it,' she says. 'Come on, Morry, you lump, get moving or I'll kick you the rest of the way.'

'Bellsy,' moans Reacher, flailing around with one hand until he catches her by the wrist. 'My dear, dear Bellsy. My favourite Bellsy. You're all that's left, aren't you?' Tears glitter at the corners of his eyes, magnified by his spectacles. 'Then that will be it.'

Arabella just pats his hand in response. Reacher resumes his ascent, and we all make it to the landing without any casualties, where we help Reacher safely into his bedroom. He makes a wavering line first to Finchley's cage, stooping to kiss the bars with a wet smack, then falls face-first on to his bed, landing at a diagonal with his feet sticking out into space. Looks as though he'll be sleeping deeply tonight.

Arabella and I continue along the landing in silence, before turning into the corridor that houses our two rooms. Tension is crackling in the air – or perhaps just in my skin. At my door, I face Arabella. Try to swallow. Offer her the candle. 'Well, I'll be seeing you in the morning, shall I?'

'Yes,' she says. Takes the light, avoiding contact with my fingers.

Disappointment washes cold over me. I'd thought after the gloves, after what had been said on the front step this morning . . . But no. That's fine. At least now I know where I stand. And next time she tries anything with me, I'll just ignore it. She can't say I didn't give her fair warning. 'All right then,' I say, taking hold of my doorknob and starting to turn it.

'Wait.' My breath catches as she puts a hand to my elbow, just brushing the wool of my jumper. 'May I show you something?'

It's the usual chaos in her bedroom. Discarded threads tangle together in a web of gaudy colours. Arabella places the candle on a stack of hat boxes. She's still in her grey church suit, but she casts the jacket off now, throwing it haphazardly on an armchair that's already covered in rumpled clothing. The cream silk of her blouse seems to shine in the gloom. Crossing the space, she rummages around on her overcrowded shelves, careless of several dislodged items that fall to the floor. 'Here you go,' she says at last, pulling out a scrap of cloth.

I move closer to look, taking it from her when she indicates I should. It's another of her needlepoint pictures – me, of course. In this one, I'm up a ladder, viewed from behind as I reach to fill a bird feeder. It must be from the other week, when I invited Peggy and Ellen into the gardens.

'I was too cross to give this to you before,' she says, but I know she means jealous. 'Anyway, I wanted to apologize. It isn't any of my business with whom you choose to spend your time. You are entitled to have other . . . friends.' The pause ringing with implications. She toys with her necklace, anxious for my reply. Finds the chipped bead.

'Look, I might as well tell you: I only did it to get back at you.'

The twitch of a smile; she's pleased to hear this. 'Oh?'

'That night with the playing cards. I heard what Reacher said about me, after I left. And not a word from you in my defence. Hurt my feelings a bit, that did.'

Arabella swallows. 'Then I am sorry for that as well. I only agreed to shut him up, but that doesn't mean I was right to do it.'

'No,' I accept. 'Well, thank you for this. I'll add it to the collection.' Fold the needlepoint embroidery and tuck it into my pocket.

Arabella is standing now with her back to the shelves, leaning partly against them. One of her hands fiddles with a small wooden toy behind her – a camel, I think – as she speaks. 'They're silly really, aren't they?'

'Not at all. Your work's beautiful.'

'I would have liked to be an artist.' She knocks the camel over, glancing back at it a second in surprise, as if she hadn't realized she'd been playing with it. 'My brother Harry went to the Slade School – this was before the war, of course. He *adored* it. And what stories about all those bohemian types! I had a notion I would follow him there, but my parents didn't like the idea. Especially after . . . Well, then Mummy and Daddy died, and it was just one blow after another.'

I remember Harry from the Epstein bust. He of the fishy lips.

Arabella sighs. 'He did such lovely watercolours. You'll have seen them around the house? He died during the war. The bloody Krauts hit his troop ship. All that talent, gone. And for what?'

'But you still have talent,' I say, nodding at her. 'Why waste it here – on me, of all people? You could go to the Slade now. What's stopping you?'

'Oh no, it's too late for me.'

I can't hold in my disbelieving laugh. Impossible to imagine having all of this – privilege, title, a great big house – and being too scared of my own shadow to make the most of it. I just don't know what can be going on inside her head. 'You're always saying that,' I tell her. 'It's ridiculous. You're still young, Arabella. No – you *are*. So why are you so afraid to live your life?'

She looks away from me. 'I've already told you.'

'The curse, is it?' When she doesn't reply, I take a step away, shaking my head. I'd thought we'd been having a proper conversation. But it's my own fault: I should know better by now. 'Every time I think we're getting somewhere, you and I . . .'

She looks back to me, eyes wide in alarm. 'No, Vee, come back.'

I don't come up close again, but I pause my retreat.

'I *need* you to understand about it,' she says. 'It isn't an excuse, or something I have made up. It is as real as the brick and mortar of this house. Since that night with the hare, every three years, the owner of Harfold has died suddenly and unexpectedly. You must have seen them for yourself in the graveyard today. Freak accidents, unprecedented illnesses. First my father and mother, then Rex, then Harry, Stephen and Charlie. It's followed the line of inheritance exactly.'

'Arabella, I—'

'You're not listening,' she interrupts. 'Charlie died in 1923. Next year will be three years since then.' She's looking at me with such intensity, her whole body leaning forward and her eyes unblinking, fixed on my face. Desperate for me to hear her. 'It will be my turn.'

'Arabella,' I try again, stepping once more into her space. 'I'm so sorry that's all happened to you. I can't even imagine what it's been like. But I promise you, it's just a string of horrible, horrible coincidences.' I reach out to take one of her hands, pressing it gently. Look into her eyes. 'There's no such thing as curses. Or if there is, they come from our own imaginations. You think you're cursed, so you live like you're cursed. But that means that *you* can decide to change it.'

She sighs again, dropping my hand. 'Believe me, I want nothing more.' Her pupils flit down. Looking at my mouth.

I raise my eyebrows. Heartbeat in my throat. 'Nothing?'

She lunges at me, almost violently; grasps my face and pulls it to meet hers, mouth landing hard on mine. Her breath is fast in an animal desperation, nails digging sharp into my cheeks. The urgency of a moment we have both been dancing around for so long. I put my hands to her shoulders and shove her back against the shelves. Ornaments rattle in panic. She gasps, then the shock on her face turns to a grin. I kiss her again, press my body tight against her. The slide of silk under my palms. Her mouth open, teeth on my lips.

We've both been so lonely, in our own ways, but we've found each other now. A shared decision to let this in. 'Forget the past,' I whisper against her. 'This right here is all that matters.'

We must sleep, because I wake in Arabella's bed – alone, but with the sense that she's only just left me. A hollow of warmth where she lay. The room is a pre-dawn dark, our candle long since gone out. I get up, shuddering when the cold bites at my naked skin. Kick around on the floor at random until I feel fabric. One of Arabella's housecoats. I pull it on, the material falling chill and heavy around me. A waft of stale sweat and mildew.

I tiptoe out into the corridor, moving carefully to avoid the many barely seen obstacles. One hand to the wallpaper as a guide, its surface rough and smooth, both at the same time. Painted by hand in China, I've been told at some point.

'Arabella?' I call softly, but she's not here either. Peek into my room, finding it empty but for the glint of reflected moonlight from the dead eyes of Charlie's teddy. I pause to listen outside Reacher's door too, in case she's gone to see him. But no: I can hear his beastly snores even from out here. Finchley the chaffinch is silent tonight. As I move on to the landing, instinct makes me turn my head to look into the closed wing. There – the faintest twinkle of yellow light.

What business can Arabella have in there at this hour? And – trying not to feel too insulted – what's important enough for her to abandon me in her bed?

Creeping softly into the disused corridor, beyond where I've been before in Arabella's company, I feel the air temperature drop even further. The light whispers from around a door down the far end, which stands slightly ajar on its hinges. Every now and again, the beam is disturbed by a moving shadow. I approach, holding my breath, and press my eye to the crack.

As with the chamber of the dead Lascy parents, this room is mostly bare, just a few objects of furniture shrouded like spectres in white sheets. Bare floorboards. Walls covered in peeling blue-and-white paper. Brown circles on the ceiling from historic damp. A lamp has been placed on the floor by the shuttered window, and Arabella kneels beside it, facing away from where I stand. Whatever she's doing down there is obscured by her torso. There's a wooden rattle, then she stands upright, brushing her dust-thick hands on her nightdress.

'You're not as stealthy as you think,' Arabella says, causing me to jump nearly out of my skin. She turns to me with an amused smile. Gestures to the space around her. 'This used to be mine.'

Taking this as an invitation, I step inside. 'You slept here, did you?' Desire for old comfort bringing her here tonight. The glow of past festivities when her family were all still alive.

'I come here sometimes to remember. Childish, really.'

Now she's upright, I can see the small, low cabinet behind her, the dark gloss of its wood reflecting back the lamplight. Whatever she'd been doing just now, it must have involved whatever's inside this. I nod to it. 'What's in there, then?'

She glances behind her, frowning as if confused. 'In there? Nothing, as far as I can remember.'

'I thought you were . . .' I trail off.

'Oh, I was looking for a favourite book, that's all. No idea where I've put it. Maybe you were right about having a tidy.' She speaks easily, her movements loose and relaxed, but I'm sure there's something she's not saying. Tight strain at the very corners of her eyes.

My toes are turning numb against the bare wood floor. I cross my arms, fighting back a shiver.

Catching this, Arabella purses her lips in concern. 'Sorry, I didn't mean to wake you. Will you come back to bed?'

She floats toward me, reaching out to wrap me in her arms. Her body feels coal-hot. Despite my suspicion, I can't help but soften, letting her kiss first my cheek, then my lips. Her fingers stroke, soothing, against the back of my neck, and I slip my arms about her waist. Pull her closer.

When I open my eyes, I can still see the cabinet over her shoulder. Our legs reflected in the dark wood, elongated and warped into one combined mass.

PART FOUR

ARABELLA, 1914

16 February 1914

HOW IS IT that tragedy can strike so suddenly, without a warning? Perhaps, after what happened to Mummy and Daddy, I should have learned this lesson already; but how could I have ever imagined that such a thing would happen to us again?

One moment Rex was here, puffing at one of his awful Mexican cigars as he strode up and down the driveway, telling Mr Bruce off for raking it unevenly. I was sitting out in a lawn chair with a book, trying to make the most of the surprise bout of winter sunshine. I remember thinking that I wished he would keep the noise down so that I could concentrate. Then he did fall silent, and I was pleased. God, I am so <u>ashamed</u> to have felt that.

It was not until Mr Bruce said something or other that I looked up, and saw that Rex had come to a halt and was swaying slightly, one palm pressed against his chest. He had dropped the cigar.

'What is it, Rex?' I asked, standing. As I drew closer, I saw that he was sweating profusely.

'Do you not see him?' he asked. His voice rattled, as if he could not catch his breath. There was terror on his face. His gaze was fixed on a point further down the driveway, but there was nobody there. 'He's waiting for me.' At that, he fell to the ground. He was dead long before the doctor arrived.

It was a sudden heart failure, I am told. But Rex was so young for it; only thirty-two. Where is the sense in that?

Later, I told the others about what Rex had said before he collapsed. Charlie thinks he must have been talking about Daddy – his ghost returned to guide Rex to the other side. But then why had my brother looked so scared? I can't help but wonder if he was instead remembering . . . Sorry, I must put my pen down here before I start to cry again.

VEE, 1926

TEN

'HOW DO YOU ever find anything you need?' I ask.

Arabella looks about the mess of the study as if the problem hasn't occurred to her before now. 'Well, I suppose I just hope it will be wherever I think I last saw it.'

'How's that been working for you, then?'

A quick laugh. 'Abominably.'

We've taken it upon ourselves to organize Harfold's historic accounts, but it's been enough of a challenge to locate them in the first place. They are scattered all over: stuffed into crates; stacked on every surface, pinned down by glass weights; crammed into the pages of books; overflowing from desk drawers; confused by reams of duplicates and illegible notebooks with thoroughly battered covers. It seems like each piece of paper has simply been stored wherever it was last cast down. I didn't realize when I offered to help that it would be such a task to sift through the stew of information.

Mrs Allen has been pitching in when she has the time, mostly cleaning up the grime we uncover whenever we move something. Patches of mould, dead insects, dried-up mouse droppings. She tackles all of these without comment, though I catch her shaking her head occasionally, as if there's another housekeeper who's responsible for the negligence that's led to this point.

We've made the study our centre of operations – a room on the ground floor with wood-panelled walls and windows on two sides. Arabella's influence is less present here, although several extremely large vases of ostrich feathers adorn the corners, and a copper bathtub inexplicably filled with seashells almost blocks the doorway. Still, this is normally Reacher's territory, and his hand's visible in the glass case of delicately coloured birds' eggs on the windowsill, the relative cleanliness of the desk and shelves. I would've assumed it was Reacher's job to keep all the papers in order, but clearly – for all his complaining – he's no better than Arabella when it comes to household organization. Well, this will be a nice surprise for him when he's back from whatever his business is in London this week. Arabella says he's only pretending to work, but really bothering the lads round Piccadilly. I'm not sure if this is true, or just another of her jokes at his expense. Still, I don't blame him if he *is* off looking for warm company: unlike Arabella, he doesn't have an option so nice and close to home.

I lean over Arabella now to deposit a fresh folder's-worth of documents on to the desktop, brushing against her arm on purpose so that she smiles at me. It's been a few weeks since Christmas Day, and Reacher can hardly have failed to notice our new proximity. I spend more nights in Arabella's bed now than I do in Charlie's. But this isn't the only change at Harfold. Since our conversation that night, Arabella has turned over a new leaf – she's taking her destiny into her own hands. There have been no mentions of the curse, and she's even taken to heart my suggestion about clearing the place up. This paperwork is just the start: by the end of the year, we'll have Harfold looking like a habitable house. At least, that's the intention.

Arabella holds up a time-worn sheet of paper, browned to the colour of a strong cup of tea. 'Would you look at this,' she says, 'the deed to Harfold. I did wonder where it had got to.'

'We'll make a secretary of you yet,' I tell her, sorting a statement from Barclays Bank into the correct pile.

She examines the deed a moment longer, lost in thought.

Mrs Allen comes in at this point, carrying a basin of water and a handful of rags. 'I'm done in the other room,' she says. 'I'll get those windows while I'm here.' I move aside to let her through. She has to weave round a particularly vibrant array of ostrich feathers before she can start scrubbing at the glass panes. Under her breath, she's singing 'Rock of Ages' – 'Wash me, Saviour, or I die' – which strikes me as a little blasphemous.

Arabella gives a reflective hum. 'I always thought it would be interesting to have a job.'

Mrs Allen pauses her tune to snort, and I try and fail to hide my own smile.

'What is it? What did I say?'

'Nothing,' I reassure her. 'You just tickled me there. *Interesting.*'

'Is it not interesting?'

Mrs Allen stops singing. 'That doesn't matter either way.'

'You're not doing it for the entertainment,' I elaborate. 'It's always about the money.'

'Oh,' says Arabella. 'That bloody stuff.'

'Can't stand it,' I say, giving her a nudge.

'One never has enough, does one?' She pats a stack of letters from the bank, sorted by us into their own pile over the course of the morning. Many of them had been sitting unopened for God knows how long before we got to them. 'Nothing but debts. I knew we were struggling, but dear Morry has kept me from the extremity of our position. I hope you aren't expecting to move back into that cottage any time soon.'

'Well, my current accommodation *is* pretty shabby,' I say. Then, leaning closer to whisper, 'The landlord's making me share a bed!'

Arabella pats me on the rear. 'And more besides.'

Of course, there's no real need to keep this exchange out of Mrs Allen's earshot. She's the one who washes the sheets, after all. She hasn't commented on our new arrangement directly, though: the closest we've come to talking about it was one morning, early on, when she caught me leaving Arabella's room. I'd tried to stammer out an explanation, and she'd held up a hand to silence me. 'Not my business,' she said. And that seems to be the sum of it.

Arabella clears her throat, then plucks up one of the letters, holding it out to me. 'But look, this one from Mr Gerrish makes a change.'

The name sounds familiar, but I can't place it. 'Who's that, then?'

'Gerrish? He's the man who owns those fields over the river. Farmer Watts's boss. He bought the land from Daddy when everything had to be sold off, but he isn't at all interested in agriculture himself, as far as I can tell: he runs it all from the safety of Warminster and leaves Watts to do the grunt work for him.' She glances again at the lines of handwriting. 'Looks like he wrote this last year to enquire about buying the back paddock from us. He wants to convert it into further farmland. Extend the empire, as it were.'

'There you go,' I tell her, 'that's good, then. Something to line the pockets. And it's not as if we're using the land, without any horses.'

Arabella wrinkles her nose. 'No, that patch is simply too close to the house: one wouldn't have a moment's peace or privacy with farm hands roaming around. I couldn't live with it.'

Surely there can't be any harm in at least entertaining the option, though. When she's not looking, I take the chance to slip the letter into Reacher's in-tray. Just to see what he makes of it. Later, Mrs Allen heads off to make tea, and I find a stash of old photographs mixed in with the kitchen receipts. One of a chubby little boy in spectacles – Reacher – held in the lap of an unfamiliar woman.

'That's Morry's mother,' Arabella tells me, 'Auntie Edith, my mother's sister. He came to live with us after she died.'

'What about his father, then?'

Arabella raises her eyebrows. 'You should take another look at the genealogy one day. His supposed father – Auntie Edith's husband, Arthur – died a clean twelve months before Morry was born.'

I feign outrage. 'An affair!'

'Neither Edith nor my parents would ever acknowledge it – in fact, we have always celebrated Morry's birthday in August rather than November. But the genealogy doesn't lie.'

'I'll have to take a look again,' I say.

I've been back to the closed wing once since Christmas Day. I know it wasn't strictly right of me, but the curiosity had been gnawing at my mind ever since I caught Arabella there, until I was desperate to know what she'd been doing, what she keeps in that wooden cabinet. So, as soon as I had a chance, I silently borrowed the keys and slipped into the disused corridor, creeping my way to her old bedroom, every creak of the floor a gunshot in my ears. The way the boards moved underfoot, it sounded as if there was another tread following directly behind me – enough to make me glance back over my shoulder. In the semi-gloom as daylight filtered through the shutters, everything was so still, so lifeless, like a tomb. But then I noticed that the thick dust that coats the floors in this wing was disturbed by a clear passage along the corridor to Arabella's old room, between the door of that room and the cabinet, as if someone had been walking this way with regularity.

I don't know what I thought I'd find there. A hidden fortune, maybe. Old love notes from a previous flame. A written confession to a deep, dark, terrible secret. More needlework portraits of me. But when I pulled back the cabinet door, heart swaying in anticipation, there was nothing in there. Empty. I put my hands in to be sure, felt around. Just the smooth gloss of dark wood. The must of furniture that's stood dormant for too long.

Still, I'm sure Arabella was putting something back in there when I caught her. Perhaps she realized after that I would come looking, and moved whatever it was to another hiding place. None of my business, but I can't help speculating . . .

We fish out another photograph, this one showing a young Arabella with a boy and a girl of about the same age, all of them dressed in Shakespearean-style costumes: the girls with wide skirts and ruffs, the boy in hose. Arabella has her face powdered white, her lips slashed dark with paint. They are outdoors and, from the props scattered around them on the grass, I assume they're putting on a theatrical performance.

'Ah,' says Arabella, 'that's Dotty Gaskell and Dicky Manvers.

The children of family friends. The three of us were such good chums, once. But then they went and fell in love.'

'With each other, you mean?'

A grimace. 'Dotty and Dicky. A ghastly combination of names, isn't it?'

'What are their children called? Dilly and Dolly.'

'And a dog called Dippy.'

We both laugh at this for longer than it deserves, and I can't look away from her face, the way it glows with joy. That's because of me, I think, my heart floating light. Eventually, I place the picture back down. 'Is that when you lost touch with them, then? When they took off together?'

Arabella pulls a face. 'To tell you the truth, I had gone to bed with each of them on different occasions in the past, so I was rather cross when they chose one another over me. Oh, I see that's surprised you—'

It's so easy to forget that Arabella wasn't always such a recluse. Of course, I'd assumed I wasn't her first love affair, but I'd never thought much on the details of who'd come before me.

For my part, there was a girl in the laundry when I was fourteen. Not one of the other sorters, as I was at the time, but an assistant in the receiving office, who I caught only in glimpses at first. Later, I worked up the courage to ask her name, and soon enough we thought we were quite in love, until she left to go into service. After her, I had a couple of moments with Gladys in the Land Army. Thought there might be something there. I'd always liked the contrast of her husky voice with her exaggeratedly feminine style. Then she met Lou, of course, and that was that: anyone could have seen they were perfect for one another. Unlike with Arabella and her friends, we three never let this come between us. Used to laugh about it, in fact. Something like: 'When Vee took me dancing, she paid for my ticket.' To which Lou might say, 'Really? I'll ask her instead of you, then!' I wish they weren't so far away now.

'Do you miss it?' I ask Arabella. 'Your life before, I mean. It sounds like you were a firecracker.'

At first I think she hasn't heard me as she doesn't respond, but at last she sighs, rubbing her neck. 'Of course I do, but it hardly feels any longer like that was *my* life. It's as if all those wild stories happened to another girl, and I have just heard about them second-hand. As if she could even be out there still, free of all cares, having the most brilliant fun.'

'Well, *I* can see her right here,' I say, worming out a finger to prod Arabella in the chest. 'And this cleaning up is the first step to getting her back.'

'Do you really think so?'

I kiss her on the cheek in response.

Putting aside Arabella's photographs, I flip through a book of cheque stub receipts next – these fairly recent, from the past couple of years. Several of them are missing even so. Mice again? But I've noticed something similar a few times now. Gaps in the accounting. Ledgers missing pages. Records of land sold, but no evidence of money coming in on the banker's statements. And of course debts to the rafters – not all of them explained by the materials in hand. Perhaps the relevant papers are just hiding in other, as yet undiscovered spots around the house. Anyone's guess how Reacher keeps track of them all when they're in such disarray. Still, hard to believe he's never spotted these curiosities. It makes me wonder . . . But I don't have the best head for mathematics. Must be missing something obvious.

Arabella and I escape the study at lunch for a walk in the brisk, fresh air. The snow has come to Harfold, and the gardens look straight out of an enchanted winter kingdom. A crisp blanket over the lawns, disturbed in places by our passage: Tom's heavy tread, my long stride, Mutton's erratic dance of paw prints. Arabella and I head through the statues first, laughing at the piles of white that have settled on them – a lack of dignity in it. Albert the gargoyle's arse has collected a hefty drift, what with all that surface area going spare. The poor nude woman – Peggy's favourite – looks positively hypothermic.

When we reach the lake, it's full ice from bank to bank, a dark shadow at the centre hinting at frigid water beneath. I wouldn't risk it. Mutton's not so worried, though: I can see his tracks where he's been running over it. No fear of death on that hound. At the edges, though, the ice looks solid as bricks. Tom and I will cut some up soon to stock the ice house.

Arabella turns away from the lake, looking out over the lawns. The tip of her nose has turned red as a cranberry, and I have to fight the urge to lean over and kiss it. She has a distant expression, thoughts far off somewhere beyond the cold. Wonder if she's thinking of her parents – the drowned Lord and Lady Lascy forever haunting these waters. 'I haven't a clue about money,' she says, almost to herself. 'You may have noticed.'

I make a diplomatic decision not to answer this.

'As soon as any of the stuff comes in, it has to go back out right away, and yet it still doesn't seem to make the tiniest dent in our debts. How can that be the case? This house is an endless cash-hungry pit. I have given up on knowing what to do about it.' She sighs, her breath puffing white. 'It can't continue like this for much longer.

'Would you ever leave?' I ask.

She shakes her head, loose hairs shushing over her shoulders where all the morning's work has pulled them from her braid. 'All of my memories are here, my heritage. Generations of Lascys have been born and have died in those rooms. I can't abandon that.' Her tone regretful, as if she would like to, if only it were possible. The same answer as Tom; the weight of history a web they're both caught in.

'Well,' I say, nudging her leg with my boot, 'it will end with you and Reacher anyway, won't it? If your predictions are true.'

She considers this. 'Yes, there is always that.'

'So why not end it on your own terms? Sell up and move away. It's all the same in the end, surely.'

Another shake of the head. 'This place is probably worth less than the cost of selling it. There's simply too much that needs doing, between the damp, the rot, the subsidence. It's falling apart more and more each day. You would be better off knocking it flat to start again.'

It's true that Harfold has seen better days, but she must be exaggerating here. Someone with cash to spare could fix its flaws, make it grand once more. Or you could get the National Trust in: open up the lands to the commons in exchange for their help to preserve the building. 'Can't you get a bank loan to tidy it up?' I wonder aloud.

'Morry and I are up to our eyeballs in unpaid loans already,' Arabella says, watching a wren as it hops over the lawn. 'They wouldn't lend me a pot to piss in.' She sighs again. Then, after a moment, frowns. 'Now, I have just had a thought. But it may be nonsense . . .'

'Promise I'll tell you if it is.'

She moves closer to me, and her hand snakes over to touch my elbow. 'I was thinking, they won't give me or Morry any more money. But they might loan a little to you . . .'

'Me? Have you gone daft?' I scoff, scaring away the bird. 'They don't go round giving out great wads of cash to gardeners, Arabella!'

'Not as a gardener, of course. I meant if you owned Harfold.'

'Oh, I see, and I'll call myself the Queen of Sheba while I'm at it, shall I?'

But Arabella presses my arm tighter. 'No, I am serious, Vee. If I signed Harfold over to you – don't look so alarmed! Just on paper, temporarily – then you would have all this collateral against the loan. The bank would *have* to accept your application.'

A nervous laugh bubbles in my throat. 'I don't think that's how it works, Arabella.'

'Yes, the details are more complicated than that, I know, but I am speaking in broad strokes. Daddy used to do a similar thing all the time. It's really just your name that I need to borrow. The solicitors can sort the rest of it out for us – don't worry, I hardly expect you to grasp all the finer points of property law.'

I don't think she intends this to be mean, but there's an implied dismissal in it that I don't appreciate hearing. 'I'm sure not,' I reply, a little waspish, and turn away from her. 'Anyway, I'm getting cold. I'm going back in.'

'Oh, don't be like that, Vee.' She comes creeping up behind me, pressing up to my spine and placing her lips gently against my shoulder. 'I didn't mean it in that way.' Winds her arms around me and squeezes. Her breath tickles the nape of my neck, sending a thrill right through me. 'Would you just think about it, at least. As a favour to me?'

My body melts by reflex in her embrace and I'm helpless against her. 'All right, I'll think about it.' The plan has no hope of working, but if it brings Arabella a sense of security in the meantime, why not let her believe it might?

Reacher returns the following day, the Singer crawling its way slow as a glacier up the frozen driveway. Tom's been shovelling it clear, but the ice left over is vicious as anything; you could break your neck easily if you didn't watch your step. Reacher himself almost goes over as he finally climbs out of the car. Strangely, he isn't as appreciative of the tidied study as I thought he'd be. After taking in the results of all our hard work – the orderly shelves, clean windows, new chronological system – he seems at first panicked, as if he's come home to the scene of a burglary. Even after Arabella and I explain our plans to him, he only pouts and says he wished we'd warned him first. 'What if I need something, and it isn't where I left it? I don't see why you had to meddle so. A man's business is his business, after all. It isn't as though I have any other authority in this house I can lay claim to.'

'Quite right,' says Arabella, rather pointedly.

Well, some people just don't know how to say thank you to a good deed! If Arabella's right about what Reacher gets up to in London, I'd say he hasn't had much success this time around, and it's put him in a temper. This isn't the demeanour of a man who's spent a few days in pleasant company.

But then I think a bit more, about all that missing paperwork. Money that doesn't total anywhere near what you'd expect. The blip of alarm on Reacher's face at the first moment, when he realized we'd been mucking around in his stuff. What if the messy accounts are intentional? Could Reacher be skimming Arabella's finances without her knowing? Just a theory, with no real evidence to prove it. Still . . . maybe I should be keeping a closer eye on him.

In the meantime, there's still plenty more to do, and I turn my attention to the hazard of the stairs over the next few days. I'm still not clear why Arabella decided to store her newspapers there – or why she hangs on to them in the first place. Surely the point of current events is that they're current. Who wants to read about what the weather was like in Cumbria six years ago? But when I ask Arabella to explain the reason for keeping this archive, she just gives me a confused look, as if she can't see why I expect her to know the answer. 'You won't throw them out, will you?'

'So you *are* keeping them for a reason?'

She scrunches her nose. 'I don't know. Preserving the past, maybe. I hate to imagine all the days just disappearing. What if I want to revisit one?'

'Right. Well, can I tidy them away? Maybe you have an empty cupboard in the closed wing?'

She shakes her head. 'No, that won't do. You could put them in the cellar, if you really want to.'

The main door down to the cellar is in one corner of the kitchen, though there's another access hatch outdoors, in the vegetable garden. I've passed both entrances enough times, but never yet seen inside. Never had a reason.

Thinking I'd better check my route first before trying to transport anything, I light a lantern and enter via the kitchen. There's a set of stone steps on the other side of the door, proper old, like something out of a castle. Some people are scared of cellars – the dark and damp – imagining that the earth will close in on them, or that something's hiding down there in the roots of the house. But I don't mind being underground – it's where all the good things come from.

At the bottom of the stairs, I set the lantern down on the floor. Sparse daylight shines through from a narrow slot right at the ceiling. A wooden ladder hangs down below it: the outdoor access hatch.

Around me, rows and rows of wine racks, all empty as a beggar's purse. I wonder if their contents have been drunk and not replenished, or if they were even sold off in the past, given the state of the Harfold finances. Assorted foods stored on shelves against one wall: chutneys, fruit jams, pickles, cordials, dried herbs and seeds. Garden produce from years gone by. Cobwebs hang in ropes from the ceiling. Underfoot, the evidence of rodents: shrivelled droppings and gnawed-up grain husks. Examining an empty shelf, I find a desiccated mouse carcass – presumably a victim of the poison that Reacher had me scatter around. Still, I can't let myself get upset over it. I remove its body, then shift the food up higher until I've created a fair bit of free space. The perfect new home for Arabella's print archive.

Leaving the lantern where it sits to guide my way to and fro, I fetch bundle after bundle of newspapers, depositing them in stacks from the bottom shelf up. I'm soon warmed through, leg muscles twinging from taking the stairs over and over. Newsprint smudging my fingertips so I have to be careful where I touch. Carrying my next armful through the kitchen, I happen to glance down. Nearly drop the lot. Struck with horror. There in clear print: 30 October 1923. TWO PLEAD GUILTY OF ATTEMPTED MURDER.

No. This can't be happening, I think. Not when I've worked so hard to leave that day behind me, when I've finally found a new place to belong. People who want me here. Arabella.

My heart's racing like a hare over the fields. Try to calm myself. *Think.* This newspaper's been on that staircase for years, buried and forgotten. Nobody at Harfold would have a reason to connect the story to me . . . Then again, you never know what detail might jog a memory. Has Reacher read this? I should never have let him see those letters to my parents. I rip out the top page and fold it, tucking it into my shirt. Better not leave it lying around, just in case. After depositing the rest of the stack in the cellar, I head to the morning room, where I know a fire will be burning already. Luckily, no one's around when I get there. I kneel beside the grate and feed the scrap of paper into the blaze. Watch it lick over the curling lines of print. I won't let that day ruin what I've found here.

I breathe out slowly, calming myself. I'm safe again. Safe for now. Dusting soot from my overalls, I stand back up and – not looking where I'm going – almost collide in the doorway with Reacher. My heart starts racing again. How long has he been here? How much did he see?

'I thought Bellsy wanted those newspapers in storage,' he says. Tilts his head in curiosity.

'That's what I did with them.'

'Then what were you burning just now?'

'This one had mould on it,' I say, the excuse coming to me only as I open my mouth. 'I didn't want it to contaminate the rest. You know how it spreads.'

Does he believe me? His expression suggests not. But the paper's already burnt to ashes, and there's nothing he can do about it now.

I have the sense that I've backed myself into a trap of my own making, and I'm not sure how I'm going to get out of it. When I applied for this job at Harfold, I thought I could escape what I'd done. Hide in the English countryside. Start fresh. But what you're running from always catches up with you. And Arabella's not the only one cursed by the past.

ELEVEN

THE FIRST SNOWDROPS are pushing up on the west lawn over by the lake, legions of tiny green soldiers standing to attention. Spring's around the corner and this morning I'm preparing the kitchen garden seed beds, digging in a fresh helping of compost and pulling weeds as I go. I plan on more variety in the vegetable crops this year. While I appreciate that Mrs Allen cooks for us all, there's only so many helpings of plain celeriac a woman can eat before she has to put her foot down. My mouth waters just thinking of what's to come: crisp lettuce, sugar-sweet peas, radishes, beets, pungent bulbs of garlic, tomatoes so plump they burst like sunlight on the tongue. All the better for the care that goes into growing them. Never one to be left out of things, Mutton has found his way to my side and is helping to dig – when he's not chewing the handle of my fork. He lives a charmed life, that dog, and he doesn't even know it. I give his rump a scratch with the fork tines.

Heading round the front of the house to access the potting shed, I notice that Tom's preparing the Singer for Reacher to take out. 'Back to London, is he?' I ask.

Tom shakes his head. 'Just Warminster.' Doesn't elaborate, which is unlike him. Wonder if he has something else on his mind.

I still have questions about Reacher's odd management

of the Harfold finances, and I'm conscious that if he's off to Warminster, it'll be for a business engagement. So, while I'm moving things around in the potting shed, spotting the tin of rat poison I bought last time, an idea strikes me: if I ask Reacher for a lift into town, maybe I can get a glimpse of whoever he's visiting. I pop down my bits and bobs and scoot round the side of the manor until I come to Reacher's study window. Peering through the array of wild bird eggs on the sill, I can spot him at his desk, shoving things into a file. I tap the glass until he looks up. Wave him over.

'All right, Mr Reacher?'

He fights with a stiff latch to get the window open. 'Hello, Miss Morgan. To what do I owe the pleasure?'

'Tom says you're off to Warminster this morning. I wondered if you could give me a lift? I have some seeds to collect at Wheeler's.' Give him a smile.

'Don't they deliver?'

'I'd like them today, while the weather's good for it.'

He adjusts the lapels of his bottle-green suit jacket. 'Well, I shan't turn down the offer of company. But don't go getting any ideas: you're not driving *my* car, understood?'

So a quarter-hour later, I join Reacher in the Singer. It's a very different driving experience to the Renault: she takes her time to get up to speed, and never passes much over thirty-five downhill, the engine grumbling the whole time. Whenever Reacher hits the brakes, they let out a sharp, piglet-like squeal. Still, it's a fresh, sunny day and I let myself enjoy the unfolding countryside, more visible than it was on that previous drizzled drive.

As we pass places with quaint names like Codford St Peter,

Ashton Gifford, Tytherington, Little Sutton and Bishopstrow, Reacher nudges me with one elbow. 'You and my cousin are getting along jolly well.' His expression is hard to read, his eyes roving over the road ahead and a slight scowl of concentration from driving.

'Looks that way,' I agree.

'Who'd have thought . . .' We pass an old tollhouse, coming into Warminster now. 'Do you ever miss your last place? Where was it you were – in Cardiff the whole time?'

I glance at him. Why the sudden interest, I have to wonder. Is this just casual talk, or is he needling for information about my past? Could he have made the connection to that newspaper article? 'That's right,' I say. Tell myself not to panic. 'No, not really – I like it here just fine.'

Both a truth and a lie. That deep heart-ache for what I used to have: my parents, my home, the easy friendship with Lou and Gladys, running round the Reeses' lawn with sweet little Kenneth. But all of that was already long gone by the time I applied for the job at Harfold. And there's so much to love here. The beautiful, green countryside. A garden that's all mine to shape. Tom's solid cheer and Mrs Allen's growing warmth. Funny old Mutton.

Arabella. That swooping in my chest when I'm around her. The knowledge that someone wants me.

Of course, I'm trying to keep sight of reality when it comes to the two of us. Our affair is a comet in the night sky, fierce and bright, passing in a flash. No expectations beyond that. Even if I weren't her employee and from a completely different world; even if she could forget her paranoia and I could escape what happened in Penarth – even then, we'd still both be women, wouldn't we? Not that it can't be done. Lou and Gladys. Others: women I know, women I've heard of. Best not to get carried away in dreaming, though. The star will shoot by. But in the meantime, I tell myself, why not look up to the heavens and admire its passage?

Reacher interrupts my thoughts. 'Was it a large house?'

'Fairly.' I cast around to change the subject. 'And how about you then, Mr Reacher? D'you prefer Harfold or London? I'll bet you get better company up there.'

Reacher gives an expressive sigh. 'Alas, no. The men are all spoken for, ugly, old, or disappointingly *normal*.'

'More's the pity.'

'You don't need to tell me! No, Finchley is the only fellow to share my life. Ah, here we are.' We've arrived in the marketplace, and Reacher finds a place to park the car nearby. Cuts the engine, leaving my ears ringing with silent absence.

We agree to meet back in an hour. As we part ways, I pretend I'm heading for Wheeler's, then dart behind a stationary hackney, the horse rolling its eyes at me. The driver gives me a look himself, so I bend over to tighten a bootlace, using the activity to conceal my peering out after Reacher. Wait for enough distance that I can risk following.

I've been expecting him to head for a business engagement, so at first I'm not surprised when he makes a beeline for the Savings Bank just up the marketplace. But then, to my interest, he overshoots, turning instead into the pub that's one door down – the Three Horseshoes, it's called. I sidle up to the entrance, trying to peer in without it being obvious. Catch a flash of green suit. Reacher's inside, greeting another man at the bar. Then they both move out of my sightline.

I wait a few minutes, now pretending to be winding my pocket watch, then stick my head in. A handful of men – the sort of drinkers I'd expect to see before noon on a weekday. One of them eyes me, wary. Expect they don't get so many women in pubs out here as we did in Cardiff. No sign of Reacher. Searching all round with my gaze, I spot a door to a backroom. A private meeting, perhaps. The man watching me screws up his nose. It's clear that if I go in, there'll be no hope of my enjoying a quiet drink undisturbed while listening at the door.

Stepping back into the street, I see that to the side of the pub – the other side from the Savings Bank – is a covered entrance, which must lead round the back. I try this and find a yard with stables and, at the far end, what look like residential cottages. And yes, there's the rear of the pub itself, a handful of windows at ground level. Crouching down, I peep into some of these until I find one that looks into a wood-panelled room, with two people inside it. Reacher and another man. The cadence of their voices seeps through the glass. Considering our earlier conversation in the car, it does cross my mind that this rendezvous could be of the amorous variety, but the other fellow is really getting on in years, with a receding head of grey hair and the bushiest moustache I've ever laid eyes on. He doesn't strike me as Reacher's type.

Thinking it won't do to be caught eavesdropping, I light a cigarette and lean against the wall, keeping my ear pointed at the window. Now if anyone comes through the covered entrance or glances out of the cottages, it will just look like I've popped out of the taproom to have a smoke in the fresh air. Or so I hope . . . It's not always possible to make out full sentences, but I can catch what Reacher and the other man are saying in bursts. Enough to get the gist. To realize that this stranger is Mr Gerrish, the man who wants to buy the back paddock to add to his farming portfolio. Now this is interesting because, as far as I know, Arabella is still holding her position against giving over that land for agricultural use. I haven't personally heard Reacher raise the topic since I slipped the letter into his in-tray, and I flatter myself in thinking that Arabella would've mentioned it to me if he'd discussed it with her in private. I have to assume, then, that this meeting is happening behind her back.

Gerrish and Reacher are certainly discussing the paddock: I hear that word mentioned several times. The tone of the conversation is friendly, excited. It sounds like the pair are in agreement on most points – at least, there's no argument that I can pick out. Gerrish says something and Reacher responds with his characteristic squawking laugh. Reacher makes a suggestion and I hear several enthusiastic yeses from Gerrish. My forgotten cigarette spills ash on my boots.

Later in the conversation, I distinctly hear Reacher say, 'Let's call it a deposit,' then a flurry of numbers are chucked back and forth between the two men. I risk a swift eyeball to the window and see Gerrish counting out a fair number of bank notes. Dart away again.

Has Reacher promised the land to Gerrish, without Arabella's knowledge or permission? Maybe he knows that Arabella will stubbornly refuse to part with it, but will be grateful for the money once it comes in – an overriding of authority for the greater good. After all, hadn't I done similar by putting the letter into Reacher's tray? Both Reacher and I contriving to pull Harfold out of its bog of debt.

I'm holding my breath in an attempt to hear what happens

next, when a woman comes out of one of the yard cottages. She's wearing a white apron and a look of suspicion. Her hands on her hips, like a schoolmarm. 'Who're you?' she demands, in a way that tells me she isn't asking to be friendly.

'No one,' I say. Wave my long-extinguished cigarette end around. 'Just enjoying a fag.'

'Well, you can enjoy it elsewhere,' she tells me, 'unless you want me to call the police.'

Does anyone ever want that? I smile ever so politely and give a salute, before turning for the marketplace, casting a final, regretful look at the window as I go. Only then do I spot that the room beyond is now empty. The meeting must be over.

Not wanting to miss anything, I go quickly back into the covered entrance and loiter there, trying to angle myself so the woman won't see I'm still close by. After a couple of minutes, Reacher and Gerrish both emerge into the street. Reacher carries a brown paper package that he didn't have with him before: this must contain the money that was handed over.

The two men shake hands outside the Three Horseshoes' door, Gerrish offering a string of thanks, before they part ways. Gerrish heads in the direction of East Street, and Reacher, this time, does go next door into the bank.

The coast now clear, I step out into the marketplace and, looking up at the building Reacher has just entered, I have another realization. I've been elbow-deep in the household accounts after all, tidying them up. Arabella banks with Barclays – *not* the Warminster Savings Bank. So whatever Reacher is doing with this money, he isn't paying it into his cousin's account. I try to convince myself that there could still be a charitable interpretation. Maybe Reacher deposits all Harfold's income into his own account, then transfers it later. Yet this doesn't feel right to me . . . When I was winding my pocket watch earlier, I accidentally moved the hands out of sync, so I'm not sure how much time has passed since Reacher and I parted, but I reckon it should be coming up to an hour now. This must be his last errand. Probably safest to head back to the car and wait for him there.

Ten minutes or so later, Reacher strolls over to where I'm idling by the Singer. I search his face for a sly look, a flash of guilt, but there's no evidence of wrong-doing to be found. 'Ready to go?' he asks me.

'Yes, sir.'

He pauses a moment, cocking his head, and I worry I've overlooked some damning evidence of my own little secret mission. 'Did you get your seeds, then?' he asks.

'Oh, yes,' I say, patting my empty pocket. 'It's only a small packet, but they'll make all the world of difference to the garden – just you wait and see!'

'Wonderful stuff,' he replies.

'And you managed to do everything you needed?' I ask, bold at his easy acceptance of my lies.

'Yes, thank you. A productive outing for all.'

I need to decide whether to tell Arabella about what I've seen. Instinct tells me not to. *Not yet.* I have to play this strategically. I don't have any real evidence against Reacher so far, and I don't know what suspicions – if any – he may hold about me and my past. Each of us waiting for the other's poker face to crack. No: if asked to choose between his word and mine, Arabella may still pick him – even now. He's the only family she has left. Best keep my cards hidden a little longer, at least until

I know I have an upper hand. Though I wonder if this game is more like Old Maid: impossible to win; the only hope that your opponent will lose first.

I'm still pondering all this later in the day, back at Harfold, when I see Tom come stumping past with a basket on his way to the wood-store. When I call out to him, he doesn't return my greeting. Maybe doesn't hear me. Then a little later, on his way back, he passes me once more without saying anything. Unusual for him to miss the opportunity for a chat, and I think again of his subdued mood this morning.

'What's up with him, then?' I ask Mutton, who doesn't offer much in the way of helpful insight.

Mrs Allen brings me out a cup of tea a little later. 'Tom all right?' I ask her, blowing on the hot liquid. 'He seems a bit down in the dumps today.'

She makes a sympathetic tutting noise. 'Don't mind him, he always gets like this round this time of year. It's the eighteenth of February today, George's anniversary.'

'The day he died, you mean?'

A nod. 'He'll be all right again tomorrow.'

It's strange to know that Tom walks around all the time with this secret grief still heavy on his chest. He's usually so cheerful, so open. His good mood can be relentless. I wonder for the first time how much of it's a mask. A person can't really be happy every waking minute. Not sure what to say next, I take a sip of tea. The flavour's weak – probably made from sweepings. Another of Harfold's embarrassed economies.

'He likes having you around, you know,' says Mrs Allen, in a sudden tangent. 'He's friendly to everyone so it's hard to tell the difference, but he does think the world of you. It's nice for him to have another person to talk to; Bruce was never much of a chatter.'

'Tom's been very welcoming to me. That is, you both have.'

Mrs Allen shakes her head with a rueful smile. 'Well, now I know you're a liar!' Then she sighs, her breath white in the winter air. 'I didn't mean to be rude to you, when you started. I only wanted to warn you. But I never had a hope of getting you to listen, did I? And now here you are, just as tangled in her web as the rest of us.' Her eyes flick in the direction of the manor, where a light burns in the morning room.

'I wouldn't put it like that,' I say, after a moment.

'If you'll let me give you one piece of advice, Vee: keep your wits about you. The Lascys . . . Tom's always singing their praises, but nobody else round here's forgotten how it was when Lord Lascy sold off all that land. And that's without mentioning Miss Yates – the children's old governess, that is. Lovely woman; I still write to her from time to time. Well, I don't believe for one minute those hidden cocaine tablets were ever hers, not after she'd come crying to me just the week before about some nastiness Lord Lascy had tried on with her. He just wanted an excuse to kick her out after that.'

'That's dreadful.'

Mrs Allen purses her lips. 'As for Lady Lascy and Mr Reacher . . . well, the apple doesn't fall far from the tree. Look what they did to poor Bruce when he couldn't work any more – evicted him from that cottage without so much as a parting goodbye. Oh, he's too much of a gentleman to complain about it, but that doesn't make it right. So I have to ask, what'll they do when Tom and I get too old to be of use?'

When Tom had told the story, I'd got the impression Bruce had chosen to leave, moving in with his sister so she could take care of him. However, playing the conversation back now, I realize that had been my interpretation – Tom never actually said it'd been Bruce's decision to go. My mind turns to Dad. The Reeses. One squint in the wrong direction and you're out. I still feel a spike of fierce anger just thinking about it. Even after everything that's happened since. 'Why do *you* stay, then?' I ask.

'Oh, I've asked Tom to leave plenty of times: set up a nice bed-and-breakfast or public house together, something like that. Own our lives. But he won't listen – all on account of George's memory.' Her mouth twists down. 'You've heard what happened to him, I suppose?'

I nod, remembering the gory details of Peggy's story.

'Tom thinks George did it on purpose. I reckon, deep down, he feels like he failed George by not noticing his pain. Leaving him behind now, well, that would be failing him all over again.'

'And what do you think?' There's a long pause from Mrs Allen, and I worry for a second I've come up against one of her walls again.

But then she leans in close to say, 'George would never have left his family like that. He loved those kiddies. And without saying a word to Tom . . .' She looks up at the main house, as if searching its windows for an answer. 'There's no way of knowing, but I think it was a tragic accident. Lord knows, we've had enough of them at Harfold over the years.'

At the top of the garden, Tom crosses the lawn with a barrow, Mutton trotting loyally at his heel. We both fall silent for a moment, watching him pass, as if afraid he will hear us across this distance.

'Well, I'd best get back,' says Mrs Allen, at length. 'You done with that?'

I drink the last inch of tea and hand the cup to her. 'Thanks.'

Turning to head in, Mrs Allen clears her throat. 'You won't tell anyone I said all that?'

'Course not.'

'I don't mean to give the wrong impression: there's plenty of good here as well. Just . . . watch you don't make Harfold your whole life like Tom has. Like Bruce did. It won't give you anything in return.'

Later in the evening, I find myself still thinking about George.

'Did you know Tom's brother, then?' I ask Arabella.

We're in her bed, sweat cooling on bare skin. Her head resting on my chest so I can run my fingers through her hair. I love these moments of calm together, away from the world, away even from the light. Here, we could be anyone. Everything feels possible. Arabella doesn't reply for so long that I think at first she's fallen asleep, her face hidden from me. Then she finally says, 'George Allen? Not well, no.'

'Mrs Allen was telling me it's the anniversary today, of when he died.' I tuck a strand of hair behind her ear, letting my touch linger on her jaw.

Arabella hums in thought. I feel the vibration through her skin. 'What's today – the seventeenth?' So like her, not to know the date. Always in her own world.

'Eighteenth.'

'Oh,' she says. 'Well, he would have died on the night of the seventeenth. The eighteenth was just the day they found him.'

We lapse into silence for a few minutes, then Arabella wriggles away from me and props herself up on an elbow. All I can see of her is an outline. 'Why are you asking?'

'No reason,' I say, truthfully. 'It was just on my mind.'

'Hmm,' says Arabella, flopping back. 'It all seems so long ago.'

But the loss is still here, haunting Harfold as much as any other.

I won't go so far as believing that the manor is a cursed place, but I have to admit there's a dark weight over it. *A tragic accident. Lord knows, we've had enough of them at Harfold over the years.* I wonder why Arabella has convinced herself the tragedy only falls on her immediate family – what about George? Or Reacher's mam, further back again. Why does her imagined curse start only with her parents' deaths? I think of the genealogy, the stitched lines of ownership. The reversal of years of good fortune; the hare's curse leaping from name to name. A creeping sensation moves up my spine. On the other side of the mattress, Arabella's breathing is slow and heavy, as if she's already deep in sleep.

The next morning, I take my daily walk-around to check over the gardens. Bump into Tom, who chatters away as if yesterday had never happened. It's good to see him with the spring back in his step. I start at the front over by the house, inspecting the yew dogs. All traces of their former shapes long forgotten. Now that I think of it, for all the fuss that people round here make about hares, I've never seen any of the buggers nearby. Badgers, foxes, deer, rabbits, plenty of Reacher's beloved birds – but not a single hare. Makes me wonder if they even live in this part of the country at all. I cross the east lawn to the paddock, passing the old cottage on my way. I'm not sure when I stopped thinking of it as *my* cottage. But I feel no lingering emotion for it – it's just a sad, empty husk. I can't imagine I'll ever return to it. The main manor is my home now. I turn to face it, looking over its familiar red-brick front, the clinging ivy. For just a moment – only for the fun of it – I let myself imagine what it would be like to be owner of a house like this. No landlord to pay, no camp bed on a pal's kitchen floor, no servants' quarters with the knowledge that my employer can send me packing on a whim. Trundling up my drive in my motorcar.

Over by the woods, a cherry plum has started to unfurl its white, star-like blossoms. Soon the green buds will be returning in force. I head through the statue garden, patting Albert on his stony arse as I go past. Check in the conservatory: rows of sleeping pots, just waiting to jump to life. In the orchard, a branch has come down in the wind – only a small one. I'll ask Tom to move it later. Cross the west lawn, and . . . Come to a halt. The snowdrops at the lakeside. I drop to my knees to examine them closer. A silvery froth fuzzes at their bases. Grey mould. How long has it been there? I don't remember seeing it yesterday, but there's so much of it, it seems impossible that it's all grown up overnight. A creeping sickness.

Working slowly and carefully, I inspect the area to find the reach of the damage. It's got to all the snowdrops on this section of the lake bank, but doesn't seem to have spread any further yet, though I'll be careful to keep checking over the coming days. In the meantime, I need to remove the existing threat.

First off, I fetch Tom's barrow and a spade, then start digging up the infected plants, heaping their corpses all together. Need to make sure not to drop any scraps, not to leave behind any sick material. Then, once everything is gathered, I take it to the bonfire heap for burning. I won't be able to plant more snowdrops on that spot for years to come – not until I can be sure the earth is free of contamination.

TWELVE

ARABELLA AND I spend most evenings together in the drawing room these days, discussing our plans for the manor or just sitting in companionable silence, enjoying each other's drowsy company. I find the stuffed animals in here less unnerving, almost homely, as the firelight plays over their pelts – with the exception of Miss Moppet whose bug-eyed, vacant stare will never be anything but demonic. It's a wonder nobody's ever 'accidentally' placed her too close to the open flames. Sometimes we play cards together – games for two people: cribbage, German whist, Truc. Other nights, I read whichever books I can safely salvage from the death-trap that is Harfold's library, while Arabella writes in her diary or works on a new needlepoint design. Her current project is much more ambitious than the little scraps she's shared with me before – a winter view from the front lawn of the manor and gardens. Between the yew hedges, chalk lines represent where Tom, Mrs Allen, Reacher and Mutton will eventually be sewn in. Beyond them, in the front doorway, two women already stand close together, almost touching.

Reacher doesn't normally sit with us, perhaps feeling like a spare wheel now Arabella and I are so tight-knit. One evening, however, he unexpectedly asks me to join him in the study for a drink. I try to tell myself it's just a friendly invitation, yet I can't help leaping to the worst possible conclusions: that it's about Mam and Dad, about the Reeses. But I shouldn't work myself into a panic until I know for sure, I try to tell myself as I follow him into the room, stepping carefully around the copper bathtub of seashells that still stands pointlessly in the doorway. Reacher gestures for me to pull up a collapsing damask armchair opposite the desk. The space is lit low by a single lamp, and the dark wood panels absorb the light in a way that makes it look somehow both smaller and larger than it really is. Cave-like. The curtains haven't been drawn, and the two of us are reflected back in the black windowpanes, the play of light and shade like a chiaroscuro painting. Since Arabella and I gave it a tidy, the place has remained looking neat enough, papers still held in their smart bushels on the shelves. For all Reacher's fuss over our interference, even he must mark the improvement.

'Scotch?' asks Reacher, heading for the drinks cabinet. 'Or I could make highballs. Do you like ginger ale?' Now that I look at him properly, he doesn't seem quite well. The pinch of stress around his eyes, skin washed in a chalky grey. Roots of his hair showing where he hasn't applied henna of late. I wonder what's weighing on him.

'Lovely,' I say, relaxing back into the chair in an effort to put myself at ease.

Reacher fusses about with ice from a bucket, then dashes out the measures very roughly. No wedge of lemon. Maybe I should try growing them in the greenhouse. 'Here,' he says, plonking the glass down in front of me, before crossing to take his seat at the other side of the desk. He's brought the whisky decanter with him and, as it catches the light, I see it's been engraved with a set of initials: HL. Catching my gaze, Reacher looks down at the scratched letters as well. 'Uncle Henry,' he says. 'This used to be his study, of course. Before . . .' Doesn't finish the sentence.

I let the silence stretch out, taking a sip of my drink. Heavy on the Scotch. The ice-cooled glass nips at my fingertips.

'Harfold is the only real home I've ever had,' Reacher says, the honesty of his tone taking me by surprise. 'My mother moved us around a lot but every summer we would return here.'

'I suppose Arabella was like a sister to you, was she?'

Reacher snorts. 'No. She always made it very clear that I was an interloper. A sort of charity case. Not really family at all.'

'That surprises me.'

'Does it?' He lifts his eyebrows. A scar still there on his forehead from the thrown teacup.

'Maybe not.'

'She used to pretend she couldn't see or hear me. You know, childish games. "Did anyone hear that? No? Just the wind" – that sort of thing. And there was one time when I was maybe eight or nine, she shut me in the ice house for about fourteen hours. The cold . . . I was completely blue by the time they found me. And I had pissed myself, of course.' He taps a thumb against his own glass. For a moment, I can see back through the years to the little spectacled boy in the family photo. 'She still brings that up, you know. "Don't wet yourself, Morry."'

'God.' I don't know what else to say.

His eyes flick over me, running something through his mind – I can see the decision in progress. At last, he sighs and knocks back a swig of his cocktail. Looks at me again. 'And let me tell you the irony of it all: I really *am* her brother. Biologically, that is.' He waves a hand, as if he expects me to protest the matter. 'My mother never admitted it, nor Uncle Henry, but Auntie Caroline told me once she thought I was old enough. The secret of her husband's infidelity.'

'With her own sister, you mean?' I remember the genealogy upstairs, Arabella telling me to check back over the dates. Only three months after the husband had died.

'Bellsy has never accepted it,' Reacher goes on. 'She doesn't want to admit that Uncle Henry would have done such a thing. But why would Auntie Caroline have told me, unless it was true? It would be some lie to tell.'

I've allowed myself to be caught up in the gossip, but now I come back to myself. 'Sorry, Mr Reacher,' I say, sitting up straight, 'but why are you telling me this?'

Reacher squares his shoulders. 'My *point* is that, despite her flaws, Bellsy is the only family I have left. Her wellbeing is a concern to me, as is the future of Harfold.' A challenging lift of the chin. 'Therefore, you can imagine how worrying it is for me to hear that you have convinced her that she needs to—' He breaks off, frowning. Clears his throat. 'To sign the manor over to you.'

It all becomes suddenly clear. I straighten up even further. 'Now, wait just a minute, sir: that's not what's happening here. I don't know what Arabella's told you—'

'She wouldn't have told me anything if she'd had her way, but I found the contract she had written up at your request.'

'It was *her* who asked *me*!' I can hear my voice climbing in volume. Try to reel it back in. *Stay calm, Vee.* 'She had an idea about it being only for show, just to help you get a loan to fix this place up. And I already told her no. It's a daft plan – it makes no sense.'

'But where did Arabella get the idea? You really want me to believe that you weren't the one who put it into her head?'

'No! I mean yes. What am I, on trial now? Fucking hell!' I'm sweating, angry prickles forming in my armpits. Can feel my temper getting away from me.

Reacher scowls at my language. 'I didn't want to accuse you of anything, Miss Morgan, but you must appreciate that you look rather like a cuckoo in the nest. You cannot blame me for feeling suspicion as to your motivations. Then, to compound matters, you have always been markedly silent about why you left your position in Cardiff. It makes me wonder if this isn't a habit of yours, and you got caught out in something similar there . . .'

He wants to get a rise out of me, but he's chosen the wrong thing to say. Revealed how little he knows. A calm confidence washes over me. 'No,' I say. 'You know that's not the case, sir: you had my references, didn't you? I came here for the job, plain and simple. I was hardly expecting to start anything with Arabella. That's just how it turned out.'

'So you expect me to believe you actually care for her?'

'I do.'

His tone until now has been firm, almost condescending, but now a meaner edge appears. 'Well, I am sorry, but she doesn't give a rat's shit about you.' I smile, all polite. This is the same behaviour I saw that night of the card game: Reacher's friendship extended only until the moment his position in the social order is threatened.

'I have evidence to suggest otherwise.'

Reacher claps his hands at this, the noise almost loud enough to make me jump. 'Ha! Well, if it really wasn't your idea, then I suspect that she is playing you right back! Do you really believe this is about clearing a debt?' He pulls a face of mock pity. 'I know you are from a poor background, Miss Morgan, but even you must know that's not how property law works.'

The same thing Arabella said, now from the other side. I turn from him for a moment, eyes falling on a knot of cobwebs under the desk. A spindle-legged spider lurks at their centre. 'Oh, I see what this is about all right,' I say. 'You want her all to yourself, don't you? I've always known you were jealous. You can't bear that she'd want to spend her time with someone like me.'

'No, that's not—' Alarm in his face.

Another flickering realization comes then. 'Wait, I get it: it's Harfold, too. You think you're the rightful inheritor. Next brother in line. It should have gone to you, not to Arabella. Is that it? God, you must be pissing yourself at the possibility it could be mine before it's yours!' Reacher's expression darkens when he hears me twist his earlier vulnerability against him. 'You're just worried you won't be able to leech off her any longer,' I go on. 'If anyone's a fucking cuckoo, Reacher, it's you.'

'Fine,' he says, standing up so quickly his chair squeaks over the floor. 'Don't say I didn't try to warn you.'

'And maybe *I* should warn Arabella about what you're up to with Gerrish,' I say.

That puts the blood out of his face all right. But then he swallows, gives a thin smile. 'Am I supposed to be afraid of your threats?' He looks down his nose at me, disdain clear on his face. 'You don't belong here. You are *nothing*. Sign the deed, don't sign the deed. You should know by now that people "like you" – as you put it – can't win against people like me.'

I don't wait around to hear any further insults. Standing

sharply from my own chair, I go stomping out of the study, slamming the door behind me, loud enough to set all the picture frames in the corridor rattling. Can't bring myself to care – let them fall, let them smash! My pulse is roaring in my ears, like a storm at sea. I push through the next door into the drawing room.

Arabella is curled up on a nest of cushions in front of the fire, reading a slim book. Tennyson. She doesn't look up as I enter, just turns a page and says, almost to herself, 'How was it?'

'Your cousin! I swear to God, I could kill him.'

She glances at me, one eyebrow raised. 'Goodness, what did he say?'

I shake my head. 'Where's that property deed, then? I'll sign it right here and now.'

If Arabella's surprised by this sudden change of heart, she doesn't show it, just dog-ears the book to mark her place, then sets it down. Hauls herself up from the cushions. 'I left it in the library, I think. Shall we go through?'

Without a fire on the go, the room has a deep chill to it. I catch a damp, musty smell – paper gone to rot. Arabella lights one of the reading desk lamps. As she rummages in the drawers, my spitting rage cools into something more calculated. I have time to wonder if I'm being thoughtless, letting Reacher's words goad me into a decision that I otherwise wouldn't have made. *She doesn't give a rat's shit about you.* But then I picture his smug, toadish face. Anything to wipe that mocking smile off it. I do belong here.

'*Voilà!*' says Arabella, pulling out a fountain pen and a crumpled sheet of paper, before moving aside some clutter to set both on the desktop.

'Let me have a look, then.'

Instead of moving for me to pass, she steps closer, reaching up to brush a thumb against my cheek. 'You know, you *are* adorable when you're fired up like this!' Her smile is all teeth. 'Remember that first time you walked in here, practically frothing at the mouth because you thought I was about to dismiss you? God, I wanted you right then and there. I think that's what they call love at first sight.' She must see a change in my expression, as she hesitates, withdrawing her touch. 'What?'

'You just said love.'

She turns her face away quickly, a rosy flush rising in her cheeks, like the arrival of dawn. 'No, I didn't.'

Placing my hands around her waist, I bring her close, pushing my face up to hers. 'Yes, you did!' I'm smiling now, enjoying seeing her like this, her shell cracked open to reveal the warm innards.

'Well, I didn't mean to. And I shan't say it again.' A deep breath. 'But yes . . . I do, as a matter of fact.' She meets my eye, then pushes me away, holding her hands up over her face to shield it. 'Oh, stop looking at me! You are making me embarrassed.'

Despite her words, she's struggling not to giggle as I catch hold of her wrists, moving them down. I lean in to kiss her on the chin, the forehead, the mouth.

And in the back of my mind, a small voice asks: *is* this love? Being around Arabella excites me. She's like a blazing fire under every inch of my skin. Like a beast trapped in my abdomen, trying to gnaw its way out. Like the shuddering feeling of holding your breath till the moment you think your lungs are about to burst. I love the way she looks at me – hungrily. I love her careless laughter. The animal smell of her body. Her nails against my skin. The quiet triumph she can never keep from her face when she's about to take a trick at cards. How she makes me feel wanted. No longer alone. Is that the same as *loving* her?

Arabella pushes me away again, straightening her cuffs where they've ridden up her forearms. 'Come on then, Faustus, sign away your soul.'

'Funny,' I say, shaking my head. Pick up the fountain pen and start to read the deed. Still not convinced this will stand up before the bank. 'Shouldn't we have a witness?' I ask.

'Don't worry about it. I'll send it to my solicitors tomorrow and they can sort out that side of things. Like I said, they used to do this all the time for Daddy.'

I hover the pen nib over the paper.

'Wait,' says Arabella. Confused, I look up at her. A struggle is happening behind her expression. But then she shakes her head, swallows. 'No – never mind. You go ahead.'

So I sign my name. Well . . . I sign *a* name. And now, however temporarily, Harfold Manor belongs to Miss V. Morgan. The Lascy family claim swept away as easily as cobwebs in the morning.

PART FIVE

ARABELLA, 1911

6 February 1911

I HAVE PUT off writing as I don't know what to say. We have been living through a nightmare. Perhaps if I set it down in order, like telling a story, I will finally be able to make sense of what happened – or maybe I will wake up after all.

Two days ago, just after breakfast, Mummy and Daddy went out for a walk around the grounds. They had seemed in a perfectly ordinary mood that morning, reading snippets from the paper aloud to us all. Daddy grew particularly passionate at the news that Amundsen had arrived in the Antarctic: 'The nerve of the man! Does he really think he can beat us to the Pole? Well, I will be first in line to shake Captain Scott's hand when he returns victorious.' Then he put on that ugly old flat cap that Mummy hates so much, saying he wanted to see if the daffodils were out yet, and would I like to join him? But I said no, as it looked like rain and I had just used the irons on my hair. Mummy said she would go with him instead. I can't help thinking that if only I had been less bloody vain . . . Come lunchtime, we realized that our parents still had not returned, and all the horses and motorcars were accounted for so we knew they had not taken an impromptu trip into town. After another half-hour, we children were all traipsing about in the drizzle to try to find them.

Rex put himself in charge, as always: it was under his command that I went to the lake.

At first, I thought it was a pair of logs that I saw floating at the centre. Then I spotted Daddy's cap, left at the water's edge.

Mr Allen arrived within moments of my shout and, before anyone else had got to us, he was pushing out in a boat. I could barely stand to watch as he worked the oars. Every moment that passed was an agony. I almost dived in myself, but thankfully Charlie reached me at that point and had his arms around me to keep me back.

When Mr Allen at last pulled them from the water, I already knew it was too late. There was something in the way my parents' limbs refused to move, how much of a struggle it was to get them flat. Even so, Mr Allen began to apply pressure to Mummy's chest in an attempt to resuscitate her, the boat rocking so much I was sure they would all go overboard. Then he tried the same for Daddy.

Finally, Mr Allen sat back and lifted his head to look at Charlie and me across the distance. Then he took up his oars and began rowing back. This time, there was no urgency.

We brought them up to the house, and after that, everything was a commotion. Each person that returned from the search had to be told what had happened; I felt the deaths anew every time I saw the heartbreak on one of my brothers' faces. I kept thinking over and over, 'I am an orphan now.' It just does not seem possible.

Later in the afternoon, the police came to speak to us all, and I had to tell them exactly what I had seen and show them the lake. They concluded that it must have been an accident: one parent had slipped on the damp ground and fallen into the water; the other had gone in to rescue them. But I do not understand how that can be the case. Daddy in particular was such a strong swimmer. He was always out in that lake in the summer and never once had a problem. Perhaps he hit his head as he fell in, and Mummy couldn't manage his weight when she tried to pull him out. But there wasn't any sign of such an injury when the police checked. Harry says it could have been on purpose, but I think that is just the artist in him speaking. Why would they both decide to . . . And Daddy wouldn't have been talking about meeting Captain Scott in the future if he had been planning <u>that</u>, would he? I cannot help but remember all the similar speculation after George Allen's death – also ruled an accident by the police, nevertheless.

We have all been at a loose end these past days. Bloody Morry keeps breaking into tears as if it is his own parents he has lost. I would give him a good slap for it, if not for the fact that he would only enjoy the attention: he just can't stand it when the spotlight is not on him. Even the Allens have been miserable, but then they are almost a part of the family themselves – more than Morry is, in my opinion. I wonder if all this also reminds Mr Allen of what happened to his brother. The commotion, everyone searching for answers. It seems a cruel twist of fate that this came almost three years to the day after that unhappy event. And just like with me and my parents, poor Mr Allen will never know exactly what happened to his brother that night.

VEE, 1926

THIRTEEN

WELL, HERE I am, mistress of Harfold Manor. On paper, at least. Arabella tells me she's sent off all the documentation now, and we'll soon hear back about this loan. Then I can just imagine it: Harfold returned to its past glory. Made better than before, even! Brought kicking and screaming into the twentieth century. A roof that doesn't leak into the bedrooms. Piped water. A central heating system. Perhaps – dare I think it? – electrics.

At the start of March, my twenty-sixth birthday sneaks up on me. I haven't said a jot about it to anyone at Harfold, but I was hoping I might get post from Mam or Dad. No such luck. They'll write one day, when they're ready. I have to believe that.

I do get a note from Lou and Gladys, though. It sounds like they're doing well. Happy. Gladys has a new job as a shop girl, which is just perfect for her; her favourite part of the Land Army was always the standing around and chatting, not the muddy work in between. She describes the uniform in detail – sophisticated black silk, a white lace trim – although she isn't allowed to wear it outside the premises. For her part, Lou has purchased a bicycle with a little bonus she got at Christmas, and has spent the past months zipping round the streets of Cardiff in cycling shorts and a turban, terrifying anyone unlucky enough to cross into her path. They both write that they miss me, but I can read between the lines to know that life is easier with me out of the way. I expect the neighbours have finally stopped leaving poisoned rats on their front step, for one.

Arabella finds me in the hall, where I've paused to read this letter. 'What's the occasion?' she asks, meaning that I never receive post normally – not something I realized she's noticed.

'Oh, nothing,' I say, hiding it quickly behind my back.

She raises one curved eyebrow at me, mischief glittering in her smile. 'Well, now I am even more intrigued.' Takes a step closer. 'Go on: tell me.'

'Did you never hear about curiosity and the cat?'

Arabella is right up square to me now. 'Ah, then what luck that I am no feline.' She darts her face close to mine, then, while I'm distracted, makes a snatch behind my back.

Laughing, I manage to pull the letter away from her in time. 'All right,' I say, 'if you really have to know: it's my birthday today.'

'Your birthday! But I had no idea. Why didn't you tell me?'

'It's not important.'

'Of course it is. You will have to have the day off.'

'I need to do the watering, Arabella!' It's been an exceedingly dry week or so, and my spring plants are all gasping from it.

'Well, after that, then,' she says, pouting. 'As your mistress, I order a day of leisure.'

I give her a prod in the side. 'Aren't I the mistress of Harfold now?'

'Then all the more reason to take a break! I shall think of a delightful activity for us to do.'

So, once I've finished saving the garden from shrivelling up, I down tools and return to the main house, where I find Arabella waiting for me on the doorstep. She's changed into a deep blue cardigan with a white trim, paired with a white neckerchief to create an outfit reminiscent of American sailor uniforms. On her head, she wears a straw cloche hat that would be better suited to summer weather. The thinking behind this ensemble soon becomes clear when, taking my hand, she pulls me through the statue garden and up the steps to the west lawn. 'I thought we could go boating,' she says.

'On the lake?'

'Why not? The sun is out, it's warm enough.' She leads me over the grass with a girlish skip in her step. 'Have you ever been in the boathouse?'

I haven't; I wasn't even aware it was still in use. The wooden hut straddles the lake at its southernmost point, next to a short, unstable-looking jetty. My guess is that it was a Victorian whim, intentionally quaint with its decorative turret and open balcony on the upper storey. The outer walls have a grubby, half-rotten appearance, and lichen clings green to the more sheltered surfaces. 'Come upstairs first,' says Arabella, running up the steps to the balcony.

It's good to see her out of the house, cheeks flushed and merry in the sun. The optimism of the new year has stayed with her; if anything, it's even more noticeable now than it was in January. This is helped in part – at least, in my opinion – by the fact that Reacher has been away this past week, having taken off in a foul mood after I signed the deed. Arabella wanted to be the one to break the news to him, but that didn't stop me from listening in at the door. After all, I've earned the right to gloat. It would've been hard to miss the moment he found out anyway: he hooted like a distressed owl, before launching into a powerful rant, loud enough for me to hear as clearly as if I'd been in the room myself. 'I swear, Bellsy, I am done with you! I know you think this is going to save us, but I am telling you now that you couldn't be more wrong. When you realize that, you had better not come crying to me. I wash my hands!'

I'm not sure when he'll be back, but Arabella and I have been enjoying the time to ourselves meanwhile.

Following her into the top room of the boathouse, I'm made even more certain that it hasn't been in use for some time. There's a strong smell of damp, the various seat cushions chill to the touch. My fingertips come away with a khaki dusting of mould.

Arabella rummages around in a wicker chest, pulling out various items at random: a tin cup, a moth-eaten shawl, a lone sandal. 'We used to go out on the lake every summer,' she tells me. 'You should have seen Morry – he was such a coward about it. All you had to do was rock the boat the tiniest bit and he would go green as a cucumber.' Her tone is light-hearted, but the words make me remember what Reacher told me the other day, about how cruel she was to him as a child. Is there a vindictive air in the way she chuckles at it now? 'Then he'd complain that his arms hurt and he couldn't possibly row, so you would have to do all the hard work if you had the misfortune of being paired up with him. Still, it was all great fun.' She pulls out a man's straw boater. 'This was Charlie's, I think. He used to be in the rowing club at Oxford . . . Here, you should put it on!'

I try to wave her away, but Arabella's too insistent, and the hat eventually makes its way on to my head. 'Very fetching,' she laughs, cupping my chin and standing on tiptoe to kiss me. Nudges one knee between my legs, but when I bring my hand up to the top button of her cardigan, she slaps me away. 'Naughty. Not before we take the boat out.'

I'm not sure where this sudden obsession has come from, but Arabella is clearly hell-bent on the idea, so I follow her down the ladder to the storage room. In here, three wooden scudders are lined up in a row, dusty tarpaulins draped over them. We free the nearest one, which requires chasing away a fat wolf spider first of all. I snatch off swathes of cobwebs.

'When did you last use these?' I ask.

Arabella is quiet for a few seconds – long enough to make me glance up at her, see the twist in her mouth. 'Not since . . .' Her parents. 'Oh, I'm sorry, Arabella. I should've thought.'

She shakes her head. 'No need to apologize. I'm the one who suggested it. It is high time I stop being afraid.'

Once the boat's clear, I drag it to the water's edge. It looks old and tired, but I can't see any obvious damage, so with luck it will still be able to float. 'Here goes,' I say, kicking it in.

We both watch intently, then laugh at each other's seriousness: it's bobbing along just fine.

'Do you think it will hold us?' I ask.

'Of course,' says Arabella. 'You can get in first, though. Seeing as it *is* your birthday.'

'Charming!' I step in. A moment of panic as it shifts under my weight, but then I'm in the seat and still dry as ever.

Arabella passes the two oars over to me, then takes my hand to climb in herself, moving with far more grace than I'd managed. Once she's all settled, I untie the rope and we push off. I've never rowed before in my life, and Arabella's obviously out of practice, so for a while we flounder around in circles, colliding with the jetty and not making it much further than a few feet away from the shore. An alarmed duck beats its wings in our direction, quacking in protest. But at last, we're able to pick up a rhythm and set off, hugging the side of the lake at first, passing along the west lawn, the ice house, the orchard wall with its treetops peeking over.

'Let's go to the middle,' Arabella says after a while, and we splash about until we've changed direction for the centre. The water here is dark and unfathomable. It's nearing midday by now, and the sun is warm overhead, bouncing back off the surface so that I'm part dazzled. I'm reminded of summer days on Penarth beach: Mam and Dad taking me as a girl so I could learn to swim, cup of tea on the pier after. Then, later, returning when we worked for the Reeses. I'd sometimes take a sunset stroll on the promenade, or just a pause to watch the waves from their garden – you could see right down to the sand from one end of it. Little Kenneth used to collect seashells, I remember in a flash. Kept them lined up on his bedroom windowsill, sorted by colour. I'd forgotten about that.

We down our oars now and Arabella carefully manoeuvres round to come alongside me, leaning back and stretching her legs out over her own seat to balance the weight. I shuffle down as well until I'm lying next to her, careful not to let my body dip in the middle: the footwell below us has gathered a shallow pool of water, possibly from a leak, possibly from our poor sculling. Arabella removes her neckerchief, rolling it behind her head as a makeshift pillow, and starts to hum – not a tune I know. I tilt the boater hat down to shade my eyes. Between the rocking lull of the water and the warm light on my face, I'm completely at peace.

'I was the one who found them,' Arabella says, out of the blue. When I turn to look at her, she's still staring up at the sky, face in profile. Her eyelashes cast spiked shadows over her cheeks, making her expression hard to read. 'Mummy and Daddy. That was fifteen years ago, now.'

'What were they like?' I ask. 'Tom always speaks highly of them.'

Arabella's lips quirk up in a smile. 'Tom wouldn't speak poorly of someone if they stole the shirt right off his back.'

'That's true.'

She thinks for a moment, then rubs a hand over her brow. 'Daddy could be a fierce man. Very protective, very proud. And Mummy was rather old-fashioned at heart, I suppose. They weren't the sort to show a softer side, but we knew that they loved us, all the same. They always put us first – no matter what. Even when . . .' Her pupils dart sideways to look at me, though her head remains still. 'Well, as I am sure you can imagine, I wasn't always the easiest of daughters.'

'You?' I say, feigning surprise. 'Go on, you're a walk in the park, you are!'

'And *you* are a horrible liar,' she laughs, slapping me gently with one hand. I catch it and hold it out before me, tracing a finger over her lifeline. 'What do you see?'

'Long and happy,' I say, planting a kiss in the centre of her palm.

'Hmm.' She pulls it away, and I realize I've said the wrong thing, reminded her of the curse fixation that she's been doing so well to forget. 'Of course, their death was when the chain started. If only we had known back then what was ahead of us . . .'

'When did you' – I pause to look for the right words – 'first *think* there was a pattern?'

Arabella frowns in concentration. 'Let me see . . . Well, it was Morry who suggested it first, actually.'

'Was it, now?' Try to keep the shock from my voice. Reacher has previously told me outright that he's never once encouraged the delusion. I should have known that was a lie. Yet another way that he's been taking advantage of Arabella over the years: of course it suits him perfectly to keep her housebound in fear for her life, to keep her attention turned away from whatever he's been doing with her finances. Locked in a little cage like poor Finchley.

But that doesn't matter any more: there's a sea-change happening at Harfold. Because now I'm here to protect Arabella from her cousin's schemes. When she handed that deed to me to sign, knowing how strongly Reacher objected to it, it was all the proof I needed that she's chosen me over him. I've won. And he knows it too – that's why he's gone slinking off to lick his wounds. *You should know by now that people like you can't win against people like me.* Well, this feels a lot like victory to me.

As if hearing my thoughts, Arabella twists her body so that she's facing me. Smiles, showing her teeth. Puts out her hand again and traces – just with the fingertips – up my arm, elbow to shoulder. 'Anyway, I don't have to be afraid of that any longer, do I? Thanks to you.'

'I didn't really do anything,' I say, as modestly as I can.

'Oh no, Vee; you have done *everything*.' She scoots closer and presses her hand to the back of my neck, beckoning me forward to kiss her again. Her lips linger on mine for several heartbeats, soft and unmoving. 'Thank you,' she whispers.

A sudden splash interrupts us, and we both shoot upright, looking round in confusion. There, by the shore: the tip of a grey nose, two wide eyes. A froth of foam.

'No, you silly beast!' shouts Arabella. 'Go back!'

But Mutton won't be told; he continues paddling toward us with an expression of determination.

'Come on then, Muttsy,' I shout.

'Don't encourage him!'

'Who's a good boy?'

The dog draws nearer, mouth gaping in anticipation, until he's alongside us.

'Don't you dare,' says Arabella, though it's not clear if she's speaking to me or to Mutton.

I give her a wink. 'Come up, then, boy.'

Arabella just has time to shriek in disapproval before Mutton's large paws are on the gunwale and he's desperately trying to scramble aboard. The whole boat goes rocking beneath us, and I jump back in an attempt to redistribute the weight. Realize I haven't quite thought through what the addition of a creature of his size would do. There's a split second where the angle is so extreme that I'm sure we're about to go tumbling into the lake, but then Mutton is up and safely aboard. He gives a tremendous bark of triumph, water streaming from his matted fur.

'He's going to—'

Arabella's warning is lost to another scream as Mutton performs a full-body shake.

Back on dry land, we towel off and eat lunch, then Arabella digs around until she finds an old picnic gramophone and collection of records. None of the songs are more recent than a few years ago, so I assume that these are yet more relics of Arabella's brothers. Even so, Arabella picks each one up with exclamations of fond recognition, as if she knows them well and had simply forgotten she owned them. 'I love this one,' she says, brandishing a copy of 'Paddy McGinty's Goat', before promptly dropping it, the disc shattering into pieces as it hits the floor. 'Oh, drat. No, it's fine, there are plenty more.'

I pick up the fragments of shellac, shaking my head. 'Poor goat.'

'Just like him to cause a nuisance.'

It takes a little more searching to find the spare needles, but eventually we're set up to play music.

'You choose,' says Arabella, charitably presenting the collection of records to me.

I pick out 'And Her Mother Came Too', since I know the words to that one. Give the gramophone a wind. Pop it on and wait patiently through the dead hiss and crackle for the brass to kick in.

'Ivor Novello is a Cardiff man, isn't he?' asks Arabella.

'I think so.'

'And a homosexual.'

I wiggle my eyebrows. 'I hear they're everywhere these days.'

Arabella laughs and begins singing along. As I listen to her throaty rendition of the song – a young man complaining that he can't get a moment alone with his girl without one of her family members turning up for the ride – I can't help thinking: at least his girl's relatives aren't still interfering even from beyond the grave!

'Shall we dance?' Arabella asks.

I haven't in years, not since before the trial. I'd go out to the halls in Cardiff then with the Land Army girls, or occasionally with the Reeses' younger maids, if they had an evening off. Obviously I couldn't dance too lovey-dovey with whatever girl I had an eye on: we'd have to make sure to giggle and clown about like any other female friends would. Normally, I'd end up dancing with a random lad before the night was through. I didn't mind this so much – I normally found it funny – but some would get ideas and expect us to go with them next time we saw them as well. Although that was more a problem for Gladys, who was always glamorous as a film star, whereas I didn't tend to get sought out again in a hurry.

My steps are a bit rusty, but it must have been even longer for Arabella, so I let her take my hands and we have a spin around the drawing room, dodging the taxidermy and usual bric-a-brac and having to stop every few minutes to change the record over. It's perfect, nonetheless. I don't believe in birthdays as grand occasions – there's no particular achievement in clocking up another year of life – but even so, I feel my heart lifting in optimism at this one. Once we've had our fill of dancing, Arabella suggests we go upstairs for a bit. She takes the staircase at a gallop, laughing as she goes, calling me to follow.

I head after her, not really paying attention to the steps now that they're not barricaded with obstacles. This is a mistake. Toward the top, I lose my footing – the wood surface is smooth and polished now that Mrs Allen can get at it to clean. There's a moment of shock as my heel skids from under me, then my face smacks against the banister and I'm tumbling, each step pummelling me along the way.

I come to rest at the foot of the stairs, twisted partially on to my side. I lie there for what feels like an age. Taste blood in my mouth. Then the pain catches up to me and I groan, roll on to my back. Open my eyes. Blink away the tears that arrive of their own accord.

Upside down in my view, Arabella stares back at me from

the landing, as if too surprised to act. Then she seems to gather herself. Picks her way down toward me. 'Are you hurt?' she calls.

I've bitten my tongue and there's a dull, bruise-in-progress ache all up my left side, but I don't think anything's broken. My fingers and toes move when I tell them to. Gingerly, I prop myself up to a sitting position.

Arabella crouches at my side. Her fingers brush over my face, my scalp, my ribs. 'All in one piece,' she says. 'Show me your teeth? Yes, still there. You know, if you had not made me move those newspapers, you would have had something to cushion your fall.'

'Fuck off,' I manage, pulling a face.

Arabella pats me on the knee. 'I'll fetch ice.'

As she disappears to find the Allens, I experiment with turning my neck to and fro. Not too painful. When I look in the direction of the drawing room, I notice an object on the floor. Recognize the so-called lucky hare's foot. We must have danced more enthusiastically than I'd realized earlier, knocked it down from its pin above the frame.

Reluctant to move, but knowing it will cause hell if Arabella finds it first, I get to my feet and limp over to pick it up. I scramble to fix it back on the pin before Arabella can return. My fingers come away dusted with dark powder and I almost drop it again in disgust. The reverse side, normally hidden from sight where it sits against the wall, is completely black with mould.

FOURTEEN

FOR DAYS AFTER his return from London, Reacher slinks around like a wounded animal, shutting himself up in the study, or in his room with only Finchley for company. I don't think he expected me to call his bluff on the deed, and now that I have, he doesn't know what to do with himself. Whenever I enter a room that he's already in, he'll find an urgent excuse to get up and leave. Won't eat his meals with Arabella and me. He's just as angry with her over the whole business as he is with me.

'He always was a sulker,' Arabella reassures me. 'A true master of the silent treatment. But he will see sense once the loan is secured. In the meantime, shall we play a merry piano track over his movements, like in the cinema?' But the piano is wedged in a corner, missing several keys since its outing at Christmas and covered in dead orchids, so we decide against this trick.

The two of us normally take an afternoon tea break in the drawing room, Mrs Allen leaving out a tray of bread-and-butter or sandwiches for us after she's started the fire in there. It's coming up to that time, one day in late March, when I spot Mutton creeping across the east lawn as I'm scraping off my boots. Something in his gait makes me stop to watch: he seems off-kilter, like when you've spun round and round in circles and can't walk in a straight line any more. A drunken sway to his step.

'All right there, Muttsy!' I call out to him.

He lifts his head slowly, looking around till he spots me, then starts to approach with the same slow shamble. As he draws closer, I hear a low whine in his throat. His eyes are large, showing the whites.

'What's the matter, boy?'

He can't answer me, but cringes when I try to touch his flank. It's hard to tell with a dog, but I think he's in pain. The whine heightens in pitch when he moves.

'I'll go and fetch Tom,' I tell him. 'You stay here.'

When I find Tom, he's out by the boathouse, chopping up a tree that came down earlier in the year from the winter winds. The axe is dull-bright in his thick hands.

'Mutton's not himself,' I tell him.

The axe blade falls with a thunk, sending chips of wood flying. He pauses, propping its hilt against the remainder of the felled trunk. 'How do you mean?'

'I don't know. Come and see.'

Back on the east lawn, Mutton has disappeared. Can't have made it far, though, not at the speed he was moving. I have a walk-around, and eventually hear scrabbling coming from the old cottage. Must have gone in there to hide.

Inside, it's hard to recognize this as the place I'd called home six months ago. The door – swollen from the flood – has never closed properly since, leaving the interior open to the elements. Pools of stagnant water sit on the floor, alongside piles of mulch where vegetation has blown in to rot. The stench of fox piss. One of the chairs had toppled over, nibbled at by something. And here in the middle of the scene is Mutton, cowering at the foot of what was once the armchair. He's been sick: yellow-pink vomit glistens by his head. When I get closer, I see flecks of blood floating in the pool.

Tom rushes over, squatting to examine the dog. 'What's happened, boy?'

Mutton looks up at him, his panting laboured. A plea in his canine gaze.

'Mutton!' He reaches out to touch the dog's back, but Mutton flinches away, then yelps at the pain the movement causes him. Tom hesitates, then tries Mutton's face. This is tolerated: Tom caresses his snout, his brow, his ears, gentle as a mother with a newborn baby.

'I don't know what happened,' I say. 'I just found him like this, walking funny.'

There are tears glittering in Tom's eyes, and when he speaks again, his voice is rough, choking. 'His ears are all cold.'

I come closer, and that's when I catch it: a faint smell of garlic on the dog's hot, heavy breath. Nothing so strong that you'd normally notice it, mind, but it's enough to send ice shooting up my back. That scent haunts my nightmares. Underpins the stark memories of that terrible day in Penarth – just after Dad was let go. I can still see the Reese family clearly, each member hunched over in pain. Mr Reese, Mrs Reese, the old woman, the nanny and Kenneth. A sudden illness striking them all like the biblical plagues. Their faces contorted in agony. Moaning, squirming. Clinging to sick bowls. That garlic mingled with bile and shit. Blood in the bed pans. All of us helping to fetch and carry – even Mam called up from the kitchens, even me. Fresh water, blankets, lavender-scented cloths to wipe their foreheads. The little boy in his nursery bed, shaking in a seizure. Eyes rolled back in his skull. Blood as he bites his tongue. Child's pulse sputtering like a trapped bird. His little hands so cold, so very cold. The doctor delivering his verdict.

'Arsenic,' I say. Mutton must have got into the rat poison. But it's kept high up on a shelf in the shed. The tin is sealed, the door locked. He couldn't have got at it. Unless he found and ate one of the dishes left scattered around on Reacher's orders. Tucked out of sight to tempt the vermin.

'You greedy bastard,' Tom sobs. 'Why'd you do that, Mutton?' The dog only whimpers in response.

'What do we do?' Tom looks up to me, putting me in charge.

But I don't remember what the doctor did for the Reeses. I don't remember any medicine passing their lips at all. 'Let's take him inside,' I say at last. I fetch a blanket and we roll Mutton on to it as if it's a medical stretcher. Carry it between us as gently as we can. Still, the dog cries at every tiny jostle. Tom and I take him through to the kitchen.

'Put him by the oven,' Mrs Allen tells us, after I explain things, touching a wobbling hand to her mouth. 'That's his favourite spot.'

So we lower him with great care on to the floor. Somewhere he can feel safe and warm.

The commotion on the lawn must have reached the main house, as Arabella and Reacher appear shortly, stepping tentatively into the servants' quarters. Strange to see them here, where they don't belong, but Mutton gives an exhausted wag of his tail when he hears their voices.

'Should I drive up to town to fetch the vet?' asks Reacher once I've filled him in, our quarrel momentarily forgotten in the face of this shared disaster. He looks stricken, his face pallid with concern.

'I don't know,' I say. Try to remember the doctor in Penarth. What had he said? No antidote – that was it. Just bedrest, taking plenty of fluids. Time and waiting. 'I don't think there's anything a vet could do,' I say. 'He's already thrown up. We should try to get some water into him.'

So Tom has a go at dribbling water on to Mutton's mouth and nose with a damp rag. The dog twitches his tongue, but makes no effort to drink. Arabella taps her fingers nervously on the kitchen table. Reacher blows his nose loudly. Otherwise, we all sit in silence, not really noticing the cups of tea that Mrs Allen sets out for us. The feeling of keeping vigil. The Reeses all recovered in the end. Even Kenneth . . . after a fashion. I heard – afterward – he was never quite the same. Not so bright. Struggled to remember things. The poison creating a permanent barrier in his unformed mind. But I don't know how true that is; I wasn't allowed to see him for myself.

Warm in his blanket and surrounded by his family, Mutton flutters his eyes shut and falls asleep. One paw twitches. Goes still.

After what feels like hours, I set down my still-full mug and stand, stretching the cramp from my back. Night is falling outside. I go over to Mutton and tuck the blanket over him, covering his slack face, the peep of white that glitters hollowly from between his eyelids. 'I'll put him outside.'

'Not in the cold,' says Tom.

Mrs Allen rubs circles on her husband's back. 'We have to, love. We can't leave him by the stove. Look, in the morning we'll dig him a proper—'

Tom closes his eyes. 'Don't say it.'

Reacher sniffs loudly, clears his throat. 'Poor old boy.'

'We'll find a nice spot tomorrow,' I tell Tom. 'I can plant something over him.'

'What if the foxes get him?'

'All right,' I try, 'how about the larder, then? He'll be safe in there.'

Bargain struck, I tie the blanket closed and carry the stiffening dog through to the slate-lined room. The difference in temperature sends a ripple of gooseflesh up my forearms. As I bend to place Mutton on the floor, I spot one of the little dishes I'd set out for the mice. Wiping my eyes on a sleeve, I crouch down to check on it. A little of the poison is gone, but not disturbed as it would be by a large dog – only the rodents have been at this one. But suddenly I have to know which dish did it. Because it must be my fault. I've carelessly left one out where he could access it. Taken in a frenzy, I check all the dishes that I can remember setting out. Some full, some empty, but none with the look of having been found by Mutton. The potting shed, then? The door is still closed tight when I get there, but I check inside anyway. Everything as I'd expect it to be. The dried plants hanging from hooks. Fresh pots of germinating tomatoes, chillies, aubergines and sweet peppers. Sacks and crates. The yellow and red tin of poison is still on its high shelf, lid in place. No – wait. I step closer, feeling the frown grow on my forehead. The tin's moved. Hasn't it? A smidge to the right – I can see by the ring of dust at its base. As if another person has been in here. Not Mutton's doing, obviously. But somebody other than me. I shake my head. No use being paranoid. I haven't looked at the shelves in a while: this could have happened any time. Could have been Tom, looking for something, moving things around. Could have been me, and I just forgot. Still . . . where *did* Mutton find that arsenic?

The next day, Tom and I dig a grave for the dog out in the orchard. The weather has warmed up, so the ground isn't too hard – a small mercy, as he was a big old boy and we have a fair job to do. Might as well be digging the grave for a man.

Everyone comes up from the house to see him off. Reacher has put on a black mourning suit, which may have seemed like cruel satire if it weren't for the fact I know he loved Mutton as much as the rest of us. Tom lowers the blanketed bundle softly into the open hole, then sprinkles a handful of earth over it with great ceremony.

As my companions swap memories of the dog, my mind drifts, running back over the bowls of rat poison. I must have missed one in my sweep. The certainty chafing at my conscience. *Think.* Did I check the drawing room? I can't remember, but as I stand listening to the fond reminiscences I become more convinced that I overlooked that one. So, once the small funeral is done, and after Tom and I have mounded the remaining dirt back into the grave, I head inside. Knock my boots on the scraper and enter through the back door. Down the passage, into the main hall, then the drawing room.

A crunch underfoot. I look down and see a china plate, fissured under my toe. More plates around. An upturned tea-tray. Of course: Mrs Allen would have left it out for Arabella and me yesterday but, with the chaos over Mutton, we forgot all about it. Nobody will have been in here since. The tray would have been left on this side table – at the perfect height for a dog's curious nose to knock it down. The food has been gobbled up, just breadcrumbs remaining, a greasy smear on the rug where it must have fallen.

I look down at this all with a slow horror in my guts. Tell myself not to rush to a conclusion. Double-check the dish of rat bait. It's undisturbed, the same as the others. So this tray was Mutton's last meal. Which means that it must have been the source of the arsenic. Yet the meal hadn't been set out for him. No, this was meant for me and Arabella.

Again, I try to reel myself back. This doesn't necessarily mean anyone was trying to poison us. Food can become contaminated in all sorts of ways. Besides, no one but Harfold's inhabitants would have had access to the drawing room: me, Arabella, Tom, Mrs Allen and Reacher. My stomach churns. I think of Reacher's fury the other evening. He's desperate to inherit Harfold. But what would he have to gain from it now? After all, Arabella has already signed the manor over to me, and sent off the deed to be formally recognized. If I die without a will, I imagine that means the house would pass to my next of kin – to Mam and Dad. Unless Reacher really is sure that the deed's invalid; that, in the event of Arabella and me meeting a tragic demise, it will be ignored, and Harfold will go to him as it always would have.

Or maybe it's not about Harfold at all: could it be as simple as petty revenge? Someone's wronged you and, in the heat of the moment, you want to hurt them back. Nothing in your mind but the desire to inflict suffering. And it's so easy to slip a little arsenic into a plate of food. Mix it with the butter, stir it into the milk jug. Multiple ways to do it. It takes less than you'd think to kill even a human. He could have crept into the kitchen while Mrs Allen was away, or else waited till the tea-tray was already sitting vulnerable in the empty drawing room. Then what? Encourage the police to rule it a double suicide . . . Or place the blame on the Allens. Suspicion would immediately turn to the person who prepared the food.

I can picture it clear as day, but surely Reacher isn't so desperate that he'd harm his own cousin . . . Then I have another thought. Arabella's food, always sliced into tiny, harmless chunks. Reacher would've been able to target just me.

Well, I'm not going to wait around for him to try again.

It's a full moon tonight, so Arabella will be off out to look for her hare. I wait till she leaves to confront Reacher. Don't need her overhearing this just yet.

He's in his study when I find him, skulking like a rat in its nest. He doesn't stand as I enter, but does lift his eyes over me. Notes my thunderous expression. How I shut the door firmly behind me.

'Go on, then,' I say. 'What's your next plan?'

He opens his mouth. Smooths his collar. 'Whatever do you mean?'

'Smother me in my sleep, maybe. Or is that too hands-on for you?'

'Miss Morgan, what *are* you talking about?' The act isn't quite convincing. A bead of sweat on his brow. The study curtains have been drawn against the night, and only a single lamp burns on the tabletop, sending his shadow looming up the wall behind him. The decanter of Scotch is already out today, standing off to one side with an array of glasses.

Without waiting to be invited, I walk over and take the armchair opposite, leaning forward to fix him in my gaze. 'You've been stealing from Arabella for years, haven't you? That's why she has no money; it's all been syphoned off into your own bank accounts. Hidden behind fake invoices, investments you've pretended aren't paying returns. A secret deal with Gerrish.' Under the table, the spider has caught something – a silverfish, I think. Spinning it up in a neat little bundle, round and round. Ready to drink up its innards. 'You've made sure she hasn't noticed by keeping her dependent on you, by propping up this bloody curse delusion. She told me, you know, how it was *you* who first put the idea in her head. Who encouraged her. And now here I am, standing in your way, and you can't bear that – so now what? You're trying to kill me! To keep her all to yourself?'

Reacher blinks at me, then swallows. Stands up.

'What're you doing?' I ask, immediately on edge.

'Calm down, I am not about to knock you over the head. I simply want to make sure that we are speaking in private.' He sidles past me, scooting around the copper tub of seashells to crack open the door and peek out. A sickly sweet, unwashed smell crawls off him. 'Bellsy? No?' Closing it again, he turns the key in the lock.

'You've forgotten something,' I say, as I cast around for a way to defend myself. The decanter looks good and heavy.

'Oh?' Reacher settles back into his seat, crosses his arms idly over his stomach.

'The deed's already in my name,' I remind him. 'So it's pointless to kill me – Harfold wouldn't pass on to you either way.'

He makes an uncertain humming noise. Opens one of the desk drawers and roots around. Pulls out a crumpled piece of paper and places it down, directly under the lamp so it seems to glow. Even upside down, I recognize the deed to Harfold.

'How'd you get that?'

'This?' Reacher taps the paper with one finger, then shrugs. 'Bellsy never sent it off.'

'What do—'

A mocking smile. 'You may be tending to Arabella's garden, but that doesn't make you a member of the family.'

This taunt misses its mark, since I know how insecure Reacher is about his own position in the genealogy: *he's* the one who wants so desperately to be a legitimate Lascy, to claim his inheritance to Harfold. 'Trust me, I wouldn't want to be,' I tell him.

'Really?' Eyes narrowing, shrewd. 'It's funny, isn't it, how you are always sending letters to your parents, but they never write back to you.' A pause, tilting his head to watch me. Knowing he's caught me. 'Why is that?'

I open my mouth to tell some story, but nothing comes out.

'Hmm, that's odd,' he says, interrupting my silence. Leans forward to examine the deed. Then with mocking theatricality, he removes his spectacles, gives them a polish, and places them back on his nose. Looks again. 'Yes, that is right. I am afraid it doesn't look like your name *is* on here, you know. It is made out to a Miss Vee Morgan.' Smiles up at me. 'But that's not you, is it? You are Vera Owens.'

I have the sensation of a terrible machine bearing down on me. Headlights rushing closer on the road, too fast for me to move away; my body frozen in place anyway. A sudden image of that struck deer the first night I came here. My surname, Owens, Reacher had already learned from when he picked up those letters to my parents. But where did he hear 'Vera'?

'I realized, of course, that you were lying about your family working for the prison service,' Reacher says, voice conversationally light. 'I imagined perhaps they were incarcerated themselves. *Well, no business of mine*, I thought, *Miss Morgan is a good little worker all the same.* But how odd it is that her criminal progenitors never return her letters. I was always under the impression that even inmates may send mail. I'll admit I was curious, so I called in one or two favours with some fellow birders based in Wales – I know all sorts of useful people; you would be surprised. It wasn't much work for them to find the story.' He places his hands on top of the deed, one resting in the other. 'So, a little thought game for you, Miss Owens: if Arabella drops dead from arsenic poisoning—'

'Arabella?' My confusion moves me to interrupt.

'Yes. And who do the police believe, then? Her loving cousin? Or the daughter of two convicted criminals who attempted to murder their employers in the very same way? In fact, the woman who *purchased* the poison in the first place.' He plucks up the deed, holding it aloft like a proclamation. 'And see this, she has even tried – no matter how inexpertly – to manipulate Lady Lascy into signing Harfold over to her! It's just *so hard* to believe that she didn't know anything about her parents' crime.'

'Look here,' I say, fighting to keep my voice steady, 'I don't know what you've heard, but my name was clean in that business.'

'Still, rumours stick, don't they? I assume that was what drove you out of Cardiff.' A smug smile when my expression tells him he's right. 'Now, I am not sure if you have heard of the law of forfeiture, but it means that a person found guilty of murder can't profit from their crime – which means that the ownership of Harfold would revert back to its rightful heritor.' He taps the table. 'Me, in case that was not clear.'

A cold sweat drips down my back. I feel like I'm in court again, hundreds of eyes burning into me as I'm hit with a torrent of questions, each one designed to trip me up. *Why did you purchase the poison? Did your mother or father ask you to buy it? Did you go into the store-shed that day? How did you come to have the keys? After you'd been in the store-shed, did you go into the kitchen? Did you see your mother prepare the food? Did she put anything in it? Did you have any grudge against the Reeses? Were you aware that your father had been dismissed the previous day? Is it true he is a socialist? What did he think of the Reeses? Was he there in the kitchen? Why were you there?*

'Drink?' Reacher sloshes out two Scotches – neat this time. 'We are out of soda, I'm afraid. Now, I still haven't been able to find the answer to my question: why is it that your parents refuse to write to you? Is it because you appeared in court as a witness for the opposition? I noticed that tidbit. They must have felt very betrayed. Still, I admire your mercenary attitude.'

I breathe slowly. Try not to remember Mam's and Dad's faces as I took the stand. 'What do you want from me, Reacher?'

He raises his glass. 'To Mutton. I really did love that stupid dog.' He takes a sip and sighs in appreciation. Presses a thumb to the corner of one eye, then the other. It's possible the tears are genuine. 'And I do like you. I would have been sorry to throw you into the crossfire, but I wasn't left with much choice. Although . . .' He pauses in thought. 'There is an option that could benefit both of us. What if Bellsy were to kill herself? Poor old girl, so terrified of this lunatic curse theory of hers: it all just got to be too much.' He nods at me. 'You remember her saying so to you, don't you, Vee? How she just wanted it all to end? And in return for your sharing that with the police, I shall rip up this silly deed and forget all about it. You can go on your merry way. I can even put in a good word with some friends to help you find a new situation. How does Kew sound?'

I don't believe the nerve of him. 'You really think I'd betray Arabella like that?'

'She doesn't deserve your loyalty, my dear. Why do you think she made you sign this in the first place?'

If I moved quickly, would I be able to snatch the deed away from him, unlock the door and run?

Seeming to sense my thinking, Reacher places a palm flat over the paper. 'It's because she thinks Harfold is cursed. She was trying to push you in front of her in the firing line!' With the other hand, he slides the decanter until it sits directly between us to illustrate the point.

'That's not true.'

'Pew!' He pushes the decanter's neck, but catches it before it topples. 'You know, I wonder if she didn't have this planned the whole time. I just could *not* understand why she wanted so badly to bring in a new gardener from all that way away, then why she invited you to live in the manor with us, to share our meals, to play our games. But now I realize she was leaving a little breadcrumb trail, and you have come along gobbling it up.'

I scowl at him. 'That's you, who uses people. She's not like that.'

A long, slow smile. 'Ah, but of course: you don't know the whole story behind the curse... Tell you what, no point in hearing that from me. You would only say I was lying. Why don't you go and ask Arabella about it? Or better yet, read that bloody journal of hers. Then you will see just what sort of a person she is. And I already know what sort of a person you are, so you know where to find me when you change your mind.' He takes another glug of Scotch, then looks at me, one eyebrow raised. 'Well, go on, then.' Makes a shooing motion.

'You're letting me leave, are you?'

'I was never stopping you!' He gives a self-satisfied wink. 'Now, you won't say anything to Arabella or the Allens, will you? Not unless you would like them to learn what happened to that poor family you used to work for. The child . . . Oh, it breaks one's heart.'

Kenneth. My throat stings as the memory is forced fresh into my mind. His hands so cold, as if they'd been plunged into a drift of snow. But how *dare* Reacher use what happened to that little boy against me? As if the tragedy is nothing more than a trump card to be laid out on the table. I grit my teeth, hearing the squeak of bones meeting echo inside my ears. He's got me all wrong, and I *will* make him pay for this. First, though, I need to warn Arabella.

Cautiously, I rise from my chair and edge back toward the door. Step around the seashells. Fumble with the key, not wanting to take my eyes off Reacher. Finally get it open.

Reacher's voice follows me down the corridor: 'Don't forget to ask Bellsy about that curse!'

FIFTEEN

WHAT HAPPENED TO little Kenneth is one of those guilts that will follow me around for ever.

It was the day after Dad had been sent packing and my blood was full boiling over it. I'd half a mind to go up to Mr Reese and tell him where he could shove it.

'Just you leave it,' Mam told me, catching my scowl as we walked to work. She was always in before the crack of dawn to start breakfast for the other servants. As an undergardener, I didn't need to be at the house till much later in the day, but I normally went with her anyway and just waited in the kitchen, keeping her company as the morning loaves rose doughy on their trays. When I didn't reply to her snapped words, she grabbed me by the wrist and pulled me back to face her. 'I mean it, Vera. At least we two still have our jobs. Let's keep it that way.'

I couldn't stand that: being told to be grateful that Mr Reese had so *kindly* only fired one of us. But I kept my mouth shut and sat nicely at the kitchen table like an obedient dog.

The morning continued almost as normal after that. When it was time for me to start, I took myself out to the garden and continued with the tasks that Dad had left for me the previous day. Tried not to think about how another head gardener would be employed soon, coming here to order me around. Might not take kindly to having a girl work under him. That it would be a *him* was never a question.

After breakfast, Kenneth came out for his eleven o'clock runabout. He tried to get me to play hide-and-seek with him as I sometimes did, but I wasn't in the mood. Not cross *with* him exactly: it wasn't his fault that his father was a no-good, dirty, cunt-faced reptile of a man. Still, that didn't mean I was going to play with the boy that day. Instead, I chatted with the nanny a bit, and she told me they were off to a tea party that afternoon at a friend's house. I wouldn't learn until much later that the other child came down with the mumps at the last minute and the appointment had to be cancelled – leaving Kenneth and the nanny taking tea at home instead.

After that, I went into the store-shed to have a tidy. There were many tools kept there that belonged to Dad, which he'd brought with him when he started at the Reeses', so I thought I'd put them aside to take home. It wouldn't have been right for Mr Reese to keep enjoying the benefit of them, after what he'd done. Moving things around, I found an old tin of rat poison that I'd purchased the previous winter, when we were having a problem in the kitchen garden. I could tell by the weight there was hardly anything left in there, really.

I stopped for lunch in the servants' hall with the rest of the staff. Mam looked utterly miserable; in fact, everyone was subdued, Dad's absence felt keenly by all. Welcomed by some, mind, who'd never liked working with a 'conchie'. The footman was a particular one for that – he often left white feathers scattered round the garden for Dad to find. The first time it happened, I'd wanted to confront the bastard and show him just where he could stick them, but Dad insisted on taking the matter to Mr Reese to sort out instead. Of course, all he'd done was tell Dad to ignore it. Funny how that was the advice until it was one of Mr Reese's friends with a complaint about Dad's conduct.

When it was coming up time for Mam to get tea for that lot upstairs, I thought I'd play a little joke. Cheer her up, like. So I took the tin of arsenic out of the store-shed and brought it into the kitchen, and clowned about like I was going to put it in the milk jug. But Mam didn't see the funny side of it. 'You put that right down this minute, my girl!' she shouted, brandishing the rolling pin till I did as she said. I muttered something about only having a laugh, and popped it safely on one of the shelves over the kitchen worktop.

At that moment, Dad came in. He'd never been much of a drinker, but I could tell he had a few in him when I saw him that day. His speech was slower, the syllables all jumbling together.

'What the hell are you doing here, Gethin?' cried Mam. 'You two will be the death of me. *You*' – me, this was – 'get back into the gardens now, and will you leave that bloody tin alone! No, don't take it with you. Just stop mucking about with it. And *you*' – now turning on Dad – 'take yourself home this instant.'

Dad wove his head about – I think meaning to shake it. Frowning in anger, or perhaps just concentration to get a full sentence out. 'I'm going to have a word with Mr Reese.'

'No, you're bloody not!'

'I'm going to show him what's what. If he thinks he can get away with this . . .'

And then there was a bit of arguing to and fro, but the long and short of it was that I went back outdoors, leaving the poison behind up there on that shelf. Saw that wretched footman on my way out, who said, 'Your daddy shouldn't be here,' so I stuck my tongue out at him. Of course, he'd later be the one to come forward and say that he'd seen Dad go into the kitchen that day. Seen the state he was in. The anger on his face.

Later, the courts speculated that there were two things that *might* have happened next. Maybe I hadn't balanced the tin properly. It could have toppled over, and the lid, old and rusted, could have sprung open. Sprinkled powder down on to the kitchen worktop, where the tea-tray was waiting to go upstairs. A horrible accident.

Or maybe someone emptied it intentionally into the milk.

When the family all took sick and the law came by, I knew how it looked. I was frightened. I felt like such a grown-up at twenty-three, but I wasn't really much more than a child, looking back on it. The police kept asking me where I thought the poison had come from, until I was sure they thought I'd done it, that they were going to lock me up for the rest of my years. So I panicked. Desperate to turn their attention away, I told them how, when I'd left the kitchen, Mam and Dad had both been worked up over the Reeses. That Mam had sent me away from the argument . . . and that she had told me to leave the arsenic behind.

If I hadn't said all that to the police, the story may have turned out differently. A terrible misfortune caused by a poorly balanced tin. But instead, I'd been so worried about the blame falling to me that I'd pointed the finger right at my parents. I knew that they would never have done such a thing. I tried to speak up for them later, in court: tell the judge that it wasn't in their natures, that it must have been an accident. But I couldn't change my story too much without turning suspicion back on myself and, thanks to my testimony, Mam was found guilty of administering poison with intent to murder, and Dad of conspiring to commit the same. Those were the terms the judge used. As for me? I was just an innocent bystander.

With the benefit of hindsight, the ridiculous thing is that if the blame *had* fallen on me, Mam and Dad would immediately have come to my rescue, if I'd only have left the choice up to them. But I betrayed them to save my own skin . . . and for that, they still haven't forgiven me. It's been nothing but stony silence from them both ever since.

Mam and Dad received their sentences in October 1923 – a little over half a year after the Reeses were poisoned. Dad remained at HMP Cardiff, but Mam had to be sent away to a women's prison in Aylesbury. Since the jury decided there was evidence of intent to murder – rather than just to inflict harm – Mam was served with a life term, and Dad with the full possible penalty of ten years as her co-conspirator. I suppose the judge felt he couldn't afford to be lenient, given Dad's previous history of incarceration, and for fear that angry servants all over the place would start trying to bump off their own employers if they thought they could get away with it.

In between the arrest and the trial, I was evicted from our home in Penarth. Naturally, I'd found myself swiftly unemployed after Mam's and Dad's arrests, and hadn't exactly been keeping up on the rent. So there I was, parentless, jobless and homeless all at once. Most of my friends had stopped speaking to me – Lou and Gladys alone were kind enough to answer the door when I came knocking. I'd only ever meant to stay with them a short while, just until I was back on my feet. But then I never got back on my feet. Nobody wanted to hire me and, even if I'd had money, nobody would have let me a room either. My name had been splashed all across the local papers. People would stop me in the street to tell me they knew I'd had a hand in it. *How could you do that to a little boy?*

After almost two years of this, I knew I had to leave, and the job advertisement for a new gardener at Harfold Manor had been my shining ticket out. If only I'd known then where it would take me instead.

The one thing in my mind is that I need to find Arabella. Get her away from Harfold and her cousin, at least until we can work out how to deal with him; she's in too much danger here. If not the poison, there are still a hundred other ways she might 'kill herself': a fall down the stairs, drowning, hanging, a farmer's shotgun under the chin. I won't let that happen to her. I know that Reacher's threatened to expose me if I tell her about his plans, but I have to believe Arabella would side with me. First, what happened to Mutton is clear proof of Reacher's schemes. And second, she told me she's in love with me. That has to mean she'll believe me. Doesn't it?

I struggle to find her. Not in the drawing room, not in the library, not in her bedroom. Then I remember: the full moon. She's off over the fields, looking for that lucky hare, in the grip of the obsession that Reacher has planted and grown within her. Though I don't care much for his hints that I'm missing a key detail here. *Don't forget to ask Bellsy about that curse! Or better yet, read that bloody journal of hers.* It's clear he's just trying to cloud my judgement. Divide and conquer: it's got to be the oldest trick in the book.

Then again . . . I have a sudden flash of memory. Arabella's reaction when I asked, joking, to read her diary. *You must never touch it.* The fleeting panic I thought I saw. Now that Reacher has put the doubt in my head, I'm becoming more and more certain that there's something Arabella doesn't want me to know.

I shake this off. Before anything else, I need to make sure Arabella is safe from Reacher. Explanations can come later. She's been out for hours and is sure to return soon – if I go out to meet her, I should be able to catch her on her way home, stop her from walking back into Reacher's clutches. Not taking the time to fetch heavier clothing from upstairs, I pull on the jacket and boots I keep in the back hallway cupboard. Slip on my gloves, their careful embroidery a reminder that Reacher's full of shit about Arabella not caring for me. I take up my trusty electric torch – heavy enough to hit someone over the head, if I need it. Keep expecting Reacher to jump out at me, stop me, but he doesn't.

I strike out into the silver garden. The night is windy, with high, thin clouds racing over the moon's swollen face as if afraid to let it catch them. Fingers of cool air hook themselves under my collar. I wish I had my scarf. Passing by the woods, I hear the trees creaking as a mournful chorus. Branches whip about overhead. It will be no use calling out to Arabella – my voice will be snatched away before it's even left my lips.

Crossing the lawn, I catch the glitter of a lantern out in the fields. Perfect timing. As I pick up my pace, I become aware that I keep looking around for something. Realize it's Mutton. A hollow feeling in my stomach. I'm so used to his pawsteps echoing my tread, I wonder when I'll stop hearing the memory of them. Another thing that Reacher needs to pay for.

By the time I come up to the river, I can see Arabella herself, much closer now, low-held gleam lighting her from below. I'm struck with intense relief, even though of course Reacher couldn't have done anything to harm her since I last saw her.

'Vee!' she calls, when she's close enough to recognize me. At least, that must be what she says – I see her mouth move, but don't hear the words.

She's right at the property border now, just across the footbridge. I walk over it, careful of the slick surface. Moonlight sparkles off the river below, giddying for a moment. Then I'm face to face with Arabella. 'What are you doing out here?' she asks. She's wrapped up tight in a patchy fur coat, clutching to her head a felt hat that's about fifteen years out of date, from under which strands of hair flail rebelliously about. The wind's bitten her cheeks red as poppies.

Without having planned to, I throw my arms around her in a hug, the plush fur making her wider than I'm used to.

She staggers in surprise, holding the lantern awkwardly to one side. 'Goodness, what's all this about?'

I release her and glance over my shoulder, as if Reacher might have followed. I'm standing right at the end of the bridge, subtly blocking her path back to the manor. 'Look here,' I say, 'Harfold isn't safe for you, not while your cousin's there.'

'Pardon?' A bemused smile on her face. She must think I'm making a joke, the punchline not immediately obvious.

'Reacher,' I say. 'I know this sounds crazy, but he's trying to kill you. The poison that Mutton ate – that was meant for you. Reacher added it to our tea-tray, and if Mutton hadn't got to it first, it would have been you we'd had to bury.'

The smile falters, only the confusion remaining. 'What . . . why are you saying this?'

It's all coming out wrong, too dramatic to seem real. It's clear she doesn't believe what I'm telling her, can't grapple with the idea of Reacher doing such a thing. But I have to keep trying – she *has* to understand. 'It's true,' I press on, 'he just admitted the whole thing to me. He wants to murder you so he can inherit Harfold, and he asked for my help to stage it as a suicide, or else he says he'll frame me for it.'

'This isn't funny, Vee.' Arabella tries to pass me, to step on to the bridge, but I take a pace back and block her, boot landing on slimy wood. She pouts. 'It's cold; I want to go inside.'

'I'm serious, Arabella. Cross my heart.'

Now she frowns. Shakes her head. 'Morry wouldn't . . . Look, you don't understand how it is for the two of us. How can you? You have been here for such a short time.'

'Arabella—' I try to take her free hand.

'Morry doesn't want to inherit Harfold,' she insists, shaking off my grip. 'He knows that the curse—' She's looking around wildly now, as if expecting something to jump out at her at any moment. Eyes wide as two full moons.

'There's no curse – he made it up!' I'm near shouting now, struggling to hide my frustration. 'He's been lying to you for *years*, so that you'll keep depending on him, trusting him.'

Again, she shakes her head.

I force myself to stop. Breathe out. Lower the race of my pulse. 'I don't want to argue. That's what he wants: to turn us against each other. He kept saying all of these things about *why* you think you're cursed, that the hare isn't the whole story. Trying to manipulate me, like.'

'He said that?' Arabella tugs at the collar of her coat, as if struggling to breathe. I expect her to deny it, to tell me that

Reacher was lying about this as well, but instead she says, 'Not the whole story . . . I suppose it isn't.'

'What does that mean?'

She ignores my question. 'What else did he say?'

I don't want to admit it to myself, but her reaction has worried me. Fed into the bubbling doubts Reacher has created. 'That you made me sign that deed to see if the curse would move on to me. To offer me up in your place.' I want her to laugh this all off, but instead there's an expression of panic. Animal caught in the headlights. It makes me hesitate – just for a moment. 'Arabella? You didn't—'

She cuts me off: 'I don't want to hear any more.'

'No, you have to listen!'

In a sudden lunge, she shoves me. I think she just means to push past me, but I'm caught fully off-guard, and there's no grip on the surface of the bridge. My boot sole skids across damp wood. A shock of intense pain as my skull connects with the railing. Roaring inside my head, like the sea. Flashes of brightest black pop before my eyes. Then I'm falling. The last thing I see through the bursting colours is Arabella's face, lit in crazy angles by her lantern, my dropped electric torch. The image so clear that it feels burnt into my eyes. She hasn't moved an inch to help me – just like that time before, when I fell down the stairs. She isn't even *looking* at me. Her focus is beyond, as if she can see something in the distance. Surprised O of her mouth. A single tear on her cheek. Then, at the final instant, her expression melts into one of relief. And I realize that Reacher was right. She really did mean to pass the curse on to me. Thought it had come to claim me that time on the stairs. And this time – as the river water meets me with a slap – I know that it has.

PART SIX

ARABELLA, 1908

18 February 1908

CHARLIE HAS WARNED me against writing this in my diary, but if I do not record the truth somewhere, I fear I will blurt it all out the moment I am asked. That, or go entirely mad. They will have to lock me up in the attic like Bertha Mason... Yesterday evening was Nellie Frye's twentieth birthday party up at Abingdon, so Charlie and I had to go, as you know Charlie is rather taken with her. I was hoping that Dotty Gaskell would be there myself. I hadn't seen her since she visited for the night last November, and as you can imagine I was eager to continue that conversation. I thought I would be a little daring and wear my new black silk dress from Liberty's.

Just as we were getting ready to leave, Mummy said that measly Morry wanted to come along as well, and we had to take him with us. Well, Charlie and I weren't having any of that: while Morry was fetching his coat, we took to Charlie's new Renault and left him behind! Nellie's do was second-rate in any case. Dotty was there, but do you know who else showed his face? Bloody Dicky Manvers. That was a surprise, since he has not returned one of my letters since our little brush last summer. To make matters worse, the pair of them danced together the whole evening and ignored me entirely. It is bad enough to take a knock from one former lover, but to take it from two at once is beyond toleration! Naturally, I spent the rest of the party getting as drunk as I could.

But look at me going on about this all as if it matters, compared to what happened later that night. I only write it down because it explains the mood I was in as Charlie drove me home: that is to say, miserable and utterly stewed.

Charlie spent the journey trying to cheer me up, but as he didn't know what had upset me in the first place, he was at a disadvantage. Finally, when we were coming up to the familiar roads around home, he asked me what he could do to help. What I wanted was a bit of fun, so I asked if he would let me have a go at the wheel. He said no at first, but I kept on pleading, and eventually he gave in. 'Just for a few miles,' he said, stopping so we could switch places.

God, it was as glorious as I have always imagined! There was a feeling of such power as I clunked up the gears. The engine growled like a terrible dragon, and with the wind washing through my hair and the hedgerows whipping past at lightning speed, I could almost believe we were flying. A full moon steeped the world in glorious silver. Charlie kept shouting that we were going too fast, that I had to slow down, but I didn't want to hear a word of it. I went up to fourth gear – sixty miles per hour! Charlie had told me that the car was based on the model that won the Grand Prix two years ago, and I could easily believe it.

Then, as we came roaring down the road to the village, something flashed suddenly into the headlights. A rush of yellow-brown fur and long, upright ears. I barely had time to understand what it was: I wrenched the steering wheel sharply to the side, throwing us out of the hare's path.

I didn't see George Allen there in the dark.

God, the <u>sound</u>. The initial thump, then a viscous, wet cracking. I <u>felt</u> it through the pedals as the car went over him.

Charlie was shouting at me, telling me to go on driving, not to stop. 'Daddy will fix this,' he kept saying. I wasn't in any state to think for myself: I did what he said, even though by this point I was shaking all over and could barely see the road for tears.

When we got home, Charlie made me halt the motor halfway up the drive, so we would not wake Tom and Nora Allen.

'Should we call the police?' I asked.

He looked at me as if I was insane. 'Are you joking?'

'What if he's still alive?'

'He isn't.'

Charlie made me wait there while he went to fetch Daddy. I don't know what time it was by then; it must have been two o'clock at least. I couldn't stop thinking, why was the churchwarden out that late? What had he been doing on the road? The scene kept repeating behind my eyes: the flash of hare, then George's bulk suddenly ahead. One of his arms had been half raised, as if to wave at us as we went past. I hiccupped back the bile in my throat.

When Daddy came out, he had Mummy and all the boys behind him, even Morry. The little creep looked <u>delighted</u> to be part of the action for once.

'We have to clean this mess,' Daddy said. He meant on the car. The grille, the wheels, the undercarriage, all spattered with it.

'What about the body?' asked Charlie.

<u>George</u>, I wanted to say, but I couldn't make myself speak.

Daddy didn't reply, just sent Mummy to fetch a picnic

blanket from the summer house. Rex and Charlie took it off with them in one of the other cars, leaving the rest of us to jack up the Renault and set to scrubbing. Stephen and Harry changed the tyres and put the old ones on the bonfire heap for the morning. One of the carbide lamps had cracked, so we had to replace this too. We hammered a bent axle back into shape. We checked up and down the driveway for anything we had missed. Then we all pushed the car silently back into the coach house.

A little later, Rex and Charlie returned. They had the picnic blanket with them, this time stained dark. They added it to the pile for burning.

By the time two policemen came up to the Allens' door this morning, we had cleared up every trace, the bonfire already blazing away. I watched through the back window as the men removed their hats, turning their faces down respectfully before knocking.

'Remember that you know nothing,' Mummy said, when she caught me looking.

'But . . . it was my fault, Mummy. Shouldn't I say something?'

'Do not be ridiculous, Arabella; people like us don't belong in prison.' Then she saw the look on my face, and pulled me in tightly to her chest with a soft clucking noise. 'You made a silly mistake, darling, but there is no reason to let it ruin your life. We are all here to protect you. You will always be safe here.'

The police are saying that George Allen had a terrible accident: he was found at the bottom of the stairs in the bell tower, having fallen all the way from the top. I could hear Mr Allen's sobs through the walls. Rex and Charlie must have . . . No, I can't bring myself to imagine. I only hope that this is the end of it, and now we can all just forget. But I fear that I'll still remember George's face vividly as it was in that last moment – skin painted white by the headlights, his shocked eyes directly meeting mine – for as long as I live.

VERA, 1926

SIXTEEN

I DID NOT drown.

I'm in a bed, its sheets crisp with age but clean, smelling sweetly of faint lavender. A patchwork quilt is tucked round my legs – yellows, blues and pinks. Late afternoon light washes through a window with a green-painted frame. Not Harfold. I remember, now, deciding to go into the village for help. But when was that?

Under the bedsheets, I'm wearing a loose flannel nightgown, riding up short on my shins. Whose clothes are these, and whose bed? That was good of someone to give it up to me. I squeeze my eyes shut again, trying to recall exactly what happened after I hit the water, but my memories are confused, scattered like dandelion seeds in the breeze. I have the sense that time has passed – a few days, perhaps. My body is slick with sweat and feels like it's been put through a wringer, but the worst is my head: as if a hot iron is being driven directly into it, right through the skull to the cringing brain matter. Forcing my mind back in time, I'm rewarded with the moment I first surfaced to consciousness. The sensation that another person had just left. A face like Tom's, but not Tom's. George? I tried to call out his name. Coughed up water instead, throat burning, limbs burning. 'George?' I tried again. No reply.

Then I woke again, later, and was able to turn my face this

time, and see the riverbank mud all around me, a weeping willow above. The daylight stabbed like drawing pins into my eyes. I was alone, of course. Whatever I'd thought I saw had just been a hallucination. I'd realized then that I was cold as the grave. My clothes were soaked through, and the liquid ground beneath me was leaching what little warmth my body had left. No feeling in my fingers, my feet. I knew I needed to move before I froze to death. Bracing myself for the pain it was sure to bring, I experimented with moving first my arms, then my legs. Nothing broken as far as I could tell. I managed to bend one leg and, so doing, rolled on to my side. Then, not stopping to let myself feel it, I twisted again and pushed up on to hands and knees. Fire shot through me and I battled down a sudden wave of nausea. Blinked until I could see. Then ordered my body to crawl up the bank, to where a haze of green promised a softer surface to receive me.

There's a gap after that, and then the next memory is of being in a meadow. Buttercups, daisies, blue-flowered speedwell. I could see the tower of St Anselm's church. I must have washed downriver past Harfold village, then by sheer luck caught on the bank. I'm amazed that I'm alive. I *think* that I'm alive.

My clothes had dried somewhat by then, although the seams still chafed damp against my skin. I'd lost a boot and sock, my foot taking on a curdled yellow colour where all the blood had fled. I pressed my gloved palms to it, but they offered no help, not being much warmer. Eventually, I found a hanky in my jacket pocket and used this to wrap my bare foot. Limped my way in the direction of the village.

In my sorry state, I must have forgotten that the rules of the city don't apply out here in the countryside. In Cardiff, I could have spent hours prowling around the streets half dressed, dripping with river mud, and nobody would have looked twice at me. This is not the case in Harfold village. I was barely two steps into the lane when I was startled by a flat-capped lad yelling 'Oi!' at me. He came up closer. 'Oh, sorry Miss, I thought you were a man for a minute there.' Even though he was right in front of me, I couldn't make out his face properly. It seemed he was swaying around, pulling his features in and out of focus like some kind of mischievous pixie. His voice, too, had a strange distortion, so I struggled to understand. 'Whatever's happened to you?' is what I think he said. 'Do you need help?' He bit his lip, looking down at my unbooted foot, where the hanky was already unravelling. 'Ain't you from up the manor? You don't look fit to be walking around like that.'

'I'm all right,' I told him, but then I tripped up somehow, though I'd been standing still. Stumbled into him. He managed to catch me before I fell. It seems that whacking my head then near drowning in a river had finally eroded my protective armour against men being chivalrous to me.

This must be the boy's home. I don't recall the journey to get here. What I remember instead is being back at the Reeses' townhouse. I was in the garden with Dad, the pair of us pruning a rosebush. Kenneth asked me to pick him a flower, so I snipped one off for him. Carefully stripped the thorns. When I tried to hand it to him, however, he took my wrist in his small hand and pulled me down to his level, as if he wanted to whisper in my ear. Opened his mouth. But instead of words, what came out was a froth of bloodied foam and he started to shake, eyes rolling back to show the whites. I tried to pull away, but his grip on my wrist was tighter than it should have been possible for any child to hold. Then I realized that *I* was the one shaking, my whole body overtaken by spasms, and it was *my* hand gripping a wrist – Peggy's. I was too muddled up to be surprised to see her.

'Arabella,' I gasped out.

'You want me to fetch *her*?'

'No! She can't know I'm here.'

Peggy became a cloud of black dots, then reassembled. 'I should—'

'Promise!'

A pause. 'All right, I promise.'

Whether from drinking too much river water, or thanks to the sore dent in my head, I continued burning through fevered dreams after that. I think that they've passed now. My thoughts sound clear in my head. No hallucinations – as far as I know, at least. And I realize that I'm thirsty, my throat parched as summer soil.

Cautiously, I slide my legs out of bed. There's a shock of sharp pain as one of my heels touches the floor. When I look down, I see that the foot is bandaged – I must have hurt it while walking around without a boot. I shuffle over to the door, trying not to put weight on that leg. Outside, I find a small landing and a set of stairs down, which I navigate by leaning heavily on the handrail. When I reach the ground floor, I'm immediately face to face with Ellen, who gapes up at me, then – with the volume and pitch that only a small child can manage – she shouts, 'Peg! Miss Morgan's up. She looks *horrible*!'

'*Ellen!*' Footsteps approach fast from another room, then Peggy arrives in a doorway. I can tell by the way she frowns at me that I *do* look horrible, but she doesn't immediately force me back to bed, so that's something. The Wights' home is lovely and cosy: small, but well decorated and whistle-clean. The inverse of Harfold. 'Come have a sit-down,' Peggy says, guiding me through to the front room. Here, there are family pictures on the walls, as well as a plate decorated with painted primroses and a countryside print that looks as if it's been cut out of a book. Assorted china is displayed in a glass-fronted cabinet, and the table has a high polish, topped with a white lace runner and a vase of dried grasses. A basket of abandoned knitting takes up half the well-worn settee. Peggy moves this, then, when I sit, pulls out a half-finished blanket to drape over my knees. 'I'll get you a bite to eat,' she insists. 'You've had nothing but broth for the past three days; you must be fucking starved.'

While she disappears to fetch some much-welcome food and drink, I'm left under Ellen's watch. She continues to gawp at me.

'Whose nighty am I wearing?' I ask eventually.

'Peggy's,' says Ellen. 'She had to take all your wet clothes off for you.'

'Did she now?'

Ellen nods. 'I've never seen you in a dress before.'

'And you never will again, if I have my way.' I give her a wink. 'How's that telegraphy of yours coming along, then?'

'I'm not old enough to use a real telegraph, silly.'

'Aren't you? Funny; I could have sworn you were the eldest sister.'

This sends her into a fit of giggles, which is still ongoing when Peggy reappears with bread and warm milk. She sets these on a low stool, then moves it within my reach, saying, 'Tuck in.'

I don't need to be told twice. The bread is delicious – the best I've ever tasted. The crust is firm enough to crack under my teeth, and the inside light as air, studded with fine-chopped seeds and nuts, and still slightly warm from the oven. I tear into it with an animal ferocity. Swig the milk, rich and creamy, with its nostalgic smell of cowsheds.

'Right,' says Peggy, when I'm done, 'are you going to tell me what happened, then?'

What do I tell her? I am still coming to terms with it all myself. If I give the truth, she'll surely want to call the police, and I have no love for *them*. 'I slipped,' I tell her, 'on the footbridge. Hit my head and fell in the water. Lucky I didn't end up with worse.'

Peggy gives me a long look. 'When Daniel turned up with you all damp and bleeding like that, I thought you'd been half murdered.' Daniel is the name of her brother, I remember her telling me. He must be the boy I fainted on to – my flat-capped knight in shining armour. 'You gave us the fright of our lives! And you wouldn't let me tell anyone up at the manor you were here for love nor money. They must be wondering where you are?' Her voice rises in a question here, seeking a reason for my strange secrecy.

I see Arabella's expression again, as she let the river take me. She must think me dead. *Of course* I am dead: the curse came for me. Even if it ended up being by her own two hands. Her logic won't allow her to believe otherwise.

A lump rises in my throat. I'd thought she loved me, that she had finally chosen me over her paranoia. That together we could be free of the past. But in the end, I was nothing more to her than a sacrifice to offer up in place. 'I had a . . . falling-out with Lady Lascy,' I say at last, looking down at my fingernails. There's some kind of green scum caught under them. 'I didn't want to see her while I was ill.'

Peggy huffs. She's clearly unconvinced by my explanation, but can't work out why I would be lying to her. 'I told you *she* was no good,' she mutters. 'So what do you want to do now?'

The betrayal is still a hot knife in my back. But I'm not so much sad, I realize, as angry. I thought Arabella was different, but it turns out she's just like all the rest of the rich and powerful. Rotten to the core. Not to mention Reacher, whose true colours are just as rancid. Once the pair realize I'm alive, there's every chance they'll deliver on Reacher's threats to call the law, or else they may just try to kill me again. Even if I promise to leave them alone from now on, I'll always be a potential danger while I know what I know. They can't let me go freely about my life after this. All to say, I can't go back to Harfold. However, returning to Cardiff is also closed to me: too many strangers who think they know me from the newspaper accounts, my friends suffering for my mistakes.

I shuffle through the few things I have in my favour like cards in a deck. The only allies I can really count are Peggy and – at a distance – Lou and Gladys. I don't think Tom and Mrs Allen would have been involved in either cousin's scheme, but I have no way of knowing, so should treat them with caution. But perhaps I can still weaken my enemies: if I was just able to make Arabella believe me about Reacher, I could drive a wedge between them. Use the crack to wriggle in. Turn them against each other, so they're too busy warring to worry about me any longer. No, that won't do it. Whoever emerges the victor would eventually remember me, and I'd be back in the same position. Shuffle, shuffle. My hand is weak, the luck of the deal not on my side. I could try to slip away, start again with another new name. I can forge a reference, or maybe ask Gladys to do me one. Find a fresh position. Hope it won't be as much of a fucking nightmare.

But why should *I* be the one to fold? Allow Arabella and Reacher to punch me down, then roll over and let them continue on their path as if nothing's happened.

I realize that what I want is to finish the game. To win it. But to do that, first of all, I'll have to acquire a trump card. I need to get my hands on whatever secret is hidden in Arabella's diary.

My plan is to return to the manor later tonight, though Peggy isn't keen on letting me go walking alone, and at such an hour. 'You're not back to your full strength. What if you have a tumble again?'

'I'm fine,' I protest. 'Look, I need to speak to Lady Lascy, that's all.'

'After your "falling-out"?' asks Peggy, quoting my own words back at me. 'You aren't going to tell me what that was about, I suppose?'

'I can't really say. Sorry. It's a personal matter.'

She meets this with a sour expression. 'So you'll be staying there overnight, will you?' A hint of jealousy in her tone. I think Peggy may be a little sweet on me! Perhaps she's guessed some details of my relationship with Arabella; God knows what I said while I was out with that fever. Well, she needn't worry about that any more.

'No, I'll be back in a couple of hours,' I say. 'In fact, if you haven't seen me by then, maybe you could send Daniel up to check for me? If you're so worried about me being out alone, that is.' Hopefully it won't come to that: I intend to be in and out long before anyone realizes I'm there. But it never hurts to have a second plan in reserve.

This time around, I approach from the back lane, where I saw Peggy and Ellen out walking just before Christmas. From the low angle, I can't say much of the house over the rose garden wall, just the chimney stacks and slope of the roof, the tops of the upper-floor windows. As I'd hoped, all the lights appear to be out, the manor's inhabitants safely asleep. I enter the grounds through the rose garden gate. I'd guessed correctly that nobody would have thought to lock it, Tom being out of the habit since I took up the duty.

There's heavy cloud cover tonight: perfect for anyone looking to pass unseen through a garden. Only occasionally, I'll catch a small glint of the moon, now waning from its fullness of a few nights ago. To help me blend in further, I'm back in my own dark grey overalls, kindly laundered by Peggy while I was under her care. I've had to borrow a new pair of boots, though.

Unlike the rose gate, the main house *will* most certainly be tightly secured by this hour, but I've thought of that, too. Back when I was moving all those newspapers into the cellar, I'd noticed the room's external hatch, designed for passing down coal and barrels and that sort of thing without having to bring them through the kitchen. I don't recall ever seeing any kind of lock on it: just a simple sliding bolt from the outside.

Keeping low in a shuffling run that makes my poor muscles twinge, I cross to the exterior wall of the kitchen, beneath which the access hatch nestles in the soil. The bolt is stiff with rust, but with a bit of jiggling, I'm able to pull it back. Squat to open the hatch. It won't budge. Try again, straining this time. Still nothing. There must be a lock after all, and I didn't notice it before.

Unless . . . Maybe it's just stuck with old dirt. I scrabble around for a stick, then run it around the seal of the door, scooping out gobbets of slime. Once I've cleared the whole perimeter, I take the handle again, lifting with all my might. The wood groans, resists, then surrenders.

Groping around, I find the top of the wooden ladder on the other side. Scurry down. It's near total darkness, but I don't want to risk a light yet. I think I can still remember the way through the empty wine racks, if I hold my arms out in front of me as a guide. Dirt crunches as I walk, and a cobweb kisses my face. My toe hits something. I tap around with my boot until I've confirmed it's the first step of the stairs to the kitchen.

When I reach the top, I pause at the door, straining my ears to make sure the Allens aren't on the other side. Even if Tom and Mrs Allen aren't involved in Arabella's and Reacher's plots – and I very much hope they aren't – I can't know what they've been told about me in my absence, and my appearing now from the cellar in the middle of the night would take far too much explanation in any case. Thankfully, all is quiet.

As I open the door, I'm welcomed by a gust of warm air, the stove no doubt continuing to throw out heat from when the evening meal was prepared. I feel as though I'm rising from the grave. A ghost come back to haunt Harfold.

Moving on tiptoe, I pass through the servants' quarters into the main hall. Now, where would Arabella keep her diary? I've never seen it lying around unattended, which is normally what happens to her possessions when she's done with them, so she must have a particular hiding place for this one. I try the study first: it's mostly Reacher's territory, but Arabella uses it occasionally to write in, when he's away. It doesn't take me long to search it over, since I know the new filing system so well. The diary isn't here, but I do find the deed to Harfold in one of the desk drawers. Hold it up to the meagre moonlight from the window to see that my signature is still there. I'm not sure why they haven't destroyed it yet, except that perhaps Arabella thinks my name needs to remain in place to prevent the curse returning on her. I tuck it away in my pocket for later.

Coming back out of the study, I'm about to use the drawing room as a passage to the library when I see – fuck! There's a band of faint light under the drawing room door. The low warmth of a single candle, by my guess. Someone must still be up. How did I not spy this earlier, either as I approached the house, or as I came into the study just now? I must have been distracted by the cat-burglar rush of my mission.

But this is all right. I can go round – back into the hall, then through the adjoining room into the library by its other entrance. Moving quickly and quietly, I take this route, and make it into the library undetected. A low illumination seeps into this room from the door to the drawing room. As I scan over rows of books, I'm almost thankful for this, as now I can just about make out the colours. I start to pull down any I find with a green spine, checking to see if they could be Arabella's diary, but each one turns out to be an ordinary print work: dictionaries, encyclopaedias, novels, bound magazines, Reacher's various books on birding. My search disturbs a large spider, which runs across my hand before skittering away. I've never minded them much, but at Harfold, the creatures seem to multiply in every corner and cranny. The crawling sensation continues to tickle my skin long after the creature's moved on.

Giving up on the shelves, I search inside the reading desk

drawers, one by one, inching them open with painful slowness and flinching at every squeak of wood. There are all sorts of things stuffed in here, but again no diary.

Upstairs, then? At least Arabella's bedroom will be empty, if this *is* her in the drawing room. I sidle up to the door and place my ear to it. Don't dare to breathe.

Yes, a very low conversation is happening on the other side – I recognize both Arabella's and Reacher's voices. So they haven't killed each other yet, then. But they *are* arguing: despite the hushed tones, there's an undercurrent of conflict. Then I catch my name, and realize they're discussing *me*. How flattering! I try pressing my ear directly to the keyhole, and now I can make out the individual words.

I hear Reacher first, the end of a sentence: '. . . still out there.'

'For heaven's sake, will you stop fretting?'

My heart hammers so hard at the sound of Arabella's voice that I think it might burst, and I'm hit with a churn of emotions. Rage, pain, grief, revulsion, love. I push them all down. Need to focus on the task at hand.

Reacher huffs in irritation. 'I am perfectly within my rights to be concerned that a *dangerous* individual is at large. You didn't hear her, Bellsy! The way she was bragging about her hateful plans, how she had it all mapped out to frame *me* for her crimes. I can't bear to think what she would have done to you if I hadn't caught her first.'

That sets a fresh fire of anger in my chest. Twisting it all up to put the blame on me. There's a silence, and I wonder if Arabella is about to defend me, accuse Reacher of lying. Then she sighs. 'I know, Morry.' Despite everything she's already done, this still has the power to hurt me. She really thinks *I* wanted to harm her? After I gave her nothing but love! Or maybe that's what she needs to believe, rationalizing her choice to kill me after the fact. A way to live with what she's done. 'But I have already told you: she won't be coming back.'

'Of course,' says Reacher, voice heavy with sarcasm. 'She *has* to be dead, because you saw a hare.'

'I did! The moment she fell in the water.'

Oh, I like that. *Fell*. So Arabella hasn't told him exactly what happened, then.

Arabella is still speaking, her tone breathy, almost reverential. I struggle to hear over the pulse thrumming in my ears. 'There it was, across the river, looking at me. Then it sprang up and I swear, Morry, it started to dance – exactly like in the story. As soon as I saw it, I was struck with this immense calm, and I just knew the curse had taken her instead, and now it was sated. I was forgiven. George had let go.' That must be George Allen – but what does he have to do with anything? Maybe I haven't heard her right.

Arabella doesn't elaborate on this last comment, instead moving on to describe how light she now feels. She starts listing all the things that she and Reacher can do now that they're free. I think I've got the picture. Before I lose my sense and go bursting in there, I make myself leave the library and hurry upstairs, reminding myself of the purpose of this covert visit.

Despite my best efforts earlier this year, Arabella's bedroom is still a pigsty. There's no hope of finding anything by touch alone, so I risk lighting one of the many half-melted candles that lie scattered around. Holding this up at an angle to avoid getting hot wax on my skin, I check over the shelves, then every cupboard and drawer. Under the mattress. Still no sign of the green notebook. I'm about ready to say to Hell with all this.

No: I can't give up. Where else would Arabella keep something special to her? Then I remember Christmas Day, when I caught her in the closed wing, with that cabinet in her old quarters. But I'd already been in there to poke around, shortly after, and found the cabinet empty, and there weren't exactly plenty of other hiding places in that sparsely furnished room. My head's throbbing – I'm not sure if that's still from my little 'fall', or from all the thinking.

I remember another piece of information, all of a sudden. The story Tom told me on Guy Fawkes Day about the former governess, the one with the alleged taste for cocaine pills. He'd said Lord Lascy claimed to have discovered her hoard in the nursery, concealed in a cabinet with a false base. I don't know which room would once have been the nursery, but what's the betting this is the same piece of furniture?

Taking the candle with me, I head out on to the walkway to cross to the other wing, cupping my hand around the small light to reduce its reach, just to be on the safe side. As I pass the corridor that leads to Reacher's room, I hear a faint *pip-pip*: Finchley, sending out his sad pinking call in the hope of an answer. I pause. Consider it. *Don't be reckless*, I tell myself. There's no point in getting caught over a petty act of revenge like this. But then Finchley pinks again, and I can't bear to leave him there. I hurry silently down to Reacher's room, opening the door with a careful hand so as not to creak the hinges. There's the cage on its stand, left uncovered with a stub of candle nearby to give the lonely chaffinch some light.

'This isn't where you belong, is it?' I whisper to him, picking up his cage and taking it over to the window, before pulling up the sash a fraction, just enough for a small bird to squeeze through. The cage door unlocks with a simple latch. I hold it open.

Finchley hops forward on his perch, tilting his head.

'Go on, then.'

In a blur, the chaffinch is gone, just the flash of white tail feathers visible out there in the night. And then nothing.

I put the cage back where I found it. How unfortunate that Reacher forgot to latch it properly, that Mrs Allen had left the window open for a bit of air.

I'm grinning as I finally enter the closed wing, noting once more the clean track in the dust underfoot. As if someone has been travelling to and from the room regularly – to write a diary, perhaps? This *has* to be it.

Happily, Arabella's old bedroom has been left unlocked, further confirming my theory that it's in regular use. I enter and cross to the cabinet, kneeling down to examine it. The last time I looked inside, I'd poked my hands all over the interior and found nothing. Then again, I hadn't been looking for a secret compartment. This time, when I take it in properly, I can see that the base *does* look much thicker than you would expect. I don't have anywhere to put the candle down, so I have to work single-handed. First, I try sliding the bottom board this way and that, to see if it slots out, but my fingers simply skid across the surface. Then, thinking of the mystery pictures I've seen at the cinema, I try looking for a hidden latch to press, a carving which doubles as a release. Running my palm along the underside of the cabinet, I find a much simpler solution: a handle. I give this a yank and, with a satisfying click, a drawer drops down.

When I slide it open, I'm faced with not one, but an array of notebooks. Of course: if this is a diary that Arabella has been keeping for many years, it makes sense that there would be multiple volumes. I don't see the most recent instalment in its greenish leather binding – the others are all different sizes and colours, no interest shown in consistency. I pick one of them up and find a date marked on the front: 1917. Flick through the pages, not really taking in the words, until something catches my eye. Arabella has a habit of underlining particular words, and I've just found 'curse' picked out in this manner. 28 March 1917. *I had not been thinking of a curse exactly, but now that Morry has planted the idea in my skull, I can't seem to shake it.* My suspicion proved that Reacher was the one to fan the flames of this delusion. Attention drifting on a few lines, I see more: *Because everything always goes back to that blasted night. To what I did.*

Arabella doesn't elaborate on this, but it must be a reference to what Reacher hinted at earlier, that there's a further story behind her belief in the curse. So how do I find it? I flick through the journals, the different dates. Arabella told me that the curse has come once every three years, starting with her parents. If this year, 1926, is Arabella's turn, then I should be able to count back through her relatives to work out that ... Yes, the parents must have died in 1911. I find the diary for that year and place it on the floor beside me. But where does George come into it? I don't recall what date of death was on his headstone, but I remember that Henry Lascy paid for it – so it must have happened before 1911. I take a few earlier volumes, going back to 1908: whatever Arabella believes started the curse, it must have happened near enough to her parents' passing that she'd connect the two events. The books are small, just large enough to hold in the palm of a hand, so I'm able to squeeze all four into my pockets. Don't want to be caught reading them here – I'll take them away for later. I mourn the absence of the latest, green leather journal. I want to know what Arabella has written about me.

Still, a thrill of pleasure to be taking something precious away from her. I have what I came for. Time to get out before I'm spotted.

Again cupping my hand around the candle flame, I pass down the corridor and out on to the wooden walk that encircles the upper storey of the main hall. In my haste to leave, I make a mistake: I don't check that I'm alone.

A flash of illuminated movement from the hall below.

I'm stuck in place, a clench of cold in my chest, as Arabella stares back up at me.

For a moment, we are both still as the figures in the statue garden outside. I try to think what to do. Run away? Attack her? Beg her to keep quiet?

Arabella speaks first: 'No . . .' The word chokes out of her, horrified and hoarse. She carries her own candle – this is what alerted me to her presence – and its light reveals a face that's bloodless, eyes round as buttons. Her hair is loose, hanging unbrushed around her shoulders. Tucked under one arm, I realize she has the green diary; she must have been writing in it this evening, and that's why it wasn't with the others. 'Not you,' she pleads. 'Not again.'

Again? I don't know how to reply to that, so I just wait to hear what she'll say next.

'George sent you, didn't he?' The candlelight flickers – her hand is trembling. 'He realized he took the wrong person.'

Bloody hell . . . She thinks I'm a ghost! Some kind of vengeful spirit, returned from beyond to punish her for the evil deed she did me. Well, I'm not going to disillusion her. Let her feel a little fear.

She takes a small step forward, drawing closer. 'I'm so sorry, Vee, I thought if I could just . . .' Her voice trails off into a sob.

While I'd love to listen to her beg my forgiveness, I should get away before she realizes I'm the same flesh and blood that I've always been. But how? If I take the staircase down, I'll have to pass her by.

Then I remember there are back stairs in the closed wing, no longer in use. What could be more suited to a ghost than disappearing into seemingly thin air? I turn and, still not saying anything, continue down the walk until I come to the one door I haven't been through yet – the one leading to the old servants' quarters. Without turning to look back at Arabella, I go in.

No matter where I go, staff rooms always have the same uniform decoration. Maybe our employers think the familiar will make us feel at home. Or perhaps that we aren't a high enough class of being to care for luxuries like aesthetics or comfort. In this dank corridor, I'm faced with peeling beige paint, rows of unvarnished wooden doors, cracked linoleum flooring. The only points of difference are the aura of decay and the occasional dust sheets hanging over abandoned furniture.

Moving fast now, I hurry through these uninspiring passages until I find, as expected, the top of the back stairs. Now I've learned my lesson, I extinguish the candle and proceed with caution, creeping down once more into the Allens' quarters. Still empty. Arabella doesn't appear to have raised any alarm. I pass through the kitchen into the cellar, then make my escape through the waiting exterior hatch, closing it behind me as I go.

When I reach the lane, my heart is still racing fit to burst, and I'm quivering all over with adrenaline – or perhaps from the exertion; I'm still not recovered from my dip in the river, after all. But I've done it! In my pockets, I have Arabella's diaries. I could whoop with joy.

Once I make it back to the Wights' cottage, I find that Peggy has been waiting up for me in the front room, working at her knitting by lamplight. The blanket's advanced by a good length.

'How'd it go?' she asks as I poke my head in. 'All fixed with her Ladyship?'

'I'd say we both came away with things to think about.'

It turns out that the bed I've been occupying is normally shared by Peggy and Ellen. In the meantime, Ellen is in with Daniel, and Peggy's been sleeping on the settee down here. Now I'm on the mend, I try to convince her to swap, but she's having none of it. 'Nonsense, you're the guest. Get on upstairs. I'm perfectly happy here.'

So, trying to squash my guilt, I head up to the sisters' room. Light the lamp to see that my sheets have been carefully remade, the borrowed nightgown folded up on the pillow, and a jug of water and a little vase of daffodils left on the bedside table. Oh, Peggy . . . I feel bad not telling her the truth when she's been ever so kind to me, but what can I do? She'd be up at Harfold with a pitchfork if she found out the half of it.

After changing my clothes, I get into bed and prop myself up against the pillow, Arabella's pilfered diaries in my lap. I start with 1908.

SEVENTEEN

DAWN IS BREAKING. The chiming birdsong draws my attention to it first, and I wonder idly if Finchley is part of this morning chorus, finally reunited with his own kind. When I look out the window I discover a bouquet of colours: marigold, cherry blossom, rose, violet, periwinkle.

I've spent all night with Arabella's words. That spidered, calligraphic hand, too decorated to read easily at first, but by now I'm intimately familiar with every loop and tail. The Arabella in these diaries – as she was between 1908 and 1911 – is scarcely recognizable as the woman I thought I'd known for the past seven months. At the start of the pages, she's far more carefree: outgoing, bold, adventurous. She has friends, attends all sorts of lavish parties, shares gossip that'd make my cheeks smart if I knew any of the people involved. Then on the eighteenth of February... Some people might believe that I'm in no position to judge Arabella, given my history, but I say to Hell with that. There's a difference between us. Besides, it isn't what happened to George that really gets to me. Arabella and Charlie may have been reckless – his death was inarguably their fault – but it *was* an accident. No: it's the mercenary way that Arabella and her family covered it up, rewriting the manslaughter as a tragic mishap or suicide that would eat at Tom for years to come. How could Arabella stand to look him in the eye every day, knowing the truth? Because she went along with it. Oh, I'm sure it played at the back of her mind; over the next three years, she continues to make occasional reference to *that night*, particularly after her parents' deaths. She becomes more subdued, more reclusive. Not quite the Arabella she is today, but closer to her, the seed of her future beginning to germinate. She sometimes thinks she sees George. With this new context, I remember now the strange things she's said in the past. *You know* he *wouldn't like it*, after Reacher and I took the Renault out. I assumed at the time she was speaking about Charlie. In any case, she squashed that guilt down and, in the end, I suppose that's why it had to sprout in her mind as a supernatural curse.

Then her solution, of all things, was to offer me up to die in her place. I'd laugh at the irony, if my lungs didn't still hurt from almost drowning. I'm in half a mind to leave her believing I drowned – let my ghost haunt her for the rest of her life right alongside George. It's what she deserves.

But I can't do that. What about Tom? He deserves to finally know what happened to his brother. Maybe it will bring him peace. Perhaps he'll even be able to leave now, get away from the Lascy clutches and live the life that Mrs Allen has been wishing for all this time. Surely the two of them deserve to find happiness.

And what result will make me happy?

I came to Harfold looking for a new start, and for a time I thought I'd found it in Arabella. But that was the problem: it was *her* life. I had only ever been a guest in it. So stupid not to have seen that earlier. I won't make that mistake again. What I need is a life that doesn't rely on anyone else. Money enough to free me from the whims of careless employers. A home that no one can kick me out of. To drive around in my own motorcar.

And, though it's not pretty to admit it, I also want to get back at Reacher and Arabella. If the law will never bring them to justice, I'll take personal revenge as a second choice.

Besides, I've been reshuffling my hand, and it looks a lot better this morning – for the first time since coming to Harfold, I can see all of the cards clearly. I know just what I have to do, but I need to strike quickly while Arabella and Reacher are still off their footing.

First, I need to get the pair of them alone for a meeting. Not back up at Harfold – that's too far from help if things go wrong, and besides, I don't know what they've told the Allens about me. No, better for it to be here in the village. I can't exactly invite them into Peggy's house for this conversation, but there must be somewhere else we can have a spot of privacy.

As I make my way into the Wights' kitchen for breakfast, my eyes catch on the keys where they hang on the wall. There, among the usual ones for all the household locks, will be Mr Wight's spare for the church. Now, *that* will throw them off their balance.

When nobody's looking, I take the churchwarden's key down, finding that it's been helpfully labelled with a tag. Next, I beg paper off Peggy and scribble a note to Arabella and Reacher. I keep it short and non-specific: *I know what you did. Meet me in the church at seven o'clock.* Don't sign my name. I don't want it to be used against me later, and anyway, I like the idea of making them sweat a little. Then I write another note, wrapping it up along with Arabella's journals before adding Lou and Gladys's address to the front. I take both of these up with me to Daniel's bedroom, where I give a soft tap on the door to draw his attention. He's more than happy to run the first message up to Harfold for me, without letting on who it's from. I also ask him to look after the parcel and, if I don't come back to collect it before tomorrow morning, to pop it in the first post. He doesn't question any of this, seemingly too in awe of me to disobey the orders.

The church closes for worship at six o'clock, and I watch out of the cottage window until I see the vicar locking up and making his way to the vicarage at around quarter past. I give it another few minutes to be sure, then tell Peggy I'm off for a walk. Use Mr Wight's key to let myself in. The absence of other people makes the space feel even smaller than it did at Christmas, the empty pews confusing my sense of perspective. A meagre trace of evening light falls through the stained-glass window at the chancel, the shadows cast by Saint Anselm and the cowering hare stretching long up the limewash walls. From this angle, the creature's face looks sly, calculating.

As I move further in, my footsteps ring behind me up the aisle, almost as if someone is following close at my back. I breathe stale air, laden with the smell of old dust.

Wanting to keep surprise on my side, I duck behind a pew to wait, unseen from the entryway as my eyes adjust to the gloom. Perch on an embroidered kneeler, this one showing a wreath of flowers. Wonder idly whether any of the designs are Arabella's. No, it wouldn't be like her to do something for the community in that way.

I don't have to loiter for long before the wooden door scrapes open, and – risking a peep over the benchtop – I see that Reacher and Arabella have arrived. They enter cautiously, scanning the room to check if they're alone.

'She's not here,' says Reacher. He speaks at a whisper, but the echoing walls carry his words clearly to my ears.

Despite the mild evening, Arabella is bundled in her fur coat, shuddering as she pushes past her cousin to look for herself. 'I have already told you, it can't be Vee, she's—'

'Then you are sure nobody saw the other night, when it happened?'

'There was nothing to see.' Arabella's features are hidden beneath the deep shadow of a frown, but the tremor is plain in her voice. 'She slipped and fell.'

Reacher grunts in frustration and collapses on to one of the back pews. He clearly doesn't buy Arabella's story about my tragic fate. There's a puffiness to his face and his clothes are dishevelled – the marks of a man who hasn't slept. Up late looking for his escaped chaffinch, I imagine. I feel that spark of pleasure at inflicting pain.

'Perhaps it is just a trick,' says Arabella, coming to stand beside him. 'Village boys having a laugh.' She touches a hand to her throat, rubbing the skin as if trying subtly to remove something. The nervous gesture reminds me of the first day we met, just over half a year ago now. She was such a mystery to me then, a knot of threads to be unpicked. But now I see her completely for what she is: a woman unable to care for anything beyond her own fears.

I step out of my hiding place. Clear my throat.

They both look up at once. On Arabella's face, the same expression of terror that I saw yesterday – wide-eyed, white-faced, frozen in place. She grabs at Reacher's shoulder. 'I told you!'

Reacher, however, is unmoved. 'For God's sake, Bellsy, she

is obviously not a ghost.' Then to me, 'I thought it would be you, Miss Owens.'

Arabella looks at me more intently, blinking repeatedly as though she's trying to dispel an after-image. A twitch in her jaw as the disbelief melts away. She has finally accepted the truth. 'Vee?' she breathes.

'Alive and kicking,' I agree, coming a little closer up the aisle. 'I guess George Allen didn't want me after all, did he?'

At the name, Arabella jumps, then glances toward the door to the bell tower, as if she expects the former churchwarden to step out of it. 'What do you know about that?'

'I borrowed a few of your diaries for a little entertainment,' I tell her. 'In fact, I found them *so* interesting that I sent them on to a friend to read too. Hope you don't mind.' I'm unable to resist the urge to gloat a little – I'm only human.

Reacher scowls at me, getting up from his seat. 'What do you want? Money? We don't have it.'

I find it funny how rich people always think they don't have money. The Reeses were like that, too, forever suggesting cost-saving economies – although these were always imposed on us staff, never the Reeses themselves. 'The only thing I want from you both,' I say, 'is for you to clear out of my house.'

He doesn't understand. Stares blankly back at me. 'What?'

'Harfold. It's my name on the deed.'

Now he laughs – a nasty, mocking sort of bark that rings up the church's limewashed walls then back down again. 'We've already destroyed that. Haven't we, Bellsy?'

Arabella bites her lip. 'The curse . . .'

Reacher's attention snaps to his cousin, nostrils flaring. 'You told me you'd—' He catches himself, exhales slowly. 'Never mind that, Miss Owens: I remind you that your name *isn't* on it, and I will be changing it back shortly in any case.'

I smile at him, all sweetness. 'Oh, you do still have it, then?'

Reacher takes a step forward, opening his mouth to reply, but then the words snag in his throat. There's a dawning dismay on his face. He must be putting it together: that Arabella really did see me last night, that I've been into his study. That I took the deed right out of his desk drawer.

I pat my breast pocket, which gives out the unmistakable rustle of paper. 'I didn't think so,' I confirm. 'I've taken the liberty of correcting the small error I made last time, when I mis-wrote my own name. It's definitely made out to Vera Owens now, clear as anything.'

Losing steam, Reacher darts another look at Arabella. 'It won't stand up in a court of law.'

'Are you willing to bet on that?' I'm trembling with adrenaline, fighting to keep my voice and poker face steady. He's probably right – it can't be a proper legal contract – but will he call me on my bluff?

'Bellsy wasn't in her right mind when she signed it over to you.'

'And was she in her right mind when she tried to kill me?'

Arabella flinches at this, face screwing up in a grimace. She's looking down at the floor. 'Vee . . .' Her voice is soft, with a wheedling note to it.

'She did push me,' I tell Reacher. 'Gave me a nasty crack on the head and I almost drowned. I can't believe I *didn't*. I guess something wanted to keep me alive.' I look at Arabella significantly here. 'If you want to contest the deed, you're more than welcome to. But that legal battle may have to wait until *after* you're through with the murder trial. And, believe me, those really are no fun at all. So I'll say it again' – take a step forward, shoulders squared – 'clear out of my house.'

Reacher takes another pace himself, squaring up to me at the distance of just a couple of feet. 'Let me make one thing very clear: Harfold will *never* belong to you.'

Coming up behind him, Arabella reaches out a hand to touch his arm. 'We have to be careful, Morry, we don't want the curse to—'

'For the love of God!' He wheels around, forcing her to stagger back. 'There is no curse, you imbecile. I made it up!'

Arabella doesn't say anything for several heartbeats. Then she shakes her head. 'No.'

'*Yes!*' Reacher presses his fingers to his temples. 'I have had it with watching you waste the life that should belong to me. You have been given everything, Arabella, and look at what you have done with it! Diddly fucking squat.' He turns back to me, and there's a wildness in his eyes. A barb of hunger. '*My* name is going on that deed, even if I have to kill you both for it.'

I jump back just in time to avoid his lunge. There's only space to run in one direction – through the door to the church tower. Up the stairs. The wooden steps slam loud beneath my thundering feet. Reacher is hot behind me, his breaths coming out as bestial growls. I know I'm heading for a dead end at the top, but I keep going, mind racing to find an escape plan. Reacher's expression just now leaves me with no doubt that he really means the threat.

Legs white-hot from the ascent, I arrive on to a narrow wooden platform. The vast hulks of bells surround me like towering ships at sea. When I let my eyes journey to the edge, the dizzying drop below twists my stomach tight.

Moments later, Reacher emerges puffing up the stairs after me, his body now blocking the only way down. The only *survivable* way down, that is. 'You have nowhere to go,' he wheezes. 'Just give me that deed and we can forget all about this. I can still help you!'

Ordinarily, his larger build means I wouldn't like my chances against him in a brawl, but he's less fit than I am, red in the face from the climb. Plus he's *angry*, not thinking right. Both of these are things I can use to my advantage.

I take a few steps away, backing up against the wall as far as I can, drawing him out on to the platform as I do so. I'm aware of Arabella far below in the stairwell, shouting up at us, but I can't make out her words. It's just me and Reacher now.

'How's Finchley?' I ask.

Confusion on his face, then comprehension. 'You!'

'Yes.'

He flies at me, fingers digging talon-like into my upper arms. I try to twist away and we struggle against each other. I force him back a step. His breath is on my face, stale and meaty. There are beads of sweat on his forehead from the climb. He thrusts one hand into my breast pocket, so violent it feels at first like a punch, and manages to wrest out the piece of paper. Holds it above his head. Takes a victorious back-step.

I'd have thought the church would've put a railing up here after what supposedly happened to George all those years ago, but then again, I suppose they didn't imagine such bad luck would repeat itself.

Reacher is silent as he falls, as if he doesn't believe it's happening either. There's just the *crack* as he hits the ground. Then a high shriek from Arabella, bouncing in echoes around the tower like the chime of a bell.

Careful as I go, I edge over to the side of the platform and peer into the gloomy stairwell below. Reacher's body has landed spread-eagled, his neck twisted sharply to the side. One fist is still balled around the paper he pulled from my pocket. A blank sheet, of course. The real deed is safe in the hands of Peggy's brother Daniel, along with Arabella's diaries. I'm not stupid. As I turn to head back down to ground level, I think I see something just at the edge of my vision – a bulky form, standing up here with me. Only my own shadow, I think. Watching in silence as it all unwinds.

That day at the Reeses', after Dad lost his job. After I refused to play with Kenneth, found the rat poison, took it into the kitchen and made an ill-received joke. After I'd been sent out so that Mam and Dad could have their argument in peace. I passed the footman in the corridor.

'Your daddy shouldn't be here,' he said.

I stuck my tongue out.

But the bastard kept going: 'And neither should you. Do you know what I heard Mrs Reese telling her husband? That she wished he'd send you packing, too, and your mother to boot. You're a bad family, the lot of you. Cowards and traitors. Criminals. She never wanted any of you working here in the first place. Just watch: you'll both be out on your arses as well before you know it.'

I don't know whether this was true or if he was just saying it to upset me, but I believed every word of it at the time, and the injustice twisted my innards. So I waited in the garden until I saw Dad leave – about ten minutes later – and I returned to the kitchen. It was empty: Mam must have gone to fetch something. Moving fast before she came back, I took down the tin of arsenic from where I'd left it on the shelf. I went through the motions in a red daze, my anger creating a sort of dream state where I was only half conscious of what I was doing. Poison, milk, stir. Put the empty tin back where I'd left it, so Mam wouldn't notice. Yes, I wanted to do it, but I wasn't thinking about what would happen next. At no point did I imagine that it would actually be *consumed*. At least, that's how I remember it.

A few seconds after I'd completed my task, I heard Mam's footsteps coming up through the corridor. Stood back quickly from the counter.

She paused when she saw me, her cheeks blooming a frustrated pink at my disobedience. 'And what would you be doing back in here, my girl?' Then her eyes drifted past me, to the tea-tray. 'You weren't spitting in that food, were you?'

This would have been my chance to confess. I could have stopped everything that came next. But I didn't know that little Kenneth was taking his tea at home. That he'd ask, as he did every day, for a big glass of milk – the majority of the milk going to him because of it. If I'd realized that, I would never have let that tray go upstairs. But how could I have known it? So I just shook my head.

I've never admitted this to Mam and Dad, but I know that they know it. That I let them take the blame instead.

I wouldn't reply to my letters either, if I were them.

EIGHTEEN

ARABELLA LEAVES HARFOLD the day after Reacher's funeral, packing the few belongings she's decided to take into a taxicab to the station. Her hand grips tight to the lip of the door as the driver starts the ignition, her knuckles showing stark white. I wonder if this is the first time she's been in a car since she knocked George down. Then she's off. I stand on the front step to watch as the car recedes down the drive, passing between my yews and finally through the gates, until it's absorbed by the waiting woodland.

The official line is that the vicar must have forgotten to lock the church that evening, and Reacher found his way inside. There's a lot of debate in the village over whether he was simply exploring and fell – yet another tragic accident in the Lascys' long history of misfortune – or if he jumped on purpose. People want to know my thoughts, of course, as someone who was close to the family. It's hard to know, I tell them, but he *was* a lonely sort of man, so dependent on his pet bird for companionship that he was just heartbroken when it escaped. Maybe he was even looking for Finchley up there?

Arabella has told everyone that she needs to get away from Harfold, start afresh. That she's left me as the house's custodian.

Tom and Mrs Allen naturally have a lot of questions. Sitting around the kitchen table after Arabella's gone, I decide to tell them a version of the truth. I explain how Arabella – convinced the curse was coming for her – signed Harfold over to me so that it would take me instead. How, when Reacher realized this, he threatened to kill Arabella and frame me for her murder, forfeiting my claim to the house in the process. That I tried to warn Arabella about this, but, too caught up in her fear of the curse, she responded by pushing me into the river, meaning to leave me for dead. When they both learned that I was still alive and could well reveal all of their secrets, the stress of it must have got to Reacher. I don't like to speculate, I tell the Allens, but perhaps he just couldn't live with that hanging over his head . . . Although it really should have come first in the story, I leave the truth about George's death until last.

'No,' says Tom, after I tell him. Shakes his head slowly, Adam's apple jumping in his throat. 'I don't know what you think you read in those diaries, but that can't be true. George fell— He jumped— He . . .' Tom presses his fingers to the corner of his eyes, as if he can stop the blooming tears this way. 'Lord Lascy, he would never have . . .'

I exchange glances with Mrs Allen. Her face is an ashen grey, a grim downturn to her lips. There's pity there as well as sorrow: she believes what I've told them without question. She's always seen the Lascys in a clearer light than her husband is able to.

'I know you respected Henry Lascy a great deal,' I press, 'but he didn't deserve it. He lied to your face for years – they all did.'

'No.' Tom slams a fist on the table as he says it, the word no longer a denial, but a shout of rage. I think this is the first time I've ever seen him moved to anger.

Mrs Allen immediately wants to take Arabella to the police, but I hesitate at the suggestion. Until now, Arabella and I have been in a standoff: if she accuses me of fraud, I'll reveal her crimes; if I reveal her crimes, she'll accuse me of fraud. But whether or not to seek justice for George isn't my decision to make.

Arabella's diaries have returned from Daniel by now, so I hand them over to Tom. It's only right that he gets to cast the deciding vote. But Tom shakes his head at the suggestion, tears shining down his cheeks. 'I don't know,' he says. 'Lady Lascy . . . well, she was barely more than a kiddie when it happened, and she was only doing what her parents told her. If anyone was to blame, it was them two – after everything I gave to them.'

'Tom . . .' Mrs Allen stands up to rub her husband's broad shoulders, as if soothing a child.

'I know what she tried to do to you was awful, Vee,' he says, turning to me, 'but she hasn't been well for a long time. I don't believe she'd really have wanted you to come to harm, deep down.'

I don't think I've ever met anyone as good-hearted as Tom. Treating Arabella with compassion, after everything she's done . . . The twist of pain is still far too raw for me. I clear my throat. 'It's up to you both what to do next. But I should tell you first, just so you have all the information: I don't think Arabella will challenge my claim to Harfold if we keep her secret for her. I'm planning to sell up – the house is falling apart, but the land must be worth something. I see half the money as yours by right. Two thirds, even. God knows, you deserve it more than me.'

'So she thinks she can bribe us,' Mrs Allen says.

'Maybe. Or she could paint it as blackmail, if we try to go to the law. Accuse us three of forging those diaries, even. I'm not saying we shouldn't try it, but it may be a game we can't win in the end. On the other hand, if we—'

'Let her get away with it?'

'Yes. You could use that money to start over. Go and set up near George's family, spend it on them. I don't know if that's what he would have wanted, but it's what I would want, if I was him. In fact . . .' I pause, not sure whether to say the next part. I know that what I saw on the riverbank was only a hallucination – the spectre of a fever. Unless it wasn't. 'After Arabella pushed me, when I came out of the water, I thought I saw something,' I tell them. 'A man. As if he'd been the one to pull me to safety. He looked a lot like you, Tom. It was probably no more than a dream, but at the time, I thought it was George.'

Tom lets out a loud sob, and I worry for a second that I've said the wrong thing. Then I see he's smiling. A look of complete delight. 'I knew it,' he says. 'I always knew he was watching us all.'

At last, it's this that seems to settle it. While Mrs Allen's clearly still not keen on letting Arabella get away scot-free, she concedes to Tom's decision to take the money and put the ghosts of the past finally to rest.

So now it's just me. Alone. I haunt the halls of Harfold, feeling the echoes of its history following in my wake. None of the rooms are off-limits any longer: I drop into them at will, touch their surfaces, move items between them as I please. With Arabella's hoards cleared out, they all seem much larger, far emptier. At night, the dark corners feel like they could be miles and miles away. Perhaps this is the real reason that Arabella crammed them so full of whatever she had to hand.

One of the first things I get rid of is the Lascy family genealogy. Lifting it off the wall, it suddenly looks far less imposing. I'm not sure what to do with it. I consider donating it to a local museum, thinking surely it will be of historic interest. But then I think, why should the names of all these lords and ladies be remembered, when nobody gives two hoots about what *my* ancestors were called. The only real difference between Arabella's family and mine is that someone bothered to keep track of hers. That doesn't mean they deserve to be remembered for ever more. So eventually, I take it out to the bonfire heap, lay it down on top as if on a funeral pyre. Strike the match. The material is so old and dry, it catches almost immediately, the flames blackening first the corners, then racing all the way across its surface. The snarl and hiss and pop of burning stitches. Just like that, the Lascys are gone.

Now that I have the deed back, I've managed to arrange for it to be legally verified with Arabella's tepid blessing – or at least, her agreement not to get in my way. She recognizes our delicately balanced situation as well as I do.

I've already auctioned off any fittings and furnishings that are worth anything, passing a good portion of profit on to the Allens. Nora – as she's finally invited me to call her – has at last achieved her dream of a bed-and-breakfast in Somerset, close at hand to George's children. The 'kiddies' are all grown up now and building families of their own. She and Tom write to me about their antics: the first guests they have to stay; the fabric they choose for the curtains before realizing it's too pale to stop the coming summer light; the local church choir that Nora joins; the new puppy that Tom can't help but carry home when he sees its face peeping out of the pet shop window. I'm welcome to stay for free any time, they say – so long as I'll help Tom sort out the patch of dirt that's currently serving them as a garden!

Peggy and Ellen visit me on occasion, take a walk round the

grounds to keep me company, let me drive them back to the village in one of the motorcars from the coach house – mine too, now. Peggy is growing bolder in her flirting, and I expect she'll make an approach in the near future. I'll be sorry to turn her down – the last thing I want to do is hurt her, after all the kindness she's shown me – but I'll be leaving Harfold just as soon as I can. Better to make it a clean break.

I'm still working on selling the land. There's no two ways about it: the manor itself will have to be torn down. Now that everything is cleared out, the decay is even clearer to see; frankly, I'm surprised the floors never fell in on us. I've been speaking to Gerrish to see if he can use it for farmland, but he seems to think it's too large an area to take a risk on. What with all the new foreign goods driving down costs, the farming community has learned the value of being cautious, one eye always on the purse-strings. However, he's tipped me off to a possible alternative: apparently I should try the War Office. Of course, they already own a great deal of land on the Plain – not to mention that aerodrome they built over by Stonehenge – but word on the grapevine is that they're looking to acquire even more. Gerrish has given me an address to write to, so let's see if that gets me anywhere.

Toward the end of May, I receive a letter from Arabella. She wants to talk, she says. I have half a mind to turn her away, but I still have unsettled business with her, so I extend an invitation.

Since the Allens left, I'm managing the household alone. This isn't too much trouble, as I only keep two or three rooms in use – in fact, I'm glad that I can finally eat food with some flavour in it once more. I hope Nora's poor bed-and-breakfast guests know what they're in for!

On the afternoon that Arabella's due to visit, I prepare the tea things and lay them out on the kitchen table for us to have there. I've found Nora's recipe for those yellow biscuits Arabella always liked and had a go at making them, even chopping them up small as Nora used to – although I suppose Arabella is no longer so afraid of choking on her food.

At three o'clock on the dot, Arabella raps at the front door. I wonder if she's been waiting outside for the hour to arrive, perhaps looking up at the face of the house and running through what she wants to say to me.

Not bothering to go to the trouble of unlocking the front door, I open the back and stick my head out. 'Round here!'

A few seconds later, Arabella appears around the corner. I don't know how to describe what's different about her, apart from to say that she looks somehow smaller than life. Her shoulders have a worried stoop to them, and she walks with her arms crossed protectively over her chest, as if cringing from the sunlight. When she looks up at me, I see dark circles under her eyes. She's never been one to look like the prime of health, but there's a frailty that's more pronounced even for her. I feel a pang of compassion, but it's mixed together with a sick delight.

We go into the kitchen and I take the kettle off the stove, fill the pot to brew.

Arabella examines each of the chairs before selecting one to sit in. I suppose she's not accustomed to using this room, perhaps has only been inside it a handful of times in her life. 'Where are the Allens?' she asks.

'Somerset.' I take the seat at a right-angle to her, so we don't have to look each other in the face if we don't want to. 'You should count yourself lucky they're not here,' I add, 'Mrs Allen would probably have torn your throat out.'

Arabella presses one hand to her neck, the self-conscious gesture so familiar that it throws me right back to how we were before. 'So you told them?'

'*You* should have told them.'

She stays silent, which I take as agreement.

'And where are you staying?' I ask.

She tells me about her current situation, living in Reacher's old London flat. The place is ghastly, she says, so tiny and squalid, then goes on to describe rooms that are nicer than any I've lived in before Harfold. She's struggling with no staff but a charwoman, although her finances aren't as dire as she'd first feared – it seems Reacher had a bit of money tucked away, God knows where from. I don't tell her my theory behind this. 'He never made a will, so it has all come to me as his only kin. Still . . . you can't imagine how much I miss the manor,' says Arabella. As we have been speaking, her gaze has been flitting all over me, as if eager to take in every feature. Perhaps calculating, perhaps just hungry. 'How about you?' she asks. 'Will you be staying here?'

Shaking my head, I pour out her tea. 'Milk?'

'Please.'

'I'll be leaving as soon as I can sell the land,' I say.

'Where will you go?' She uses the tongs to pick up a sugar cube, drops it in with a tiny splash. Stirs. 'You're not having any?'

'Maybe in a bit. I've just finished a cup.' Where I should go next is a question I've been asking myself over and over, but I'm still not sure. It's high time for another reinvention, I think. Leave Vee Morgan behind – she died at Harfold. 'Maybe Aylesbury,' I say eventually. Try to visit Mam face to face. Apologize. She'll have to forgive me eventually – won't she?

Arabella tilts her head. 'Why there?'

Of course: she doesn't know about Mam and Dad. Only in this moment do I realize that she's never once asked me a question about my history, my family – she's always just spoken about hers, as if it's only natural that I should care about their lives. I suppose I was so relieved when she didn't show any interest in my past that I never stopped to realize how narcissistic that was. 'I've always liked the regal ring of Buckinghamshire,' I say at last.

She toys with the handle of her teacup, nudging it an inch to the left, then the right. 'You seem well, Vee.' A glance up at me. 'Is that Charlie's old jacket? I like it. It suits your figure.' Her hand twitches, then she moves it forward to touch one of mine, the gesture slow, tentative.

I pull out of her reach. I'm suddenly tired, an exhaustion coming from deep in my bones. 'Why are you here, Arabella?'

'I wanted to apologize.'

That makes me laugh. 'For which part?'

'All of it. I wasn't thinking clearly. You can't imagine what it was like, to have that weight hanging over me, knowing that my time was approaching, but with no way to stop it. I would have tried *anything*.' She gives me a sad smile. 'I only wish it hadn't been at the price of what you and I had. I really did love you, Vee.' Bites her lip. 'I *do*. I would still like to—'

I can't believe what I'm hearing! 'No,' I interrupt, 'that's not how it works, Arabella. If you really love another person, you're meant to want to trade your life for theirs, not the other way around.'

'I was a coward! But Vee, don't you see?' Now she turns her gaze back on me, an excited shine to her pupils. 'It doesn't matter any more. The night you fell into the river—'

'When you pushed me, you mean.'

She hesitates. 'Yes. After I pushed you, at the same moment, I saw it there on the other bank. A dancing hare.' She's grinning now, animated with the memory. 'I stood there and watched it, and I felt this sensation of absolute freedom come over me. It was as if I had been all tied up in a web that I didn't even know was there, and now somebody had torn me loose. I thought that I had transferred the curse to you, but I see now that, when you survived, it must have passed on to Morry instead. And now it's taken him, and it's all over.'

I shake my head at this. 'Didn't you hear what he said in the church? There never was a curse, Arabella. He made it up! He was using it to control you, for years and years.'

Arabella just smiles. 'Well, that doesn't matter. Either way, the curse is gone – I have escaped my death!' Again, she tries to reach for me. 'It doesn't have to come between us any longer. We can try again.'

I twitch my hand away once more. 'I don't think so.'

'You can't forgive me?'

I look away. Clear my throat. Look back at her. The familiar high-cheekboned face; her gunmetal eyes and smirking lips. I can see in her features that same loneliness I noticed when we first met; the burning need for my approval. For *someone's* approval. But I don't need it for myself any longer.

'I'm sorry.'

Her eyes harden. A resolution. This is what I've been waiting for. 'Vee, we need to talk about what happened to Maurice. In the church, I mean.'

I lift my chin, look her level in the face. 'He fell, Arabella.'

'I know I was far away, but . . .' She lets her voice trail off. 'I would never tell anyone if you *had*—'

'Don't you believe me?'

Arabella turns away. 'Yes, of course. I must have been mistaken.'

I give her a sad smile. So that's it, then. 'Drink your tea,' I say. 'It's getting cold.'

She lifts it, obedient, then hesitates – just for a second. Looks at me. A tremor in her hand. Then she brings the cup to her lips and takes a sip.

ACKNOWLEDGEMENTS

EVERYONE SAYS THAT writing a second novel is even harder than writing the first. In many ways, I found that to be true for *A Slow and Secret Poison*, but one real saving grace this time around was knowing that I already had an incredible team of people there to support me. A massive thank you is owed to my editors Rose Green and Loan Le for polishing this book to a shine, and to everyone at Doubleday and Atria for their hard work. Thank you in particular to Georgie Bewes, Barbara Thompson, Cat Hillerton, Beverley Mave and Izzie Ghaffari-Parker.

I have also been so fortunate to have not one but two brilliant agents – Rachel Neely and Ginger Clark – whose dual wisdom and guidance have been indispensable. My gratitude is due as well to Alba Arnau Prado, Catriona Fida and to everyone at Mushens Entertainment, and to Nicole Eisenbraun and Maria Ministeri at Ginger Clark Literary.

While writing this book, my debut novel, *Spitting Gold*, was just making its way into the world, and the love and kindness from readers, content creators, reviewers, booksellers, librarians and fellow authors were such a morale boost whenever I hit a writer's block. The same is true for my amazing family members and friends, who have been relentless in spreading the word about my writing. Thanks to all of you for being so generous with your time and compliments.

A Slow and Secret Poison is set in Wiltshire, where I grew up. I naively thought that this would mean I wouldn't have to do too much research for the novel but, as it turns out, a lot can change in a hundred years of history! Thank you therefore to my Wiltshire-based research assistant – by which I mean my mum – for sharing your local knowledge, snooping into private gardens, and ferrying me around to sites of interest.

I must also take a moment to acknowledge the tireless people at Haringey Libraries, who have supplied me with countless titles over the course of my research. To name just a handful of books that have been crucial in the development of this novel: *We Danced All Night: A Social History of Britain Between the Wars* by Martin Pugh; *Servants: A Downstairs View of Twentieth-century Britain* by Lucy Lethbridge; *Keeping up Appearances: Fashion and Class Between the Wars* by Catherine Horwood; *Britain in the 1920s* by Fiona McDonald; *The Long Weekend* by Adrian Tinniswood; and *Below Stairs* by Margaret Powell (from whom Vee's anecdote about the nanny in the park is borrowed). Less directly, I have to name as well *A Curious Friendship: The Story of a Bluestocking and a Bright Young Thing* by Anna Thomasson; *Serious Pleasures: The Life of Stephen Tennant* by Philip Hoare; and *The Enigma of Arrival* by V. S. Naipaul – three books which first introduced me to the real-life figure of Stephen Tennant, on whom Arabella is extremely loosely based.

Last and most importantly of all, thank you to Ashley for your endless love, enthusiasm and belief, for fixing all my plot holes, for motivating me with baked goods, and for your advice at a critical juncture to add a chaffinch into the story. I truly couldn't have written this book without you.

Carmella Lowkis grew up in Wiltshire and has a degree in English Literature and Creative Writing from the University of Warwick. After graduating, she worked in libraries, before moving into book marketing. Her debut novel, *Spitting Gold*, was published in 2024. Carmella lives in North London with her fiancée. You can follow her on X and Instagram @carmellalowkis.